'This is not quite how Peter Dutton imagines our dystopian future: crap technology, paranoid spies, cycling activists and even dumber politicians. Set phasers to stupid. Hilarious.' –Wendy Harmer

'Ken Saunders waddled about the 2028 National Tally Room as the results came in. He has seen the future! Relax! It's awesome!' – H.G.Nelson

'If Douglas Adams wrote *The Killing Season*, it would be as absurdly funny and worryingly prescient as this!' – Sami Shah

'It's a state of peak technology, peak focus group, peak surveillance. But the revolution is coming—and it's off-line, naked and riding a bicycle.' – Cathy Wilcox

'A highly amusing, if grim, forefeel on how politics will be plagued in the near future.' – John Doyle

'A hilarious and horrifying vision of a future where parking meters are pokies and nothing's scarier than Australia Post. Saunders' novel is fizzing with ideas that are troublingly plausible.' – Dominic Knight

'I've found the Australian Douglas Adams! Imaginative and very funny stuff.' – Tom Gleeson

2028

... AND AUSTRALIA HAS GONE TO HELL IN A HANDBASKET

KEN SAUNDERS

ALLEN&UNWIN
SYDNEY • MELBOURNE • AUCKLAND • LONDON

First published in 2018

Copyright © Ken Saunders 2018

Allen & Unwin
83 Alexander Street
Crows Nest NSW 2065
Australia
Phone: (61 2) 8425 0100
Email: info@allenandunwin.com
Web: www.allenandunwin.com

 A catalogue record for this book is available from the National Library of Australia

ISBN 978 1 76063 106 2

Set in 12/18 pt Minion by Midland Typesetters, Australia
Printed and bound in Australia by Griffin Press

10 9 8 7 6 5 4 3 2 1

The paper in this book is FSC® certified. FSC® promotes environmentally responsible, socially beneficial and economically viable management of the world's forests.

To Flo, Laurie and Marina
Three generations of inspiration

CHAPTER ONE

Renard Prendergast eased the car into an available parking spot, but as he reached for the door, Autocar clicked in and straightened out his parking attempt. Normally, Autocar only took over when a vehicle was in danger; however, several months earlier, Renard had accidentally set his Autocar feature to 'Correct all' and didn't know how to turn it off. Renard didn't much care for driving, yet every time Autocar intervened, he felt diminished. Though he held an office-based data-analysis job, deep down he felt that, as an ASIO agent, he ought to be able to drive like James Bond. Autocar clearly thought he couldn't.

Renard inserted his credit card into the Parkie and opted to play for two dollars. Brisbane City Council had been the first local government to introduce Parkies, but now they were everywhere, even in this inner-city suburb of Glebe in Sydney. They brought, in a limited way, poker machines to the streets. Motorists still had to pay for parking, but now got one play in return, a chance to hit the jackpot. Parking meters had been transformed into something they had never been before: popular. The Parkies had proven a windfall for councils. Even pedestrians stopped to play the meters and many motorists readily paid/played for more parking time than they needed.

The machine made a few cha-ching sounds before lighting up with: *Congratulations! You have won five minutes of free parking. Double or nothing?* Renard punched *No*. Who would play double or nothing for five minutes? He started a new round. This time the parking meter chimed a tinkly rendition of the 1812 Overture finale. Renard stepped back in surprise.

'What did you win?' a pedestrian called out, she and her dog both stopping to look.

'I don't know,' Renard stammered. 'I've never won before.'

They peered at the screen of the parking meter and a ripple of disappointment passed through them. He'd won only fifty dollars. 'I'd have thought the 1812 Overture would be for a five-hundred-dollar prize at least,' the woman commented. 'I'm told if you win a thousand, it plays "Girls Just Want to Have Fun".'

'What if you're not a girl?'

'The Parkies have face recognition software,' the dog walker replied.

'Do they?' Renard asked. He knew full well they did. The Parkies were one of the wearying sources of information he routinely examined in his work. The thing about metadata was its meta-ness.

'Sure they do,' the woman continued. 'Remember how a Parkie helped catch the Strathfield bank robbery gang? Though the guy driving the getaway car put a stolen credit card into the parking meter, the Parkie itself was still able to identify him. Funny attitude to try to pay for parking while your friends are sticking up a bank. A chance to win, I suppose,' she mused philosophically. 'He should have worn a balaclava like the rest of the gang. Actually . . . I think it plays "Money Changes Everything" when you win a thousand dollars. That would make more sense.'

Renard squinted at the Parkie. It was still offering to play double or nothing. Renard was not going to push his luck. He pressed the button and one clean fifty-dollar note emerged from the machine.

The woman raised her eyebrows. 'I didn't think anyone under thirty used cash anymore.'

'I'm eating at Low Expectations tonight,' he explained. 'No cards accepted.'

'I should have guessed when you chose cash,' she replied. 'I go there every so often. God knows why.' She and her dog set off down Glebe Point Road.

Low Expectations had been his first assignment with the Australian Security Intelligence Organisation. Well, not his first assignment, but his first and only out-of-office assignment. This was eight years earlier, a year after he'd joined the organisation. A new director had been appointed, someone unlike any of the long-term spooks in ASIO's upper echelons. This one had hit the agency with public relations and team-building ideas never before contemplated. 'You need to be a people person to head a security agency,' he had told the cameras on his appointment, 'and our agents need to be so too.' He had launched, in the year of the same name, ASIO's '20:20 Vision'. He wanted the data analysts to get out of the office one day per week to get a feel for the public they spied on—to 'get touched', he said, adopting a catchphrase popular back then. It was not a complete break with tradition;

'meeting people' was still to be done in the traditional ASIO way of infiltrating groups, planting listening devices and intercepting messages whenever possible. The regular workload of the data analysts stayed the same, mind you, but now they had only four office days per week to do it. The initiative, just like the ASIO director himself, had not lasted the year. The data analysts had proved remarkably inept, leaving fingerprints where they should not have and, in the case of the Lustathon incident, landing ASIO utterly in the soup.

Renard's 20:20 Vision assignment had been Low Expectations, which had come to ASIO's attention precisely because it wasn't coming to their attention. ASIO wanted to know why. Officially, Low Expectations was a bookshop/cafe, yet it sold only Charles Dickens novels and all the stock was second-hand. The inside was decked out in what Renard termed 'Industrial Revolution chic': a few tables were scattered between the even fewer bookcases, while at the back, several teenagers toiled over contraptions that appeared to be working looms. There were teacups on some tables and a smell of food. On his first visit, Renard rashly ordered a cappuccino.

The owner scowled. 'You can have tea,' he rumbled, in a tone that indicated Renard ought not to ask for cinnamon chai.

The tea was weak and Renard understood why when he witnessed the owner reusing the tea bag for subsequent orders. There was only one item on the menu. Renard ordered a bowl of gruel.

The reason for ASIO's interest was that Low Expectations had absolutely no online presence. It wasn't just that it had no website and no social media accounts—it had no wifi. In an era when virtually no one carried money, the shop didn't accept credit cards.

The owner kept his accounts handwritten in ink in large nineteenth-century-style ledgers. There wasn't a laptop, a Genie phone or a Gargantuan in the place. Their only concession to modern times was that they had electricity—used sparingly, to judge by the temperature of the tea.

Any business with so low a profile must be hiding something. Renard was tasked with finding out what. However, as Renard dutifully pointed out in report after report, he found nothing to report. He could discover no subversive activities and no answer to the still more perplexing question: how could an enterprise with such an appalling business model survive?

The owner employed a gang of local teenagers to work the looms after school. Although they did their best to appear downtrodden, Renard discovered that they were paid the standard award wage. All the employees dressed in nineteenth-century clothes or nineteenth-century rags, depending on their roles. The owner sold what cloth was produced, but the quality was not high. Book sales were minimal. Customers were permitted to read novels from the shelves while having tea and gruel. The owner kept the gruel bubbling all day. Upstairs, where the new-fangled electricity flowed more generously, they ran movies and TV adaptations of Dickens' novels. A large, threatening sign on the front door indicated that customers were not allowed to use mobile phones or any electronic devices while in the shop, and when Renard tried surreptitiously, he found some sort of jamming device prevented signal reception. Despite appearances, someone in the place had technical savvy. As far as his efforts at eavesdropping went, he overheard nothing beyond local cafe chitchat and one person snivelling over the fate of Little Dorrit.

The adolescents on the looms looked the part of surly, malcontent labourers, and on Renard's first visit, one of them lifted his wallet. Renard found it necessary to protest vigorously before the owner reluctantly compelled the youth to produce the wallet. The owner then proceeded to take the lad off 'for a thrashing'. Renard was left with his gruel and the shrieks from out the back. Later, at the office, he viewed the 'thrashing' from a CCTV camera in the laneway behind the shop. There he saw the owner and the kid laughing and having a drink of something, with the pick-pocket emitting periodic howls and pleas for mercy. What sort of business operated by training your staff to pick the pockets of the customers?

His immediate supervisor at ASIO back then dated from the romantic Cold War era, when spies spied on spies and filing cabinets had secrets worth stealing. He thought Low Expectations might be a front for something and told Renard of a photography shop that the Soviets operated in Melbourne in the 1970s. The two Soviet spies filled their shop window with dreadful wedding photos: people with their eyes bugged out or looking as though they had something stuck in their teeth. The Soviet agents wanted to work without being disturbed. The photos were there to make sure they weren't bothered by customers.

For ASIO in the 2020s, those glory days of spy-versus-spy were long gone. Now the spy service defended against terrorists: addled young men who blew themselves up in public places or lonely fourteen-year-old boys locked in their rooms hacking into the electricity grid for no particular reason. With opponents such as these, ASIO was perpetually on guard and there could never be a point of victory. 'In the old days,' his supervisor reminisced, 'when we successfully turned their double agent into our triple agent, there was a moment of triumph to something like that.'

Though he was no longer required to, Renard continued his surveillance of Low Expectations. He always went on his own. It wasn't a place that could be shared with friends, let alone with a date. And he continued to spy. He'd once stolen a letter from the box where people could leave and pick up mail. (Low Expectations had introduced this service after Australia Post abandoned letter delivery in 2022.) This stolen letter, he hoped, would finally reveal whatever was going on in the shop.

The letter had been not only harmless but inane. It was a load of Elizabeth Bennet-style trivialities about who would be attending some upcoming dance, who was wearing what and who had said what to whom. He was pretty sure he knew who wrote it: one of those Jane Austen types who had begun frequenting the place. They often sat there in their bonnets writing away. Their frivolousness annoyed him. What business did they have being in a Dickensian workshop?

That was when he realised that he actually liked Low Expectations.

Now, with his fifty-dollar Parkie win in his hand, he pushed open the squeaky door. The looms were mostly quiet, and only Kate, one of the friendlier of the teenage textile labourers, was there. In her two years working in the shop, her cloth work had become skilled.

The owner came over to Renard. 'Gruel?' he asked and, after Renard nodded, added a surly, 'Tea as well, I suppose.' Renard took a copy of *Bleak House* from the shelf and searched for where he'd left off. Did it even matter? The first forty pages were about it being

7

foggy and little else. Eight years ago he hadn't liked Dickens novels. He wasn't sure he liked them any better now.

The owner was back with a large, badly chipped bowl full of gruel. 'There's a letter for you,' he announced.

'A letter?'

'Yes, a letter. Your name *is* Ned, isn't it?'

Renard's shock could not have been greater. 'Yes,' he managed.

'It looked like you weren't too sure about that answer,' the owner observed suspiciously.

'It's just—' Renard paused, thinking fast '—how did you know I was called Ned?'

'You told me your name was Ned when you first started coming here.'

'Ah, y-yes . . .' Renard stammered, reaching for the letter that the owner now seemed reluctant to give to him. 'My name is Ned . . . It's just that no one has called me that for a very long time.'

The owner considered this for a moment, then finally handed over the envelope.

A letter for Ned. A letter that had been nine years in the coming. 'No one has called me Ned,' he repeated, his heart beating faster, 'for a very, very long time.'

• • •

Autocar was a business with a single product, normally a Darwinian vulnerability in the fickle world of technology. Autocar could stave off extinction only through the most demanding of juggling acts. Its niche was in a tiny crevice of public and political indecision and, to survive, it had to nourish that indecision. Autocar was still thriving for the moment. Everyone who wanted to drive a car needed its product; indeed, it had been mandated by legislation to be installed in all motorist-operated vehicles still on Australian roads.

The history of software companies was littered with success stories that led to the abyss. One moment, everyone would be salivating for a company's product; the next, no one wanted it at all. Autocar was attuned to this perilous environment. Despite its enormous success, it was perpetually primed to shut down the business the next day, if necessary. It rented no offices and had no inventory to speak of. The only 'premises' it kept was space on a server located in Collinsvale, Tasmania—Collinsvale being the Australian town with the lowest annual temperature, hence the lowest air-conditioning costs for the server. All Autocar employees worked from home and had what was called in the industry a 'no ripcord clause': your future redundancy money was included in your fortnightly pay. You could be tossed out of the plane without a parachute at any moment, but at least you had been paid all your entitlements.

The opportunity that Autocar had wedged open was society's inability to come to grips with the benefits of the driverless car. In its first five years, the driverless car had achieved only a 37 per cent market share. Those vehicles obeyed the rules, gave way when it was correct to do so, slowed in wet conditions. In other words, they behaved like complete chumps in the minds of certain motorists still behind the wheel who didn't obey the rules or give way and who sped past other cars in thunderstorms. Knowing that driverless cars never drove aggressively and the passengers in those cars were probably doing Sudokus or sleeping, motorists asserted themselves with greater and greater abandon. Thus, while driverless cars never hit other driverless cars, the motorists out there hit driverless cars, they hit cars driven by other motorists, they hit pedestrians and cyclists and they hit lampposts. In looking at the data, it was clear to everyone that the lampposts were not the problem. The obvious response, at least to the pedestrians and cyclists recuperating in hospital, would have been to ban the motorist car. But nothing was that simple.

Seventy years of relentless car advertisements, of sleek vehicles streaking alone across the outback or ascending to the apex of some steep mountain where no car had any proper reason to be, had left an imprint on part of the population. For them, driving was a right. Driving was freedom. Admittedly, that freedom was sometimes hard to perceive, but those motorists knew it was there, if only they could roar along that deserted outback road instead of being mired in traffic on the Western Distributor. They weren't giving all that up without a fight. To the hard core of the motorist faction, most of whom couldn't help but have a Y chromosome, the driverless car was for wusses, uncoordinated gits and women. Legislators feared to antagonise so large a group of voters, but nonetheless motorists, like the cigarette smokers before them, were going to have to make concessions.

Into this historic opportunity of political dithering marched Autocar. Programmed into a vehicle, Autocar followed a driver's every movement. It still let the motorist cut people off, pass on the shoulder and drive above the speed limit at times; what it didn't do was allow critical accidents to occur. It would always seize control prior to the moment of crisis, taking over the steering when the drunken motorist was nodding off, reducing speed on the wet road before the car careened out of control.

2028

To avoid accusations that it was a tool of the nanny state, Autocar came with illegality settings whereby motorists could choose their level of disobedience of traffic laws with a maximum ceiling set at 25 per cent over the speed limit. Whatever the setting, though, Autocar would intercede if human life was imperilled. A car could still run a red light, but Autocar made sure it was only able to do so if everyone in that intersection would survive. Installing Autocar was the concession motorists had to make. It practically eliminated the death toll.

The software programming required for Autocar to work was astoundingly complex and Agnieska 'Aggie' Posniak was among the very best of Autocar's programmers. She had never met Colin Sanderson—the founder and CEO of Autocar—in person, but when she'd joined the company four years earlier, he had sent her (as he did all new employees) a copy of Isaac Asimov's *I, Robot* in which he had inscribed: *Autocar will not through action or inaction allow a human to come to harm.*

However, a company such as Autocar could not survive on programming excellence alone. It needed the political stasis, the mix of driverless and motorist-driven cars, to be maintained. To that end, Aggie was also one of what Autocar called its 'operatives'. As Autocar's mole within the Royal Commission into Road Safety, a commission of critical importance to the company, she was to alert Autocar to which way the political winds were about to blow.

No one on the commission knew she was with Autocar. Instead, she purported to be a bicyclist-rights enthusiast, representing a group called Bicyclism Australia. Bicyclism Australia was a totally phantom association. It had been created by Autocar solely as a means of manoeuvring Aggie on to the commission. This cyclist lobby group may have been conjured into existence by Autocar out of nothing, but, thanks to the company's wizardry, it had an impressive internet presence—so impressive that not only had Aggie been appointed to the Royal Commission but, fourteen months of commission hearings later, Bicyclism Australia, to Autocar's astonishment, had developed a sizeable and growing membership of actual cyclists. Aggie now found herself obliged to send out e-newsletters, rent occasional meeting spaces and produce tedious annual reports on behalf of Bicyclism Australia just to keep up the appearance of legitimacy in the eyes of the group's loyal membership.

It was a hot night to be attending Royal Commission hearings. Though she was still several kilometres from her destination, Aggie dutifully got off the train, hoisting her bicycle onto her shoulder as she climbed the steps out of the station. Attention to detail was important. The bicycle ride would be just enough distance to give her a credible film of sweat for her arrival at the public hearings.

After more than a year of hearings, Aggie thought she had the other commissioners sussed. Two were plants from the Free Drivers movement (as the motorists now called themselves). Another was an operative from the Car Share people, who were playing a very subtle game in the new motoring world order. The rest were a hotchpotch of advertising firm types and automobile salespeople, many of whom now considered the driverless car to be their Frankenstein's monster escaped from the lab. Finally, there was Sandra, a representative of the Australian Public Transport Alliance, a painfully sincere citizens group that all the other players could safely ignore. Given Aggie's guise as a representative of cyclists, Sandra had gravitated to her as a fellow outcast from the main game.

Aggie did not particularly approve of the industrial espionage, lobbying and political chicanery involved in her role as an operative. She simply had interests that overlapped with those of Autocar in its fight for survival. She had her own agenda and would be loyal to Autocar right up to the moment when she wasn't any longer. Both Autocar and Aggie sensed the temporary nature of the alignment.

When Aggie arrived, bicycle helmet under her arm, Sandra was the only commissioner seated at the table. The others were scattered around the room typing into their Genie phones. Sandra beckoned to Aggie and patted the chair beside her. 'Agnieska,' she hissed excitedly, 'there's a letter for you. Hand delivered.'

Aggie blinked. No one sent letters anymore. No one *could* send letters anymore. 'Hand delivered . . . by who?'

'By whom,' corrected Sandra, who was always un-splitting infinitives in the revisions to their commission reports, 'and the answer is, I don't know by whom. He didn't leave a name.'

'What did he look like?'

Sandra levelled her eyes on Aggie. 'Look like? I'll tell you what he looked like: he looked like a spy.'

Aggie stared at the public transport activist. Was Sandra having a joke with her? She had never seemed the joking type before. 'What do you mean he looked like a spy?'

'Like in an old movie. Trench coat, sunglasses, a three-corner hat pulled low over a four-corner face.' Sandra paused, as if hoping for a laugh, but got none.

Aggie just stared at her, baffled.

'A trench coat!' Sandra remarked. 'It's thirty degrees out there.'

'You're making this up,' Aggie suggested.

'Making it up?' Sandra repeated. 'Well, have a look at this then.'

She handed Aggie the envelope. It had Aggie's full name on it but, underneath, it read: *For Ned*.

'Who's Ned?' Sandra probed.

'I'm Ned,' Aggie replied without hesitating. 'It's an old nickname.'

'What's it about?' Sandra asked, apparently feeling entitled to know. She had delivered the letter, after all. 'Is it Royal Commission business?'

'No, not Royal Commission business.' Aggie could feel the excitement tingling through her. She could tell the envelope contained a plastic identity card. She shifted her eyes back to Sandra. 'It's about . . .' Aggie paused, 'to become interesting.' It was going to be hard to concentrate on the hearings that night, and besides, she would soon have to resign from the commission anyway.

CHAPTER TWO

Despite the confidence he was exuding, Prime Minister Fitz-williams could not help but feel that this cabinet, his carefully constructed cabinet, was an uninspiring group. They were what he called 'lifers': MPs who thought the way to get ahead was by keeping their own head down, hitching one's wagon to the strongest horse around and being very, very careful where one used one's credit card. Duration was their measure of success. Reliable, steadfast, said some. Dullards, the Prime Minister thought—with very few exceptions.

It was his own doing. Three terms as PM, and over those years he had effectively seen off any rivals to his leadership. He had dispatched them all, the lean and hungry ones, those who would have used his fallen body as the podium from which to address the nation. The most threatening of them had been Boswell, Damian Boswell: poster boy of the private schools, movie-star handsome, witty—all things the Prime Minister was not. Damian Boswell had the common touch as well. He could mix it with the crowd at a Rabbitohs match and from there go straight on to ABC Classic FM to confide his love of Shostakovich. 'I'll give him Shostakovich,' the PM had muttered darkly to Senator Olga O'Rourke. Olga soon saw to it that Damian Boswell was outmanoeuvred in cabinet and isolated to such an extent that Boswell was almost grateful to accept a posting as Australia's ambassador to Russia, just to escape. The Prime Minister was not an overly vindictive man, although he did occasionally instruct his new ambassador in Moscow to tour some godforsaken mining town in the depths of the Siberian winter.

The cabinet was a tepid crew, but they would do. It was the moment to go for a fourth term. His inner circle had been planning it for months, his final campaign before retirement. Labor was in a feeble state. The honeymoon was over for Roslyn Stanfield, their newish leader. She was perceived as vacillating, thin on policy, a lightweight whose only ideas came from focus groups. The PR and marketing firm Baxter Lockwood Inc. had confirmed this for the Prime Minister via their own focus groups. Baxter Lockwood's research had delivered Fitzwilliams three terms in power and he counted on their help to win the fourth.

The Australian Greens, meanwhile, were in receivership. In the previous election, they had campaigned hard to ban some chemical . . . Fitzwilliams had mastered the name of it back then, but it eluded him now. The Greens had stumped up and down the country crying that if the stuff got into the water table, you could kiss agriculture goodbye. They might even have been right, sci-entifically speaking. Fitzwilliams had no idea. Being scientifically correct, however, had no particular clout when it came to the terms of the Tri-Ocean Free Trade Agreement. The Australian Greens were successfully sued for compensation by the manufacturer of Dioxy . . . something or other . . . for 'unfair practices causing a diminution in trade'. The suit cost them almost a billion dollars, with the Akron, the US company, arguing that the damage to their reputation had been worldwide. The Australian Greens had no choice but to go into receivership and lodge an appeal. That the Akron company had been subsequently taken over by a German consortium which later went into receivership itself meant that no phoenix-like Green Party was likely to emerge from that legal morass for at least a decade.

Fitzwilliams' announcement of his intention to call a snap election had gone down well with cabinet. The polls were strong and already there was a taste of victory in the air. 'Total confidentiality,' he now told them. 'I'm visiting the Governor-General tomorrow at two pm and going straight into a press conference at three thirty. That way we'll capture the evening news with scarcely any time for Labor to react. At seven, we'll have a "spontaneous" rally in front of Parliament House at the Stadlet. The whole of cabinet together on the platform. From there, we'll disperse in different directions without talking to the press, telling them only that we are fanning out across the country to take our message to the people.'

The election material packages from the campaign team lay before the cabinet members, each package tailored to the minister's specific portfolio. It would contain the catchphrases, slogans, tactics and targets of the campaign to come. There were grunts of approval around the table.

'Ah, Prime Minister . . .'

The room fell silent, the interjection jarring the upbeat mood. All eyes, including the Prime Minister's, shifted to Russell Langdon, the Minister for Security and Freedom.

Fitzwilliams had always felt Langdon was born to be on the backbench. He possessed those contradictory attributes of a back-bencher: an extreme deference to the Prime Minister that barely concealed a suppressed inclination to mutiny. Yet it was thanks to career backbencher Langdon, even more than Baxter Lockwood, that they were comfortably ensconced in their present positions. It was Langdon who had won them the last election, an election that even the Prime Minister had thought they would lose. The Labor leader then was impossibly good-looking, a charismatic charmer, gladhanding his way around the country and social media, mutter-ing inanities about the need for change. He appeared unstoppable.

But in their darkest electoral hour, backbencher Russ Langdon had managed to get his leg blown off. It happened at a campaign speech in Langdon's safe electorate of Flinders (although safe, Prime Minister Fitzwilliams supposed, was probably not an accurate term in this case). A terrorist suicide bomber, a lone wolf who had objected to . . . the PM frowned . . . objected to the court ruling on prayer rooms in state schools? Three dead. Four if you counted the terrorist, but the media seldom did these days. Four and a bit if you counted Langdon's left leg.

The fifty-six-year-old Langdon was rushed to hospital where they amputated the leg and saved his life, and Langdon, doped up to his eyeballs on painkillers, summoned all his backbencher nous, propped himself up on his pillows and gave a smiling, double thumbs-up to the photographers. That photo had won the election. Suddenly everyone realised that they didn't need Labor's heart-throb with his shallow Tony Blair smile. They needed a steady hand. They needed the kind of indomitable spirit that was Russ Langdon.

When re-elected, Prime Minister Fitzwilliams made Langdon the Minster for Security and Freedom. Whether he was competent to manage such an important portfolio didn't overly worry Fitzwilliams. The bureaucrats of vital portfolios could run them no matter who was minister.

'There may be a problem tomorrow, Prime Minister . . .' Langdon now told his leader. He winced, shifting his artificial leg. The grimace irritated the PM, who sensed it was done to remind him of just what he owed Langdon. It was an uncharitable thought, but Fitzwilliams still felt it was true.

'A problem?'

'You said three thirty for the press conference and seven o'clock for the rally outside parliament.'

The Prime Minister nodded, but Langdon appeared uncertain how to proceed. 'It may be nothing, but there appear to be demonstrations scheduled at both those times—here in Canberra—right here, outside parliament.'

'Demonstrations?' the Prime Minister queried. How was such a thing even possible? He shot a glance at Olga, the veteran Minister for Communications. She looked equally surprised, but nodded at him reassuringly. It was nothing they couldn't handle.

It was not good to start off an election campaign dealing with the unexpected. He hadn't encountered a demonstration for what . . . five, six years? On the other hand, it would be ridiculous to delay when everything was poised to go, including radio and internet interviews scheduled for ungodly hours on the morning after the election call. They had bought advertising, billboards, goodness knew what on the internet, and it was all scheduled for release at dawn on Wednesday.

His face betrayed none of his deliberations. 'I think Olga's legislation will sideline any demonstrators sufficiently,' he assured the cabinet, referring to the senator's much-lauded Demonstration Protection Act of 2022. 'We announce as scheduled tomorrow.'

He redirected his attention to Russ Langdon. 'Who's planning these demonstrations?' he asked. It never paid to ignore the unexpected.

'This is somewhat surprising, Prime Minister.'

'Just tell me, Russell,' the PM urged, ignoring another wince from the minister as he shifted his leg.

'Well, Prime Minister . . . it's the Luddites.'

• • •

Events had moved at a precipitous pace for Renard Prendergast. That he was one week later in the ASIO Canberra headquarters meeting with the legendary head of ASIO, Fiona Brennan, did not surprise him. He knew the letter he'd received in Low Expectations would go right to the top. Now, he and the director were to brief the Prime Minister on the matter.

Fiona Brennan had been made ASIO director less than three years earlier, after a succession of fumbles, from the short reign of the director who had overseen the 20:20 Vision fiasco, followed by the PM's patronage appointment (who was out of his depth) and then the know-it-all one who had annoyed the Americans. Brennan had steadied the ship. A career ASIO official, she knew the workings of every ASIO office. What made her legendary was the quality least expected of an ASIO director: Fiona Brennan had cultivated a certain grandmotherly charm. She could go on television and while sipping tea delicately from a china cup explain why ASIO had destroyed evidence of its activities in East Timor or peeked at the private tax records of thousands of Australians, and people would come away feeling that, well, she had to really. ASIO found itself with a PR star for the first time in its history. As Renard sat with her now, he found that the image she projected to the public was evidently real. She was charming and . . . nice.

'You have done excellent work here, Renard.' Brennan took off her glasses and fixed Renard with such a focused stare it made him wonder what possible use her glasses could be. 'I should warn you, the Prime Minister isn't fond of ASIO and you were part of our lamented 20:20 Vision debacle several years ago.' She smiled. 'The Lustathon incident remains a sore point with him.'

Renard was surprised the director had even spoken of it. Among ASIO employees, the word 'Lustathon' was treated with the same superstitious dread Shakespearean actors had of speaking the name Macbeth. The existence of the drug Lustathon had been rumoured for years; almost always, according to the urban myth engine that propelled it, linked to United States military research. The drug was purported to create an overpowering sexual desire in anyone exposed to it. American forces were alleged to have released it in the mountains of Afghanistan against the Taliban, setting off a homosexual orgy among the stolidly homophobic ranks of Taliban fighters, thus wreaking significant psychological damage on the enemy.

Lustathon emerged from urban myth to nightly news during the 20:20 Vision project. An anarchist cell staged a dramatic gas attack in the Melbourne financial district, simultaneous issuing a statement to the media claiming to have released the libido-raising gas. No one really knew if Lustathon existed, let alone in gas form; certainly, in the Melbourne attack, the gas released was a harmless substitute. However, the disruption was enormous, far beyond what the anarchists had hoped. What they hadn't anticipated was the so-called placebo effect on hard-working financial officers and day traders who believed they were under a Lustathon gas attack. The ensuing pandemonium and sexual abandon severely damaged the reputation of many distinguished firms in the financial sector.

What had been devastating for ASIO was that the two perpetrators of the attack were ASIO agents on individual 20:20 Vision placements. Both thought they had penetrated the inner workings of the hard-core anarchist group; both, in their activist guises, thought they had converted the other to the cause and each had fallen in love with the other. None of the actual anarchists, who had deemed the plot foolish from the start, were involved.

The Prime Minister did not forget or forgive cock-ups of this magnitude.

'Expect a sneering comment at the least,' the director warned Renard. 'I have told Minister Langdon of the contents of your surprising letter. He will have gone straight to the Prime Minister with it. I'm not sure who will attend the meeting, but the Prime Minister has only a few cabinet colleagues he truly values.' Her tone was casual. 'One is the Treasurer, Alan Chandos. Chandos is an ideal treasurer for the PM. He is creative and clever, but he is content simply to be treasurer. He rakes it all in and leaves the Prime Minister to spend it wherever.

Renard had the impression the director enjoyed gossiping along these lines. He relies on his talented Health Minister, Donna

Hargreaves, but she is disliked by the rest of the cabinet. 'And Senator O'Rourke is his other ideal minister. She's held several important cabinet posts and has run them all superbly. Where Chandos likes numbers, she likes knowledge. She knows how things work, who does what, how to get results, who to rely on in a crunch and whose heads should roll, if that is what is needed. And again, the Prime Minister can trust her because she does not seek to be prime minister. Her accent, I think, restrains her from greater ambition.'

Everyone had heard Olga O'Rourke's heavy accent—or, if they hadn't, they had heard the many comedians who imitated it. O'Rourke was the senator's married name. As Olga Kurbakova she had moved to Australia with her parents from the Soviet Union back in 1985. Since then she had learned everything possible about Australia except how to sound like an Aussie. Olga O'Rourke had the accent of a cartoon Soviet-era spy. There was no way the people of Australia, even at their multicultural best, could vote that accent to be their prime minister.

'Be totally honest with her,' Fiona advised. 'She will know if you are lying. Don't expect Minister Langdon to like us much either. He may feel that the limitations of our intelligence-gathering took off his left leg. Although that did help to get him a cabinet post, it wouldn't be polite to point that out.'

'When do I . . . we—' Renard swallowed '—meet the Prime Minister?'

A light flashed on the director's desk. 'Immediately, it would seem.' She stood and clapped her hands together. 'Gather up your things, Renard. We must head over to parliament. It isn't done to keep the Prime Minister waiting.'

. . .

'Where the hell are they, Russ?' the Prime Minister asked his Minister for Security and Freedom. Three people were in the room: Russ Langdon, the Prime Minister and the Prime Minister's campaign manager, Lister St John, the man who had masterminded the PM's three election victories, although the verb was Lister St John's choice more than the Prime Minister's. Theirs was a marriage of convenience. Lister St John was capable of doing his bit as campaign manager well enough to get Fitzwilliams elected; Fitzwilliams had proven capable of hiring him to do so. What they had in common was an underlying contempt for each other.

'Fill me in while we wait,' Lister requested irritably. 'I've rather a lot on. We are launching a surprise election tomorrow, after all.'

The PM's ability to tolerate St John waned considerably whenever he adopted that tone of voice.

'Who are the damned Luddites,' St John now demanded, 'and how is it that they bloody matter?'

'You don't remember?' Langdon asked. 'The media was full of them eight or nine years ago.'

'Lister was overseas throughout 2019 and 2020,' the Prime Minister told Langdon. He turned to his campaign manager. 'It was when you thought you were too big for small-time elections such as those held in our fair land. You were going to carve a big name for yourself by helping make Senator Bolen the president of the United States.'

The Edward Bolen primary campaign in 2020 had become a textbook case for political campaigns having gone not so much wrong as straight into the pits of hell. The Prime Minister turned back to Russ Langdon. 'It was Lister here who was behind Senator Bolen's famous "I Have a Nightmare" speech.'

'You tried to help Edward Bolen become president?' Langdon whispered. 'He was a psycho.'

'Just tell me about the Luddites!' Lister snapped.

'Fine,' the Prime Minister said. Raising Senator Bolen had been a petty thing to do, but Lister St John did not have a natural affinity for humility. 'On 1 April 2019, some two thousand eight hundred and eighty-seven Australian citizens—' Fitzwilliams still remembered the figure clearly '—went into their respective state registries of births, deaths and marriages and changed their name by deed poll to Ned Ludd. They were from across the whole country, not seemingly connected to each other or politically active. One month later, the Luddite Party registered as an official federal election party with two thousand eight hundred and eighty-seven party members all named Ned Ludd.'

'A prime number,' Langdon pointed out.

The other two men looked at him, puzzled.

'What do you mean?' Fitzwilliams asked.

'Two thousand eight hundred and eighty-seven is a prime number,' Langdon repeated.

'You mean like pi?' the Prime Minister asked uncertainly.

'No, that's irrational,' Langdon replied with a tsking sound that made the Prime Minister bristle. As if in response to the PM's bristling, Langdon shifted his artificial leg and winced. 'Irrational numbers go on to infinity without repeating,' he explained. 'Prime numbers are only divisible by one and themselves.'

'Do you mean to say,' Lister St John scoffed, 'that nothing else divides into two thousand eight hundred and eighty-seven?'

'Yes,' Russ answered.

'What about seventeen?' St John queried.

'What *about* seventeen?' Langdon shot back.

'Does it divide into two thousand eight hundred and eighty-seven?'

'No, it doesn't! Two thousand eight hundred and eighty-seven is a prime number.'

'You haven't tried,' Lister St John accused. 'Try dividing it by seventeen or twenty-nine or a hundred and fourteen. Something must divide into it.'

'Nothing divides into it,' Russ answered, louder than before. 'It's a prime number!'

The Prime Minister felt he should intervene. 'Russ, what makes you think two thousand eight hundred and eighty-seven is one of these prime numbers?'

'I don't just *think* two thousand eight hundred and eighty-seven is a prime number,' Langdon said through gritted teeth. He sounded exasperated. It struck Fitzwilliams that the man had handled having his leg being blown off with greater equanimity. 'It *is* a prime number! I know what I'm talking about.'

The Prime Minister had only received a pass in high school maths. It disturbed him that Langdon, of all people, was carrying on very much like someone with a high distinction.

'Let's get back on topic,' Lister cut in. 'What have the Luddites ever done? I've never heard of them.'

'Since then—' the PM let out a slow breath '—nothing. They have done nothing other than maintain their status as an officially registered party.'

'Until today,' Langdon piped up. 'I mean tomorrow. Tomorrow, they have two demonstrations planned—both here in Canberra, one at three thirty and the other at seven. The time of the

PM's press conference to announce the snap election after leaving the Governor-General's residence and the time of the cabinet rally outside parliament. It could not be coincidental.'

Lister St John cleared his throat. 'I don't like it—but with the Demonstration Protection Act, I expect they won't be able to disrupt our plans.'

The Demonstration Protection Act of 2022 had been rushed through in the aftermath of the Melbourne GPO bombing. The Fitzwilliams government had announced the cessation of direct mail delivery for standard letters. The usual suspects—those redundant categories of the elderly and ABC Radio listeners—had mustered in one of their lost-cause protests. Unfortunately for the greyhairs present, their protest neatly fitted the category of a soft target. A terrorist blew himself and eight others up right in the middle of their desultory chant:

Megaphone: What do we want?

Crowd (out of sync): Postal letter direct delivery!

Megaphone: When do we—

Ironically, the explosive belt was delivered to the terrorist by parcel post only the day before.

The massacre created outrage and Prime Minister Fitzwilliams rose to the occasion. He spoke movingly of a nation unbowed and of the fundamental right of Australians to free speech. His speechwriter had him cite Voltaire and he vowed that his government would defend every Australian's right to protest. He concluded with an improvised clenched-fist shout of: 'Two, four, six, eight, Australians still will demonstrate!' That image had been emblazoned onto t-shirts, a rare feat for a Liberal prime minister. It was an outstanding performance considering the Prime Minister truly loathed demonstrations and demonstrators.

Olga O'Rourke, then attorney-general, had crafted the legislation. After laudable opening first paragraphs citing fundamental rights came the reams of protection clauses. To prevent terrorist infiltration of legitimate demonstrations, all participants in a demonstration had to register three weeks ahead of time and undergo police checks (that took four to eight weeks). Once approved, it was necessary to book an appointment for a Demonstration Participant photo ID. Only demonstrators with Demonstration Participant IDs could be admitted into the approved DMZ (Demonstration Mustering Zone). Placards were allowed, but had to be reviewed seventy-two hours in advance by the Protective Office to ensure that the protest signs did not contain material in violation of the Incitement to Terrorism Act of 2021. There would be x-ray security searches of all demonstrators entering the DMZ. The act contained a bewildering host of additional measures. Fitzwilliams was awestruck. Olga O'Rourke might have left the Soviet Union when she was only fifteen, but she had a Brezhnev-era flair for mind-numbing bureaucracy.

The Prime Minister had been utterly sick of ratbag demonstrators. He couldn't invite the most innocuous G20 leader to the country without budgeting for forty thousand hours of police special duty and sealing off half a city centre. The premiers always moaned about it. 'Next time you want to meet with the US president,' the NSW Treasurer had once snarled at him, 'do it in Coober Pedy, not Sydney.'

The legislation, while effusively defending the right to protest, had plunged potential demonstrators into a bureaucratic labyrinth.

So beautifully, she had done this all in the name of protecting them. Anarchists, Trotskyites, hippies—all of them were hopeless at filling out forms. Anyone wanting to organise a mass demonstration would need a staff of administrative assistants to nag these layabouts to bring in their original birth certificates, passports and one hundred points of identification. It would be practically impossible to shepherd everyone through the approval process. Since 2022, nothing controversial had marched the streets of Canberra. And Attorney-General O'Rourke had achieved all this using only the highest-sounding, most principled language.

There was a sound at the door and both the ASIO party and Olga O'Rourke appeared. Seats were shuffled about. Olga produced a package of Scotch Finger biscuits and had trouble tearing it open. Prime Minister Fitzwilliams waited impatiently.

Fiona Brennan currently had a level of public popularity that Fitzwilliams felt ASIO chiefs should not cultivate. He had planned to rebuke her with, 'I thought you'd assured me that the Luddites were just a postmodern joke,' but did not want the comment lost amid the presentation of the biscuits. Then he remembered it hadn't been Fiona Brennan who said that to him but his own appointment, ASIO Director Heinrich, the one who during Senate estimate hearings had so embarrassingly confused their allies in Central Asia with the rogue states of the region.

'There are those,' Brennan began, 'who presumed that the Luddite Party, given its long years of inactivity, was simply a postmodern joke. In 2019, nearly three thousand people changed their names by deed poll to Ned Ludd. They registered as a political party, and then did nothing further. Were they just a joke? Back then, we attempted to find out. Sixteen office staff of ASIO, Renard here among them, changed their names by deed poll to Ned Ludd and applied to join the party. All were accepted.'

'And what have they asked you to do since 2019, Renard?' Olga probed.

Renard shook his head. 'Nothing. Nothing at all. I would get one email per year but it was . . . social.' He hesitated, knowing it would sound silly. 'It was always about the annual movie night.'

The Prime Minister let out a sigh, remembering.

'Once a year we'd receive a message to watch a particular movie. There were no other instructions.'

'What sort of movies?' Langdon asked.

'Any sort. The first year it was *Planet of the Apes*, the next year a Japanese movie based on *King Lear*, then the 2021 reboot of *Predator*, followed by something with Hugh Grant and Sandra Bullock as grandparents that I don't remember the name of.'

'During those years ASIO also conducted surveillance and monitored communications of Luddite party members,' Fiona added.

'And what did you find?' Olga asked.

'I can answer that,' the Prime Minister cut in. 'They found that they spent thirty-six million dollars conducting surveillance on a group of people who did nothing other than hold an annual movie night.' There had been hell to pay for that in the closed-door ASIO review. The PM was obliged to jettison yet another ASIO appointee and distribute a bewildering array of enticements and threats to the Greens MP on the committee to stop her leaking the details.

'Thank you, Prime Minster,' Fiona said sweetly. 'He's right. The surveillance turned up nothing. The Ned Ludds did not communicate with each other in any way we detected. They use their original names for work and life. Only when officially required—passport applications, tax returns and so on—do they use the Ned Ludd name. The Luddite party had no website, did not run any candidates or campaign on any issue. They were silent. We were concerned by this and suspected a black hole connection.'

'What do you mean by black hole?' Lister St John asked.

'The black holes were a variety of unlikely small businesses that were simply off the modern radar,' Fiona explained. 'They first appeared around this time. They typically would have no website, no email address, sometimes not even a telephone. These were places where it was as though the twenty-first century and a good part of the twentieth had never happened. We suspected Compink of setting many of these up.'

No one in the room was comfortable with Compink, the corporate arm of the Communist Party of China. In Compink's early days, ASIO was still able to investigate its activities thoroughly. Since then, it had reregistered as Compink Australia, listed on the ASX and hence was protected from ASIO's prying eyes by the full weight of Australian corporate law, although Fiona Brennan still found ways around that.

'Black holes were obviously security voids,' the ASIO director continued. 'Electronic communication traffic couldn't be monitored, as there was none. Servers couldn't be hacked because they didn't exist. Anything could have been going on there.' She turned towards her junior employee. 'Renard was sent to investigate one, a small "bookshop" in the inner west of Sydney where he introduced himself simply as Ned. It was—' she decided to get the matter out of the way '—part of ASIO's 20:20 Vision initiative.'

The Prime Minister drew in a breath. Fiona Brennan had tossed that out as if she wanted him to comment. He exhaled. 'I'm glad that 20:20 Vision managed to do something other than set off an orgy in the Melbourne financial district.' He had to let something out. It wasn't good to keep such things inside.

'Was there any link to Compink?' Olga asked.

'In some black holes yes, but not in Renard's. Despite its peculiar nature—it sells only books by Dickens and serves gruel—that shop is, remarkably enough, a legitimate business. After 20:20 Vision was abruptly cancelled, Renard continued to monitor the place. On his own time,' she added, lest someone wanted to defend the taxpayer and his or her dollar. 'Nothing of interest to ASIO ever emerged from the bookshop until last week. A letter had been dropped off for Renard in anticipation of his dining there. The letter,' she said, donning her glasses, 'reads: *Prepare. We shall run in the upcoming election and we intend to win. Yours, Ned Ludd.*'

Fiona handed the sheet to Russ Langdon, who looked at it briefly then passed it to the Prime Minister.

'Since this letter arrived,' Fiona resumed, 'the Luddites have done two things—well, possibly more, but so far we have detected only two. First, they have set up a website.'

'That seems a contradiction,' the Prime Minister observed. 'Luddites aren't supposed to like technology.'

'Not necessarily, Prime Minister,' Olga corrected him. 'The historical Luddites, those in 1812 and 1813, were selective. They didn't oppose all machinery. In Nottinghamshire, for instance, they smashed only a specific new device: a wide-frame, stocking-making machine that produced a second-rate product. They feared the production of inferior stockings would ruin the entire trade.

2028

It was a form of quality control, if I might use a twenty-first century expression, conducted by the workers themselves.'

The Prime Minister gave her his how-do-you-know-these-things? look.

'High school course on Pre-Bolshevik Working-Class Movements,' she told the room. 'The Luddites may want us to see them the way you think of them—as people too inept to learn to work common devices such as Gargantuans and Genie phones—but that may be a red . . .' she paused to recall which fish the English phrase required, 'herring.'

'What's with the Ned Ludd name?' Langdon asked. 'I take it Ned is a reference to Ned Kelly. What's the Ludd part supposed to mean?'

Olga shook her head. 'Not our famous bushranger. Ned Ludd is also historical. The Luddites used to send threatening letters to the stocking manufacturers telling them to dismantle their wide-frame machines or else. They always signed them Ned Ludd. Ned Ludd did not exist and anyone could write a letter in his name. Having a fictitious leader caused the authorities great difficulty when they attempted to track down the actual ringleaders.'

'The Luddite website,' Fiona prompted, trying to nudge the conversation back into the current century. She motioned to Renard who clicked on his Gargantuan. The screen in the room lit up with the Luddite Party homepage. It had a mundane banner heading: *The Luddite Party of Australia.* Underneath was an old map of Australia, probably drawn by one of the earliest European explorers. Only the west coast of Australia was clearly defined, with the eastward projections of the continent tailing off, unknown. Across the expanse of the Australian continent were scrawled the words: *Here be dragons.*

Lister St John was someone who truly believed his time was money. 'Why are you wasting my time?' he demanded. 'Surely we don't have to respond to a party as fucking ridiculous as this.'

'What else is on the website?' Langdon asked.

'Nothing.' Fiona pressed her hands together. 'There are no tabs, no links, no party platform, no place to donate money to the cause.'

'A postmodern joke,' the Prime Minister offered reluctantly. He had never really understood what postmodernism was supposed to be. Now that retro-postmodernism was around, he was even less sure.

'Perhaps,' Fiona conceded, 'but now we come to the second thing they've done: organise two demonstrations. There has been sophisticated planning behind them. All the paperwork was correctly submitted two months ago, all the demonstration participant photo IDs issued, all the placards filed with the Protective Office for inspection and redistribution tomorrow. Without our knowing it, Ned Ludds around the country registered quietly for these demonstrations.'

'How could you not have known of this?' Fitzwilliams demanded, unsure whether he had fired the question at the ASIO director or his Minister for Security and Freedom.

'They registered at different Protective Offices around the country. No one picked up on it.' Fiona opened her hands in apology. 'Most people working in the Protective Offices are hired for their bureaucratic officiousness, not their inquisitiveness. The enrolments of any demonstration are tabulated online. These demonstrations are small. ASIO is only alerted when a demonstration exceeds twenty-five people enrolled. A cost-saving measure,' she offered lamely. 'Tomorrow there are thirteen in the first demonstration and nineteen in the evening one.'

34

Across the table, Russ Langdon blinked at the announcement of the two prime numbers.

Olga leaned back in her chair, stroking her chin slowly. 'But there are still the security searches. The kind of people the Protective Office employs can drag out the security searches at the entrance to the mustering area. They can make sure the demonstration doesn't take place on time.'

'After Renard received the letter last week, we immediately stepped up surveillance on all known Neds, those who changed their names back in 2019,' Fiona Brennan outlined. 'They still don't use email to communicate, nor do they discuss their plans on the phone. To date, we have intercepted only one message between Luddites regarding the demonstration.'

'How did you get that?' Langdon queried.

The director hesitated, clearly embarrassed. 'The message was dispatched by pigeon—insufficiently trained, it seems. Someone found it hobbling around Parramatta Park and took it to a vet. She detached the message and contacted us.'

'We're worried about a group that uses messenger pigeons?' Lister St John asked the room incredulously.

Fiona raised her eyebrows. 'The message from the pigeon indicates that the Luddites intend to march in the nude.'

There was silence. The Prime Minister immediately looked at Olga for her reaction. Her mouth was open, but her dark brown eyes were darting busily. Suddenly, she sat bolt upright and a curious smile appeared on her face. Then she relaxed back in her chair and chuckled softly. In the stillness of the room, the chuckle seemed to reverberate.

'What is so fucking funny?' Lister St John demanded.

Olga seemed almost admiring of the Luddites and their plans. 'It's brilliant. There's nothing to search. The Protective Office can have them step through the x-ray machine at most. It won't delay them sufficiently.'

'Are you saying they're allowed to parade naked?' Lister asked. 'They aren't allowed to parade about fucking naked!' he shouted at her, suspecting she was going to give him the wrong answer.

'Stop swearing, Mr St John.' She held up a finger. 'Prime Minister, I apologise. The Luddites have found a weakness in the Demonstration Protection Act I did not know was there.'

Lister St John couldn't decide between incredulity and fury and opted for both. 'Don't let this Russian tell you that they can parade about fucking—' Olga fixed him with a glare '—parade about naked,' he compromised, losing the momentum. 'That can't be legal!'

'I'll explain simply why they can and will, Mr St John,' Olga replied. 'When we framed the Demonstration Protection Act, we lavished on it all sorts of fundamental rights to cover every minority opinion we could. The obstacles we put in the way of their demonstrations were purely bureaucratic. We devised the protective clauses of the legislation to eliminate large demonstrations, the kind where you have three thousand people shouting obscenities—' here Olga fixed her eyes on Lister St John again '—throwing stones at the police and trying to storm our meeting places. The Demonstration Protection Act enshrined many rights and the act supersedes many other laws in effect, in this case the public decency laws.'

Prime Minister Fitzwilliams could not believe it. 'Surely not,' was all he could manage to say.

'One of the clauses in the opening part of the legislation concerns attire. What was in the public mind then was a fixation about burqas. Some in the community believed a person with a burqa could conceal a veritable arsenal of weapons and bombs beneath those robes. Many people, including radio host Jim Jarvis, wanted them banned you'll recall, Prime Minister. The Demonstration Protection Act did the contrary. We enshrined the right of attire. Demonstrators had the right to wear anything they wanted. What we did do, however, was make security searches mandatory, security searches that could be of such an intrusive level that no one who wore a burqa would ever submit to such humiliation. Problem solved. Bureaucratically perfect. What the Luddites have done is appreciate the full possibilities of the attire clause. They are exploiting the uni-directional nature of the pro-cedural measures.'

'I'm sorry,' Russ Langdon said. 'You've lost me there.'

'The enshrinement of the right of attire of one's choice is unconditional, broad enough that, in tomorrow's case, it covers even a total lack of attire. The procedural measures we put in go in only one direction; they are designed to make people take clothes off, not put them on. There is no security measure required for nudity. We can make them walk through the x-ray machine to ensure they haven't swallowed a bomb—or worse—but for thirteen demonstrators and nineteen demonstrators, that won't take much time.'

'Bloody fucking hell!' Lister slammed his fist on the table. 'I'm not having us call an election in front of a bunch of nudists! We have everything ready to roll for tomorrow and I won't have it wrecked by these clothes-deprived gits with their fucking dragons and fucking pigeons. The media!' he despaired. 'They're going to fucking love this!'

'Lister!' Fitzwilliams summoned his parliamentary question time tone. 'Try not to go entirely to pieces on Day Zero of the election campaign.'

Langdon shook his head. 'It won't be such a media hoo-ha. Any naturist would tell you that nudity quickly becomes quite routine. The media will find that people having no clothes on isn't all that sensational.'

The Prime Minister's inner alarm system had gone off at the word 'naturist'. Naturist? No one used that word for nudists, not unless they were a bloody nudist themselves. Fitzwilliams didn't want to think about Langdon at a nudist colony. God, he thought, there better not be any photos.

'What planet are you from?' St John demanded of Langdon. 'We're talking about public nudity. Of course the media is going to love it. It'll be a feeding frenzy!'

'I suspect Lister is right,' Fiona chimed in. While the original three thousand or so people who renamed themselves Ned Ludd are of all shapes and sizes, the thirty-two registered demonstrators tomorrow appear to have been selected for their, er, athletic fitness, shall we say. They won't be hard on the eyes,' she predicted. 'There is not much more ASIO can contribute here, Prime Minister. I have arranged the paperwork for Renard, under the name Ned Ludd, to attend the demonstration tomorrow as an additional demonstrator.'

'What?' Renard squeaked softly.

'I was going to tell you later, Renard.' Fiona smiled at him. 'After that,' she informed the Prime Minister, 'we'll be limited in how much more we can help. The Luddites will be running in this election. ASIO cannot be at the disposal of one party against another during an election. The Luddites may be utterly secretive, but that in itself is not an offence. At this point, there is nothing to indicate that they are engaged in subversive activities.'

'They are bloody well trying to subvert our event tomorrow,' Lister St John snarled.

'That is a political inconvenience for you; it is not an ASIO matter,' the director responded primly. 'Renard attending tomorrow is purely a prudent bit of information-gathering. That is all ASIO will do. The agency must remain politically neutral.'

Prime Minister Fitzwilliams felt numb. Normally, he liked to dismiss the self-assured Fiona Brennan from a meeting with a curt, 'You may go.' He let her go this time with a simple wave of his hand.

Fiona paused at the door. 'One thing, Prime Minister. I wish to stress that the Luddites appear to have known exactly when you were planning to call the election.' She smiled. 'It is not necessarily my business—but you have a leak.' She closed the door behind her.

• • •

Prime Minister Fitzwilliams wanted his last campaign to be simple. Everything was in place. His cabinet team was adequate, familiar to the electorate. The economy was solid. The howling protest of the doctors after the GP changes had finally died down. He would retire after this one. He deserved an easy election. Instead he was feeling dazed before the campaign had even begun.

There was silence in the room after the ASIO pair had left. The others were waiting for him to speak, Fitzwilliams realised. 'I . . .' he began.

'What the fuck are we going to do?' Lister demanded.

With each successive campaign, the Prime Minister had come to dislike Lister St John more. Balding, vain, crude . . . Why had balding sprung to mind? he wondered. Hardly a character flaw and Lister St John had no shortage of proper ones to list. No matter what was decided here, Fitzwilliams would be the one to decide it. Whatever Lister proposed doing, he would veto.

Another thought popped into his head and settled there. This was his last election. He was never going to need to be re-elected. He could fire Lister St John. He'd wait until a few days out from the vote, haul Lister St John into his office and sack him. 'But we're ahead,' he could imagine St John whining. 'You misunderstand,' he would reply, 'I'm sacking you not because of the job you've done; I'm sacking you because you're an objectionable human being.'

'Well?' Lister demanded again. 'Say something. You're just sitting there and this one over here—' he indicated Olga O'Rourke '—is smiling like the Cheshire cat.'

Fitzwilliams shifted into decisive mode. 'I'll delay the announcement of the election until six pm. At three thirty the Luddites will have their smaller demonstration. Nudity near parliament will be treated as a bit of titillation, and back at the networks they'll be swearing away at all the pixilating they'll have to do. Though the delay means we miss the election call being the lead story on the evening news, we get to interrupt the news at six instead.'

'That might be even better,' Langdon put in.

The Prime Minister smiled. There were times when it was good to have a Russ Langdon around. He continued, 'Following my announcement, I'll answer twenty minutes of questions and then head directly to the cabinet rally outside parliament at seven. The media will be scrambling at that point, so when a second sorry little gang of nudists shows up demanding extra time on their fifteen minutes of fame, they'll be ignored. Sure, they'll make a ripple on the internet. Any bit of nudity will, but between six and seven thirty pm, we will be the story!' Fitzwilliams leaned back, satisfied.

Lister St John was reserving the right to disapprove, but hadn't thought out an alternative plan. The Prime Minister looked at Olga O'Rourke. While the Cheshire cat allusion had been an exaggeration, Olga did have a slight smile on her face. 'What do you think, Olga?' he asked. 'You seem oddly satisfied with the turn of events.'

'Labor are an inept opposition and the Greens are in bankruptcy proceedings,' she observed. 'It was going to be a boring campaign. The Luddites are intriguing.'

The Prime Minister had been looking forward to a boring campaign.

'The actions of the Luddites show some shrewdness,' Olga observed. 'We have no idea about them as a political party. They may still be a joke.' She smiled again. 'Or we may have a formidable opponent on our hands. I might say at this point, "The game's afoot, Watson."'

'What do you think of my plan for tomorrow then?' the PM asked tentatively.

'I cannot say.' She appeared to be deep in thought. 'This is an unexpected opening move from an opponent we didn't know we were playing. Normally, one would want to consider all our options carefully before responding, but they have left us no time for that. We must move. The clock is ticking. We must ask our-selves, how do they expect us to react? Their next thrust is planned in anticipation of that.'

'Good God!' Lister St John exclaimed. 'We're supposed to be running an election campaign here and this one thinks she's fucking Garry Kasparov.'

Olga shot to her feet. Before anyone could react, she'd grabbed Lister by his shirt and yanked his face in front of hers. 'Don't you ever,' she hissed through her teeth, 'say a foul word in front of the name of Garry Kasparov again!' She released her grip, throwing him back into the chair.

Fitzwilliams' mouth was agape. He felt an entirely inappropri-ate glow of enjoyment at Olga's rough handling of his campaign manager. He snapped himself back to attention. 'Yes,' he piped up chirpily. 'That's an easy enough instruction, Lister. Don't ever say a foul word in front of the name of Garry Kasparov again. Chess grandmasters deserve respect.'

St John seemed temporarily stunned. Bullies often were when confronted, Fitzwilliams reflected. It was so perfect a moment, the Prime Minister couldn't resist closing on that note. 'Thank you all for coming,' he said, as if everything had gone swimmingly. He stood up and left the room.

It was only much later that he recalled they had not discussed the leak.

CHAPTER THREE

Renard Prendergast was in the Demonstration Mustering Zone outside Parliament House, and he was naked. The last twenty-four hours, he reflected, had been unusual to say the least.

Fiona Brennan's declaration to the Prime Minister that Renard would be joining the thirteen nude Luddites at the first demonstration had taken him completely by surprise. The discussion afterwards in Fiona Brennan's office had been surreal. The director had cajoled him, not ordered him, to do it. She had sat there like an encouraging grandparent. 'I appreciate the regular work you do for ASIO, but this assignment is something different. It's out and about. You'll meet people.' Meet people? She made it sound as if she was concerned he had no social life. He had plenty of social life. His friends would think this hilarious, his girlfriend Taylor probably less so. 'You have a fine body, Renard,' Fiona assured him. 'You shouldn't be shy about showing it off.'

He tried pointing out the obvious flaw in her plan. 'The Luddites have scheduled thirteen marchers. I may have changed my name to Ned Ludd nine years ago and joined the party, but when I show up to the demonstration tomorrow uninvited with all my paperwork mysteriously done, they're going to know I'm a plant.'

'That's true,' Fiona conceded. 'But it's a one-off thing tomorrow. Find out what you can. That's all we are asking.' Fiona believed that the Luddites had intended for their messenger pigeon to be discovered. They apparently wanted the Prime Minister to know what they had planned. That ASIO hadn't discovered the Luddite's actual communication system most likely meant they kept internal communications to a minimum. 'Those attending the demonstration tomorrow will likely only know their assignment for the day. They won't necessarily know each other.' The Luddite leadership would quickly finger Renard as an ASIO spy, but those there on the day might not. It was Renard's chance to find out something. When the director had followed this up with a 'Please?' Renard heard his own voice agreeing to do it. He would have sworn he was only mulling it over.

At the demonstration assembly point, Renard quietly joined the small group of Luddites undressing. When Fiona Brennan had summoned him to Canberra, he hadn't considered it important which underwear he shoved into his overnight bag. He was, he grimaced, wearing the novelty pair his sister had given him for Christmas with the image of Wonder Woman emblazoned on the crotch. Getting totally naked was somehow preferable to letting the world see this embarrassing pair of underpants.

The Luddites were well organised. A Luddite arrived in a van and distributed boxes for the demonstrators to store their clothing in. He also produced all the paperwork for the Protective Office. Inside the DMZ, Protective Office officials grudgingly released the Luddite placards that had been duly submitted for approval days earlier. The placards met all compliance standards. The sticks the signs were mounted on were the regulation collapsible kind that would break if anyone tried to swing one against riot police. The Demonstration Protection Act, after all, was designed only to protect demonstrators against terrorists, not against the police should the coppers decide a particular demonstration needed busting up. Renard took a placard. There was absolutely nothing written on it.

What Fiona had told the Prime Minister was true. The assembled Luddites looked like a meeting of Olympic athletes. He'd never seen such a fit-looking group of people, or a group so handsome. However, what Security and Freedom Minister Langdon had said was also true: being naked with a group of naked people made it seem . . . natural, which Renard supposed it was. He felt oddly confident and, if he were honest with himself, even excited to be there.

There was little conversation. Everyone was waiting for three thirty pm to arrive.

'Hi, I'm Ned Ludd,' one of the protestors said to him, extending her hand.

'Ned Ludd. Pleased to meet you,' he replied.

That had been it for introductions with all of them. One Ned Ludd told him she had been designated to give the speech. The others were to go up to the microphone afterwards simply to introduce themselves and say which electorate they were running in.

'Hey, Neds!' one of them called suddenly. 'Pick up your placards. It's showtime.'

• • •

Jesse Pelletier's twenty years as a parliamentary camera operator had seen a steady erosion of the profession. When he started, they had shouldered heavy cameras, cameras people respected. His current one weighed hardly anything. He was freelance by necessity, all the permanent jobs with the networks having long gone. They used to work in threes, all permanent employees: the reporter, the camera and the sound boom. Back then, they could attack in numbers, the press corps surrounding a cabinet minister with a ring of equipment and a barrage of questions. Now you had to be all three yourself, working the camera while shouting questions at the cabinet minister and wearing the silly little headband with a mini directional microphone sticking out.

Gunnar lumbered over to him. Another freelancer, Gunnar had once been Jesse's sound man. Technically, they were competitors, but they couldn't help working together.

'Something's definitely up,' Gunnar announced. 'Nobody is in the parliamentary cafeteria.' All the cabinet had come to parliament that day but had made themselves scarce, none of them venturing out of their offices. The Prime Minister had called a press conference for six.

Jesse surveyed the sky. 'At least there are no drones about,' he observed.

When Australia Post had ceased letter delivery and become a parcel-post-only service, few had anticipated that the antiquated government service would stand a chance against the big international private delivery companies. Australia Post had surprised everyone. First, they replaced their entire delivery staff with a drone fleet. If you had a parcel to deliver, a small drone appeared at your door, the largest in the fleet capable of carrying fifteen kilograms. You logged the job online and when the drone showed up, you just loaded the item onto it and stuck in your credit card.

Then came a series of major media signings for Drone Feed on Demand. For a price, Australia Post agreed to divert its drones to any news site a network wanted covered. If a train derailed, spilling diethyltoluene across the Pacific Highway, a drone carrying the package of your Aunt Emily's Anzac biscuits would divert straight to it. Drones could get to the scene of a news flash faster than any reporter/camera operator. They could dodge in and out of landslides, bushfires and floods. The networks made all their news photographers and camera operators redundant and used freelancers for indoor events. The drones were reviled by camera operators but loved by the moguls, who noted that drones never chucked a sickie because they were hungover. Then a drone found that photogenic lost child and her even more adorable puppy in the Blue Mountains while the press corps was back drinking in a Katoomba pub. It was strictly a rearguard action for the camera operators from then on as they scrabbled for meagre employment as freelancers.

Gunnar nudged him. 'What's that?'

Jesse squinted. If he had to guess, he would have said it was a group of naked people marching with placards. Both men leaped to their feet in sync.

'You beam to Network Nine and I'll take Seven!' Jesse shouted.

Gunnar looked up as he ran towards the marchers. Not a drone in the sky. He cackled delightedly.

• • •

'Chief, you better have a look at this!'

Allison Trang looked across the newsroom and did a double take. On a screen, a nude woman was approaching a microphone. Behind her was a group of nude people with placards. All of them were smiling. All of them looked—it wasn't a newsroom sort of word—beautiful. She strode over. 'What is this? That's Parliament House behind them!' she exclaimed, pointing at the screen.

'That feed is coming from Jesse Pelletier,' the technician answered.

'Get me the audio,' Allison ordered. 'Quickly!'

The woman looked improbably dignified for someone standing naked outside parliament. A crowd had gathered around the group, including a dumbfounded high school excursion.

'Hello,' the woman said. 'I'm Ned Ludd of the Luddite Party of Australia and a candidate in the Melbourne electorate of Wills. This afternoon, Prime Minister Fitzwilliams visited the Governor-General to request that parliament be dissolved and a general election be held on Saturday, 6 May. The Luddite Party will be running candidates in every electorate—'

'Can anyone confirm?' Allison shouted to the rest of the room. 'Has there been an election called?'

'The PM's office isn't answering,' someone called back.

Luddites! Allison could hardly believe it. The Luddite story had been nearly ten years ago and she'd heard nothing about the party since. Now there were nude Luddites outside Parliament House—and they were calling an election!

There was a shriek from another phone. 'Confirmation from a contact at the Governor-General's. The PM left there five minutes ago. She doesn't know what was discussed, but the PM was just there!'

Allison turned her attention back to the woman on the screen. 'The Luddites want this election to be a genuine national debate. For that to happen, we must put an end to the meaningless style of election campaigns that Labor and the Liberal–National Coalition have perfected with their carefully manicured events, their policy sifted through focus groups, their slick advertising. During an election, the major parties follow every nuance of the polls to figure out which issues and policies are working for them and what issues to downplay. Let's prevent them from indulging in that game this time.'

'She's good on telly,' the technician whispered. 'I mean, I wasn't even looking at her tits when she was speaking then.'

'I'm asking all Australians,' the woman continued, 'no matter what party you actually support, to tell pollsters you're planning to vote for the Coalition. If everyone says the same thing, the polls will no longer indicate voter intention. Neither of the major parties will be able to tell what's working for them and what isn't. If pollsters ask you what issues are important to you, tell them all issues are important. If you are asked to be in a focus group, tell them you support all the government's policies regardless of what you truly think. Let's have an election not on what the major parties' polling data indicate will succeed for them, but on what ideas they have to present to this country.'

Allison Trang could feel the seconds ticking by. She glanced over at the screens that displayed what other news stations were covering. None of them had the Luddites on. She took several short breaths. 'Interrupt regular programming!' she instructed. 'Insert this clip from the beginning of her speech and just put underneath it: *Live—outside Parliament House, Canberra.*'

'It'll take fifteen minutes to pixilate all this,' the technician protested.

'No pixilation!' she ordered. 'Send it direct. I'll wear any complaints.' She gazed again at the group on the screen. It must be their smiles. This wasn't lewd. There was the multicultural mix of all Australia standing there nude and looking . . . well, just lovely really. 'Anyone who complains about this,' she declared grandly, 'doesn't love humanity.'

The newsroom staff weren't used to dealing with such lofty sentiments, but there were nods from around the room nonetheless.

'There she goes,' the technician exclaimed, punching in the feed from parliament to stream.

• • •

'I've prepared a kit for every member of cabinet,' the PM's staffer explained. 'The kits contain every ribbon or item that will be necessary during the campaign and detailed instructions for action-related days.'

This sort of thing was important, Fitzwilliams acknowledged, but the list grew depressingly longer with each election. It was to be only a six-week campaign and yet there were twenty-seven special days that needed noting. He'd never heard of some of the charities and causes on the list. 'National Prevention of Scrapie Day?' he asked.

'A fatal disease affecting the central nervous system of sheep,' the staffer replied. 'The Minister for Agriculture will play the lead that day. You'll note that the Woolly White ribbon we've issued is made of genuine merino wool,' she added proudly. 'Most are synthetic.'

There were twenty ribbons inside the kit. The demand for colours by charities and research foundations far exceeded the visible spectrum's ability to provide them. Were 'avocado' and 'fawn' really colours? Fitzwilliams wondered. At least the kit contained no clown noses or pirate hats.

'What,' he asked with slight trepidation, 'is Walk Like an Egyptian Day?'

'Research into Tropical Diseases.'

Egypt isn't even in the tropics, Fitzwilliams noted, but supposed that hardly mattered. 'I guess I should have asked *how* rather than *what*. How do you walk like an Egyptian?' It sounded potentially offensive, perhaps racist.

'Oh, it's a bit of fun.' The staffer smiled encouragingly; she had picked up on his lack of enthusiasm. 'Like in the hieroglyphics.' She stood up to demonstrate. 'You turn your hands at the wrist, perpendicular to the forearm and make little jutting motions.' She bobbed a few times to demonstrate and gave him her best you-can-do-it-too look.

With global warming, tropical diseases research was increasingly important and the more money the public gave for research, the less the government had to. Although tiresome, it was important to pay attention to such special days. Forget one and you'd absentmindedly offend a swathe of voters. The staffer's work on this was commendably thorough and she was looking at him so eagerly. He'd give the ancient Egyptian posture a go.

As he rose from his chair and bent his wrists, an urgent clumping sounded in the hall. The door was flung wide open. There stood Russ Langdon, looking wild-eyed.

'Prime Minister!' he exclaimed. 'Come to the media room! Now!'

Fitzwilliams stared. Langdon did not usually give him orders. 'Come!' Langdon implored. 'You need to see this.'

The three hustled to the media room. The media room had twelve screens, each monitoring a different news network. Olga O'Rourke was already there. She shot the Prime Minister a worried glance.

'What's going on?' Fitzwilliams asked.

'Network Seven is broadcasting the Luddite march,' Olga answered. 'No pixilation.' She pointed at another screen. 'Nine's switched to it!' she gasped. Other screens were cutting to the march outside Parliament House. A nude woman was speaking before a microphone.

'It's four in the afternoon!' Fitzwilliams exclaimed incredulously. 'The networks can't be showing full-frontal nudity!'

All twelve screens were now broadcasting the Luddite demonstration. Even Aunty. Fitzwilliams sighed. Couldn't the ABC have been more prudish?

'Give us the audio of Seven,' Olga called to a staffer.

'. . . the Luddite Party has no fondness for public nudity,' the naked woman on the screen announced. 'We demonstrated this way today because it's the only way we, the Australian public, can demonstrate in front of our own parliament. If we had been clothed, we would still be queued at the mustering area being individually searched by the Protective Office. The Demonstration Protection Act of this government makes it virtually impossible to have your say and your clothes on at the same time.'

A soft rumble came from Olga O'Rourke's throat.

'When you vote on May sixth . . .' the nude woman continued.

'They've announced the election!' Langdon squealed. 'The Luddites have told the nation before we have!'

'We've got to account for that,' Olga said urgently. She turned to Fitzwilliams. 'You left the Governor-General's at three, yet only scheduled the press conference for six. Why wouldn't you have told the Australian people immediately?'

On the screen, another nude woman stepped in front of the microphone. 'Hello, I'm Ned Ludd, the Luddite candidate for Denison.' A nude man stepped forward. Fitzwilliams recognised Fiona Brennan's ASIO agent from the day before. 'I'm Ned Ludd. I'm not a candidate in this election, but I'll be working with Ned Ludd, who couldn't be here today, to help her win the electorate of Sydney!'

'What could the Prime Minister have been doing in the interim?' Olga put the question to everyone in the room. 'Something important.'

There was silence. 'Sport,' Russ Langdon murmured. 'The Australian people will understand if it's sport-related.'

'There's no sporting event I can rush off to at four in the afternoon,' Fitzwilliams told him.

'Not spectator sports,' Langdon answered back, becoming excited. 'You're off doing a sport. Don't you see?'

'Frankly, no,' Fitzwilliams answered meekly.

'You call the election and then go off and do this sport for two hours before showering and coming back fresh to the press conference to call the election. People will admire that!' Russ Langdon was clearly taken with the idea. 'Like Sir Francis Drake finishing his game of bowls when the Spanish Armada sailed into the Channel.'

Olga nodded. 'It's good,' she assessed. 'Not bowls; that's an old person's sport. We should not draw attention to your age, Prime Minister. Roslyn Stanfield's twenty years younger than you. Not golf either. Not active enough.'

'I like swimming,' Fitzwilliams offered, feeling he should contribute something.

Olga shook her head. 'Harold Holt. Bad connotations.'

'Tennis?' the PM suggested. 'I played a lot as a young man. I still play occasionally.'

'Tennis,' Olga agreed. 'With a cabinet colleague. Happy team. Works together, plays together—a bit competitive, but a sense of fun.'

'Russ . . .' the Prime Minister began.

'You can't play me!' Langdon exclaimed. 'Thrashing someone with an artificial leg is not a good look, Prime Minister.'

'Not you!' Fitzwilliams snapped. 'I'll play Olga. That's a good image. PM plays sport with women. Active ageing, if you'll pardon me saying so, Olga. Friendly hit around. Relaxed.' He pointed to Langdon. 'What I want you to do is leak it to the press after we get there. The media will come scrambling about, but we'll continue playing, Olga. Shake hands. Saunter over to the press and say, "Why, yes, there is an election on."'

'Francis Drake!' Russ Langdon cheered, raising a clenched fist.

• • •

54

Australia Post drones were approaching, but Jesse Pelletier knew they were too bloody late. He and Gunnar—human, living, breathing camera operators—had covered the story before they could.

The Luddite demonstration was on the verge of breaking up, but Jesse did not want the moment to end. 'Gunnar . . .' He tugged at his colleague's sleeve. 'We interview this lot ourselves. On-screen reporting. Don't go to studio link.'

The drill whenever a freelance camera found a story was to serve up the feed to a network studio and let one of their overpaid presenters interview the person remotely. The system stank.

'We rotate,' Jesse proposed. 'I interview two of the Luddites with you filming me and then I film you interviewing them. Either the networks pick up our stream or they get nothing.' He felt giddy. All the normal rules, not just the clothes, were off.

Gunnar produced an old-style microphone from his satchel.

'You still carry one of those?' Jesse marvelled.

'Always live my life in hope, man.'

'That's so fucking retro cool,' Jesse said. He hadn't felt this pumped up since he'd filmed Senator Bolen's campaign interview back when the networks still paid camera operators to travel. The American senator had drawn his gun on the interviewer. That had been live, adrenalin live.

The crowd was still gathered around the Luddites. The previously mesmerised high school students had collected their wits enough to start taking selfies. Gunnar peeled two of the Luddites away from the crowd. Jesse quickly set up the interview, stepped between the two Luddites and readied himself. It had been so long. 'How does my hair look?' he asked Gunnar.

'No one's going to be looking at your hair, man.'

Jesse focused his gaze on the camera. 'Hello, this is Jesse Pelletier coming to you live from outside Parliament House at the launch of the Luddite Party 2028 election campaign. With me is Ned Ludd. Ned, you said you'll be campaigning on behalf of Ned Ludd.'

'Yes,' Renard confirmed. 'For Ned Ludd, in her electorate of Sydney.' He didn't know whether the Luddites had a man or a woman running in his electorate but he'd said 'her electorate' before so it was best to stick with it.

'And also with me is Ned Ludd from the electorate of Wills in Victoria. Ned, you delivered the main speech at the Luddite launch. Are we right to assume that you're the leader of the party?'

Aggie Posniak, the Ned Ludd who delivered the election announcement to the nation, felt things were off to a good start. This interview was an added bonus. 'The Luddite Party doesn't have just one leader,' she explained to Jesse. 'Luddite candidates represent a wide range of views and I can't claim to speak for all Luddites. What is important is to have a parliament that represents, and can debate sensibly, the diverse range of views on important issues.'

Jesse turned back to Renard. 'Ned, the placard you're still holding has absolutely nothing written on it. Why is that?'

'The Luddite Party doesn't run on slogans. The blank placard indicates everything is open to be debated,' Renard answered without hesitation. Yesterday he'd been nervous about meeting the Prime Minister. Today, naked, being interviewed by the national media and improvising the political strategy of a party he didn't know, he felt weirdly composed. 'I urge you all to get to know your local Luddite candidate,' he recommended. 'Let your Luddite candidate know what you think.' Picking up a theme he thought he'd understood from the other Ned's launch speech, he finished, 'Let's figure out together what we want to do with this country.'

Aggie gave him a nod. 'And don't forget, Australia,' she added, 'if a pollster calls, tell them you're voting for the Liberal–National Coalition. It is vital—' Gunnar, with a camera operator's instinct, zoomed in for a close-up of the Melbourne Ned's face '—to make the polls useless to the major parties. Force them to stop trying to manipulate the electorate and to stop bombarding us with slogans and catchphrases. Let's have a campaign on ideas this time!'

'Cut!' Gunnar called.

'Cut?' Jesse cried. 'I didn't even get to sign off.'

'Stream it now,' Gunnar ordered. 'It's my turn. Quick, before the networks get a drone in place.'

Aggie grinned at Renard. The day appeared to be going incredibly well for the Luddites. She gave him a quick high five as the journalists exchanged places. Renard beamed inside. There weren't any metadata analysis days like this.

Gunnar stepped between them. 'This is Gunnar Sigurdsson outside Parliament House . . .' he began.

• • •

Prime Minister Fitzwilliams stepped onto the tennis court, racquet in hand. Olga O'Rourke was dressed all in white. Her shorts revealed trim but muscular legs. At fifty-eight years old, she was still fit and Fitzwilliams was proud that he'd kept himself trim too. There was nothing more awkward than a portly prime minister discussing the obesity crisis.

The tennis court came with an added bonus; local primary school kids, still in their uniforms, were having tennis lessons on the adjacent courts. It would make a nice backdrop.

He would feign surprise when the press told him the Luddites had pipped his election announcement. 'Well, I guess they got a two-hour jump on me,' he would tell the reporters good-naturedly.

Olga surveyed the sky for drones. 'Let's have a quick hit around before they arrive. Get a feel for how to play.' They had already texted Langdon to leak to the networks where they were. Olga arced her back and served. Fitzwilliams stroked it back cleanly. There had been nothing on the serve. He would take it easy on Olga. Playing for fun. That was the image to convey.

Olga returned a smart shot to his backhand. He got it and she sent back his return with one that stretched him to his forehand. He managed to get to it, but only to send a lob straight to her. He expected her to smash it, but she held back on slamming it down, putting it to his backhand again, this time further away. He got to it, but barely. She caught his weak return in her hand.

Olga scrutinised him carefully. 'You were very fast as a young man, weren't you?'

'I was,' he admitted modestly. Fitzwilliams had been a natural-born sprinter. Speed was his biggest asset in all the sports he had played.

'You need to position yourself better,' Olga told him bluntly. 'When you were young, you made up for your lack of tactics by being fast.' She looked at him, not unkindly. 'You are no longer young, Prime Minister. You're sixty-four. You're not fast anymore. You need to be sharper. Position yourself cleverly.' Then, as if his hurt was visible on his face, she added, 'I am just calibrating how we should play, so that we both come off looking good when the cameras arrive.'

'It's okay,' Fitzwilliams said. Olga's advice might sometimes sound harsh, but it was always professional. Maybe it was because English was her second language that she missed the subtleties of tact. Or maybe it was just how Russians spoke to each other. It was certainly how the Russian president always spoke to Fitzwilliams.

Two drones were approaching and a car also pulled up with reporters, Fitzwilliams noted with satisfaction. They didn't often leave the studios nowadays. 'Let's play,' he said, grinning at Olga.

The game was delightful. A frisky pace, some lively rallies, laughing at the occasional flubbed shot. His two bodyguards obligingly retrieved the stray balls. Fitzwilliams was surprised at how much fun he was having. More and more reporters arrived. They were calling questions to him from the other side of the tennis court mesh. He ignored them and played on. The media could always tell when they had become part of their own story and sportingly went along with it. He imagined the report: '*The Prime Minister kept the whole media corps waiting this afternoon for the election announcement while he and Senator O'Rourke battled it out on the tennis court, the South Australian senator winning two sets to one, 6–4, 2–6, 7–5.*'

They had cropped the outing by telling the first journalist to arrive that the score of the first set was 4–4, saving them eight games of effort. He had let Olga win the final set, sensing instinctively that was the best result. At the net, Olga, much to his astonishment, had kissed him on both cheeks and put a hand on his shoulder as they left the court. They had visited the primary school kids on the adjacent court, posed for a group photo, and then, and only then, had they gone over to talk to the networks.

'Yes,' he told them all. 'This afternoon I requested that the Governor-General dissolve parliament for a general election to be held on 6 May 2028. This government is eager to seek a fourth mandate. I shall meet with cabinet briefly at the new parliamentary Stadlet before we head our separate ways to take our vision for the next three years to the people of Australia.' He was pleased to use the Stadlet, a small outdoor theatre built during his administration. It had won awards for design and had Parliament House as a splendid backdrop.

He shrugged off the many questions about the Luddites. About the nudity. 'You can rest assured I'll be keeping my clothes on during this campaign.' About the Demonstration Protection Act. Fuzzy reply talking about terrorism, safety and the sanctity of free speech. About the Luddites announcing the election before he had. 'They got the jump on me today,' he admitted, 'and have had a two-hour head start on campaigning. Good on them.' He loved being off script. To think he had wanted a boring election. 'Members of the media, if you'll excuse me—' he winked at them all '—I'm in need of a shower.' Perfect!

• • •

Russ Langdon sensed the tension in the room. The cabinet had been rattled by the unexpected Luddite events of the afternoon and the Prime Minister going off script. Langdon thought the latter a triumph, but the cabinet weren't used to the PM improvising.

Not everyone was unsettled. Alan Chandos, the Treasurer, was his usual confident but disquietingly amused self. So well versed he could handle any political situation, it made him inattentive to the worries of others. Donna Hargreaves, the Minister for Health and Ageing, used to fighting her way out of tight situations, was also upbeat. But they were the most capable of the cabinet. The rest needed leadership and the Prime Minister was still not back from his tennis match.

'The weather is changing.' The Minister for Sport and Recreation came away from the window. 'Might rain.'

'Will we still have to go out there if it's raining?' the Minister for Industry, Science and Innovation asked. The Luddites were scheduled to muster at 7.00 pm, their demonstration just one hundred and fifty metres from the Stadlet, where the cabinet would be gathered. Many dreaded a close encounter of the nudist kind. Caution was giving way to fear.

'What are you?' Langdon snapped at them. 'The New Zealand cricket team? Hoping rain will get you off the hook?' They needed to stiffen their sinews. 'There's no need to be afraid of a few naturists!'

'They aren't birdwatchers,' the Minister for Sport retorted. 'They're stark-naked nudists.'

'I said naturist, not naturalists!' Langdon stopped himself. In the Prime Minister's absence, somebody had to calm the horses. Langdon looked to Alan Chandos, but he was oblivious, chuckling over something he was reading. Donna Hargreaves had fought with this cabinet too often to lead them. It would have to be him. 'The Stadlet has an auto-roof,' he reminded them. 'If it rains, the roof goes up. So,' he emphasised, 'you all need to be ready to get out there and do your job.'

'Thank you, Russell.' Prime Minister Fitzwilliams breezed into the room, Olga O'Rourke at his side. The cabinet applauded the

PM's arrival, more in relief than affection he knew, but he basked in it nonetheless. He had wanted to speak to the troops before heading out, but there was no time. 'Let's go,' he said. 'To the Stadlet everyone!'

The Stadlet, with its small stage, was ideal for more casual parliamentary events and that was the tone Fitzwilliams sought tonight. Though casual in function, the Stadlet was built with security in mind. There was a seventy-five-metre perimeter fence with controlled entry points. The Stadlet's auto-roof was reinforced, able to withstand mortar shells if necessary, with state-of-the-art security programming.

The Prime Minister led his cabinet from Parliament House across the grass towards the Stadlet. Each was let through the security point after producing accredited ID. In security matters, nothing was taken for granted.

Fitzwilliams frowned. The media were not as numerous as he had anticipated. There were drones about, but again, not that many. He shifted his gaze over to where the Luddites were gathering. Their Demonstration Mustering Zone was just out of sight, blocked by trees. The Prime Minister could make out drones, a lot of them, circling the area. The Luddites had hewn off part of the media crowd, but there was nothing he could do about that.

A few drops of rain were starting to fall. He motioned two of his staffers to the Stadlet auto-roof control console. 'Be ready to put up the roof if the rain gets any heavier,' he instructed.

At the console, the staffers discovered that the retina scanner for ID recognition was broken. 'Don't worry, Prime Minister— we'll log on manually,' one of them assured him. 'I've done it before.'

The Prime Minister started a standard speech about the team he led, the pride in what they had done in three terms in office, their commitment to Australian values, but he hadn't even got to the pride bit when there was a murmur in the crowd. He shot the quickest of glances towards the Luddites. They had started to march.

'It doesn't like my user ID,' he heard a voice say from offstage.

'Try your Federal Government Employee Number instead,' a second voice suggested.

The rain had picked up but was still only a gentle mist. 'Everyone stay in place,' he heard Langdon hiss behind him. Was the cabinet wavering? Fitzwilliams resumed his speech.

'I'm in,' the voice at the console exhaled with relief. Then: 'Christ! It wants me to change my password.'

The Luddites were clearly visible now. He could make out that they were nude and carrying placards again, just as they had that afternoon.

'Pride in—' he started again.

'Rejected!' came an exasperated voice.

'Try eight characters. Upper case, a number and a punctuation mark.'

The Luddites halted. The rain was becoming heavier. The auto-roof was nowhere to be seen. Some media made for the exit.

'Hold your positions!' the Prime Minister heard Langdon bark at the cabinet behind him. 'The Luddites are holding theirs.'

The Luddites, as if they knew they were being watched, made a sudden move. In one synchronised upward sweep, they raised the placards above their heads.

'What are they doing?' whispered the Minister for Defence.

'The tortoise,' Langdon muttered, impressed despite himself. 'The Roman legions locked shields above them like that when under missile attack.'

The Minister for Defence snorted. 'Missiles? In Ancient Rome?'

'Missiles! Like arrows, stones shot from slings,' Langdon hissed. 'How the hell did you ever become Minister for Defence?'

The Prime Minister soldiered on. Where was the roof? He shot a desperate glance at the two young staffers at the console. Langdon was right. If the Luddites held their position in this light rain, the ministers had to hold theirs. The cabinet couldn't be seen to run for cover.

'Pride in—' he began yet again, only to be interrupted by a crack of lightning.

'Try turning it off then turning it on again,' came a voice from the console area.

All hope of a roofing rescue was lost, Fitzwilliams knew. He could faintly hear something wafting across the rain. The Luddites, under their tortoise of placards, were singing.

The skies suddenly opened and the rain came down full force.

'Hold your positions!' Langdon shouted, but three-quarters of the cabinet were running for it. The Prime Minister turned to restore order in the ranks. If they had to evacuate, at least they could be seen to do so in an orderly fashion. The Minister for Regional Development let out a girlish shriek as she ran past him, covering her hair.

Russ Langdon hadn't adjusted to the change in tactics. He stepped in front of the Minister for Small Business. 'I said stay put!' he yelled.

'Out of my way!' the Minister for Small Business yelled back. 'This suit cost me eighteen hundred dollars, you fool!' He tried to push past Langdon. Langdon staggered backwards. Fitzwilliams lunged to catch him. He got a hand to Langdon's chest, but failed to grab on to anything. Langdon toppled backwards off the stage, hitting the turf heavily.

Prime Minister Fitzwilliams knew instinctively what the photograph would look like. The freelance camera operators had run for it in the rain, but the drones were still hovering. 'Bloody post office,' he cursed. The photo would look as though he'd shoved his own Minister for Security and Freedom, one-legged Russ Langdon, right off the stage. Olga, Donna Hargreaves and Alan Chandos jumped from the stage to rush to Langdon's aid. The rest of cabinet were running for the hills. The rain was pelting down. It was like the storm scene from *King Lear*, he thought.

A voice to his left announced, 'Got it!'

A deafening alarm suddenly blared. With startling speed, the full defences of the Stadlet were deployed. The auto-roof swept up and over him and down again in one great arc, sealing the stage and Prime Minister Fitzwilliams under its hemispheric bombproof shell of titanium and steel.

Day one of the campaign was over.

CHAPTER FOUR

The Prime Minister had barely had any sleep before having to make the gruelling round of morning radio interviews. Weeks earlier, he and Lister St John had plotted the course for the six weeks ahead with a precision that now appeared to border on delusion. Fifteen hours into the campaign and much of that plan was in tatters.

The night before seemed almost dreamlike. Inside the titanium shell of the Stadlet, his two young staffers, whose attempt to reboot the Stadlet security system inadvertently caused it to believe it was under attack, fell to pieces. 'We're so sorry, Prime Minister!' they stammered repeatedly. They simply couldn't stop apologising to him. He found it almost reassuring that twenty-four year olds could experience the same exasperation with technology that he did.

The security services outside needed to establish that any external threat was neutralised before the protective dome could be retracted. This involved numerous verification steps in the security protocol, even though there was clearly no security threat whatsoever. It took ten minutes to roll back the roof.

Isolated inside the Stadlet, he had missed his cabinet colleagues' rush to help Russ Langdon. Typically, a drone had been hovering about to capture the action. The 'PM Shoves One-legged Cabinet Minister Off Stage' clip had rapidly gone beyond viral to pandemic, according to one news host.

From the drone's vantage point, Fitzwilliams' body completely blocked the view of the Minister for Small Business bumping into Langdon. What its camera caught instead was Langdon stumbling forwards and what looked like Fitzwilliams shoving him backwards off the stage, three cabinet ministers jumping down to help him, the rest of cabinet scattering and the emergency dome coming down over the stage, sealing Fitzwilliams inside.

Donna Hargreaves' initial first-aid response when she reached Langdon was to exclaim, 'Oh my God!' Chandos tried to help Langdon to his feet, but Langdon shrieked in pain gasping, 'I've dislocated my shoulder'. He actually had to gasp it twice, as Hargreaves drowned out his first effort with another 'Oh my God!' She pulled out her phone. 'I'll get an ambulance. Reassure the patient,' she instructed Chandos in the first glimmer of proper first aid. Chandos turned to Langdon and said, 'Flinders is a pretty safe seat. I'm sure you'll get re-elected.' Hargreaves snapped, 'Now is not the time for jokes, Alan!' but Langdon had given a weak chuckle. 'I want an ambulance,' Hargreaves screamed at the 000 operator, the pounding rain forcing her to raise her voice. Pause. 'It's the Stadlet! It doesn't have an address!' She paused again. 'It's outside Parliament House.' Pause. 'No. Not Adelaide! Canberra!'

Pause. 'I'm the bloody Minister for Health!' she roared. It had been her own idea, Fitzwilliams recalled, to centralise the entire 000 service to South Australia.

'Let me do this,' came Olga's voice. She moved into the view of the drone camera. O'Rourke grabbed each side of Langdon's face. 'This is going to hurt a lot,' she told him, as if that was one of the attractive features of what she was about to do. Patient consultation out of the way, Olga lifted his right forearm up and back and then raised the whole arm. Langdon howled, then gasped in relief. 'It's back in,' he managed. Hargreaves shouted, 'Never mind,' into the phone. Chandos looked at Olga, obviously impressed. 'Where did you learn that?' 'Advanced First Aid Medal, Soviet Youth Camp 1983,' Olga replied, her shoulders betraying a small twitch of satisfaction.

Normally, morning radio interviews were closely controlled. The politician came prepared to talk about the chosen point of the day and the interviewer had time to raise a secondary topic towards the end. The politician repeated a key phrase on the primary topic several times, knowing that a good portion of the target audience was half asleep.

The events of the day before, however, had left a field strewn with casualties upon which the crows of the media were eager to feast. By 8.30 am, Fitzwilliams was exhausted, his mind swimming in a morass of platitudes. He thought back on just a sample of his answers:

A: This government is determined to protect demonstrators and
I make no apology for that. If the Luddites choose to offend public
decency, that reflects on them. I think the Australian people will
see it for what it was, a hollow and rather pathetic publicity stunt.

A: The Luddites have not told the people anything about what they stand for or their vision for Australia. Until they do, I don't think they are worthy of comment.

A: I don't wish to comment further about the Luddites.

A: No, I didn't hear that [Russ Langdon asking Frank Knox: 'How the hell did you ever become Minister for Defence?'] Russell and Frank are good friends [fake chuckle]. They like to give each other a bit of stick.

A: No, I wouldn't use the word 'debacle' [Fairfax Online's headline description of yesterday's events]. Yes, Murphy's Law was working overtime last night [fake chuckle] but I think the Australian people, like me, can have a good laugh about it and move on.

A: [To shock jock Jim Jarvis] No, I don't think Senator O'Rourke is a 'commie sympathiser'. She was praising first-aid training, not the Soviet system of government. I think it would be a good idea to have first-aid training added to our high school curriculum. [That had been a moment's rashness. He'd better get Alan Chandos to cost it.]

A: No, I tried to catch him. It just looks that way on the footage.

The worst moment had come on ABC radio.

Prime Minister: The Luddites haven't told the Australian people what they stand for. They seem more like some sort of postmodern joke than a political party.

Interviewer: In what way?

Prime Minister: In what way what?

Interviewer: In what way would you consider the Luddites to be postmodern?

A terrible void had engulfed the airwaves. Something had to be said. His primal political spinal cord seized control: when cornered, answer a completely different question.

Prime Minister: The Luddites said yesterday they want a meaningful debate about the future of this great country. I welcome that debate.

Interviewer: Are you saying you're willing to debate the Luddites?

Prime Minister [hesitation]: I am saying I'm keen to visit every corner of this great country to get our message across.

Interviewer: Will you debate Ned Ludd?

Prime Minister: I think I have answered that question, Jenny.

Interviewer: With respect, Prime Minister, you haven't.

Fitzwilliams hated that phrase. 'With respect, Prime Minister.' Interviewers only said that when they were sticking the knife between your ribs.

It was only a single day in a long campaign, he consoled himself. Mopping up the mess and turning shambles into spin what was needed. It was for precisely that particular skill that Fitzwilliams could stomach having hired the likes of Lister St John.

His campaign manager was waiting for him when he got back from the parliamentary studio. St John handed him a letter. 'What's this?' Fitzwilliams asked.

'My resignation. What a complete fucking balls-up yesterday!' Lister declared. 'I'm not working with your pack of clowns any longer. You don't deserve me.'

'On that we are agreed,' Fitzwilliams answered stiffly. It was crystal clear to the Prime Minister what was happening here. Lister St John's reputation could not survive another electoral fiasco, not with the skeleton of Senator Bolen lurking in his closet. He was jumping ship. Fitzwilliams fixed him with his most contemptuous stare. 'When the going gets tough . . .' he said quietly.

'What's that supposed to mean?' St John snarled. 'I got you elected three times, in case you've forgotten. It's not as though I think you're a great prime minister!'

Fitzwilliams thought he had never seen a more unpleasant face. Not so much ugly as totally repellent. But now that the time had come to tell the odious Lister St John he was vermin, Fitzwilliams found he couldn't be bothered. He waved his hand dismissively. 'Just go,' he said.

Lister St John wanted the last word. 'You're fucking doomed,' he predicted and swept away.

A campaign manager quitting on the day after the election announcement would suggest that the campaign was in disarray. Nonetheless, Fitzwilliams couldn't help but feel a sense of liberation as St John moved off. He scanned the letter. It spoke of 'irreconcilable differences', as if they had been married to each other. He noted that St John had backdated his resignation three days. It would dissociate him from the events of the day before.

Olga O'Rourke and Russ Langdon were in the media room with several staffers. Olga was shaking her head, her arms crossed, her lips pressed.

Langdon grimaced at Fitzwilliams. 'More bad news, Prime Minister.'

Langdon's right arm was in a sling. The bad news could wait. 'How's the shoulder, Russ?' he asked, touching him gently on the other arm. Langdon flinched in obvious pain. Fitzwilliams blinked. 'What's wrong?'

'I broke my left wrist in the fall as well,' Langdon informed him.

'Why don't you have it in a cast?'

'I don't want them—' Langdon nodded at the television screens '—to make more of a story of last night than they already have. I'll see a doctor when all this has died down.'

Fitzwilliams put a hand to his mouth. Langdon was rapidly running out of limbs with which to serve his party. 'What's the bad news?' he asked reluctantly.

'Show him,' Olga murmured.

On the screen, a YouTube video came up of Fitzwilliams and Olga on the tennis court. Olga had the ball in her hand. The screen Olga spoke:

'You are no longer young, Prime Minister. You're sixty-four. You're not fast anymore. You need to be sharper.'

'W-W-Where . . .?' Fitzwilliams stammered. 'Who filmed that?'

'I checked for drones and journalists before speaking,' Olga said, her voice uncharacteristically flat. 'See how low the angle is? It was one of the primary school kids on the next court.'

'Little bastard!' Fitzwilliams exclaimed.

'Probably a Kid-cam,' Olga speculated. Kid-cams were the latest in child protection, a band around the wrist providing GPS location and a video/audio feed to a concerned parent. Not only could you be reassured that psychopaths had not taken your child, you could also check on whether the kid was putting any effort into their piano lessons.

'There's no context,' Fitzwilliams fumed. 'You were talking about tennis!'

'Oh, there's tennis.' Olga advanced the clip. It showed Olga sending Fitzwilliams scuttling back and forth, stretching him further each time. Fitzwilliams closed his lips firmly. 'I am sorry, Prime Minister,' Olga murmured.

About the room, heads were down. Those young staffers who could still meet Fitzwilliams' gaze had eyes full of alarm. 'I have here Lister St John's resignation,' he told them. He let the surprise ripple around him. It was a Henry V moment. 'We are well rid of him,' he declared. 'Now let's pick ourselves up and run a campaign! There's an election to be won!'

Some staffers applauded, mistaking his optimistic bluster for strategy. 'We could use that old song!' Langdon shouted, caught up in the mood. 'The one about getting knocked down but getting up again. You know the song I mean. We use it in in our campaign promos. We splice in footage from last night. You can even put in me being pushed off the stage.'

'Don't be . . .' Fitzwilliams stopped himself. He held up a hand as if trying to control the thought. The song Langdon proposed was forty years old. They needed something more modern. Fitzwilliams knew nothing of recent music. 'I want you to find me an upbeat song,' he instructed the young staffers, 'preferably written by an Australian, indomitable spirit, that sort of thing.' He clenched his fist. 'We will use yesterday to our advantage.' Suddenly the Holy Grail of the start of an election campaign seemed tantalisingly within grasp. 'We'll claim we're now . . . the underdog!'

. . .

Colin Sanderson was the founder and sole owner of Autocar. It was a pared-to-the-bone, cutting-edge organisation, the darling of IT e-journals, on top of the world. Its days were numbered.

The driverless car would eventually become mandatory and with the last of the erratic free motorists off the road, there'd be no need for Autocar to save their lives anymore. Colin's latest computer projection was that Autocar would maintain its dominant market position for another five hundred and eleven to five hundred and twenty-four days. Autocar having manoeuvred its employee, Aggie Posniak, on to the Royal Commission into Road Safety might extend that a little, but not forever. When the optimal moment came to cease business operations, Colin knew he'd click the TERMINATE BUSINESS button on his screen without a moment's hesitation.

He'd been working for hours but was still in his bathrobe. The trouble with working from home was you let yourself go. He hadn't shaved. He hadn't done the breakfast dishes—probably, he realised vaguely, because he hadn't had breakfast. Colin Sanderson had made, if his bank balance was to be believed, 480 million dollars out of Autocar and yet his place was a dump. Big and grand and expensive, but a mess; no better than the share flat he'd had in his student days, only now he didn't have any flatmates to blame for the state of the refrigerator. He could have hired a live-in cleaner, only he always imagined this cleaner sounding like his mother, carping on about all of his slovenly habits and the state of his room. He couldn't face that.

One of his computer's tasks was to monitor all media for news items that could impact on the operations of Autocar. The message on his screen was that Autocar employee Aggie Posniak had yesterday engaged in political activity of an unauthorised nature. The computer's face recognition software had identified Aggie as the main speaker at the Luddite demonstration outside Parliament House. Colin had trawled the media to find out what it was all about. DEBACLE read one headline, but that had more to do with the Prime Minister shoving cabinet ministers off a stage. Who and what the Luddites were, the media had no idea, although to judge by the number of photos, they were highly approving of the group's dress code (or lack of it).

He opened Aggie's HR file. *Do you wish to dismiss this employee? Yes/No* appeared on the screen as it always did when he opened a personnel file. His hand hesitated over the *Yes* button. Unauthorised political activity. Membership in a secretive, unknown political party. She'd gone from trusted to dangerous in the blink of an eye.

He had never met Aggie Posniak, having only interviewed her by Halo Hologram Plus. She was an excellent programmer, but he'd sacked many of those before. He flexed his fingers. Aggie Posniak and her Luddites had erupted onto the political scene yesterday and created havoc for the government.

He breathed out. 'A CEO cannot through action or inaction allow harm to come to the company,' he intoned. He pressed *Yes*.

She was dismissed.

• • •

Renard Prendergast clutched his overnight bag to his chest, not even daring to stare out the bus window. He had met Fiona Brennan, the ASIO chief, only an hour earlier in a nondescript office of a business called Geodesic Technical Solutions.

'I have no idea what they do,' Fiona had told him. 'We rent office space from them when we need to meet someone away from headquarters.' Renard had thought he'd been summoned for a debriefing. Instead, Fiona Brennan had sacked him.

'Don't take it badly,' she consoled him cheerily. 'It's just that you told the media yesterday that you were going to campaign for the Luddites in Sydney.'

'I was undercover,' he protested, recognising it as an odd description for a nude marcher. 'I had to say something.'

'Yes,' Fiona agreed, 'and you did well. It's just that if it ever came out that ASIO had an undercover operative campaigning for a party, we'd be in deep trouble.' She gave him her pleasant smile. 'So I thought it best to fire you.' She pushed a bulky envelope across the table.

His eyes opened wide when he looked inside. The envelope was filled with fifty-dollar notes. There were thousands of dollars in the packet.

'We'll still pay you,' she explained. 'We just need to have you off our books for a while. Best not to deposit in a bank for now. It would look suspicious.'

What she had done was backdate his sacking to December, putting it well before the appearance of the Luddites. With the assistance of a compliant big-four bank, ASIO had reversed his pay since then, taking them out of his bank account to leave no trace of there ever having been payment. ASIO, Fiona promised, would hire him back officially a discreet period after the election.

Renard had never held more than a hundred dollars cash in his hands. Not even drug dealers used money anymore. 'What am I supposed to do until then?' he asked.

'What you said you were going to do,' Fiona replied. 'Work for Ned Ludd in Sydney. Find out what you can. Let us know anything important.'

There was close to five months' pay in the envelope. He couldn't hide it all in one place. He would have to divide it into smaller sums and spread them around. His parents could keep one. Taylor, his girlfriend, another. An important detail popped into his head. He cleared his throat. 'What was I officially fired for?'

Fiona looked at him sympathetically. 'I thought it best to put down inappropriate sexual conduct,' she answered. 'We needed something that attracted a summary dismissal. At the Sydney ASIO staff party last December,' she elaborated. 'You know Geraldine Nesbitt? I put her as the complainant.'

Renard had danced with Geraldine at that party. If anything, she seemed interested in him. Taylor did have a tendency towards jealousy. She didn't like Geraldine, and Renard hadn't told Taylor about dancing with her. 'Don't worry,' Fiona said, 'it will all come off your personnel file in time.'

On the bus back to Sydney, he gradually realised he ought not to clutch his overnight bag so suspiciously, as if it had . . . well, nearly five months' pay in it. He relaxed his grip and let the bag rest on his lap. He tried looking at his Gargantuan like everyone else on the bus. Luddites and Liberals were all over the news. Nothing much new had happened. The Prime Minister had pledged to make first-aid training mandatory in high schools. It seemed an odd issue on which to start an election.

Two young women were taking turns looking around at him and, after a few pokes, the aisle-seat passenger came back to Renard's seat. 'You're Ned Ludd, aren't you?' she said. 'You're on all the networks.' She made the eye motion to indicate that Renard should ask her to sit down.

'Would you like to sit?' he managed, his arm going instinctively to his overnight bag. Physical money was completely unnerving.

'I didn't recognise you at first,' the woman said, shooting a quick glance at what Renard thought was his overnight bag, but realised, from her smile, was his groin. 'I've got nothing against nudity,' she said. This would have struck Renard as a promising beginning to a conversation had he not been in a relationship. 'But was all that yesterday just a joke?' the woman asked. 'Are the Luddites for real?'

The advantage of aligning with a political party whose only website item was an assertion that there were dragons in Central Australia was that you could wing it. Luddites run as individual candidates without a party platform, he informed her. 'The Ned Ludd of Sydney will discuss issues with as many members of the electorate as she can,' he promised, 'listen to what people have to say, and then take the best of those ideas to parliament.'

Her window-seat friend came down the aisle to join the conversation. Renard heard, 'It's Ned Ludd,' whispered among the other passengers.

'Hey, Ned,' a man with a deep Jamaican accent called to him, 'you got my vote.'

He explained that he was not the candidate in Sydney, only working for her.

'We live in Pyrmont,' the two women—sisters it turned out—told him. 'We'll help with Ned's campaign.' They each touched their phones to Renard's to transfer their phone numbers. The Jamaican man also signed up and a boy asked for an autograph. When the bus reached Central Station, two Australia Post drones were waiting, someone in the bus having tipped the media he was coming.

Renard gave two short, stiff interviews while grasping his overnight bag in front of him with rigor mortis-like firmness. A message arrived on his Gargantuan. *I AM WAITING FOR YOU AT YOUR PLACE.* Taylor and he had been going out for six months. She had never used uppercase with him before. He made his way home with trepidation.

• • •

'Well?' Taylor demanded when he opened the door.

'Well what?' Renard answered, a lacklustre opening return admittedly. However, there were a number of things Taylor's 'Well?' might have covered. He didn't want to answer on one she might not know about.

'You told me you were going to Canberra for work.'

'Yes.' Not a sparkling reply.

Taylor said nothing for a moment. Words were being weighed and when she spoke next, her voice was very controlled. 'When I called your office today to see if you were back, Geraldine answered and she told me that you didn't work there anymore and that you hadn't worked there since December.'

Renard said nothing. 'Yes,' seemed an unhelpful answer.

'Who is she?' Taylor suddenly demanded.

'Geraldine?' Renard shrugged. 'Data analyst like me. You've met her.'

'Not Geraldine!' Taylor shrieked. 'Who's *she*?' She flipped open her Gargantuan and dramatically projected the image onto Renard's living room wall. It was Renard and the Melbourne Ned being interviewed yesterday.

'That's Ned Ludd,' he replied weakly.

'Oh . . . just Ned Ludd! This nude woman you hang out with in Canberra!'

Taylor throttled back a few decibels and reverted to her controlled voice. 'Renard, you have never mentioned the Luddite Party to me before. You never told me you had changed your name. You never told me you lost your job. You slip off to Canberra, lying to me that it is work-related, and what do I find on the networks last night? You cavorting with your nude political friends in front of the whole nation!'

Her voice had accelerated during the short speech and appeared readying to shriek again. 'You've lied to me for months and . . . and . . . will you put that fucking bag down while I'm talking to you?' she roared.

Renard sensed this was not the moment to ask her if she could take a month's worth of his pay in fifty-dollar notes and hide it somewhere in her flat.

'You have nothing to say?' The roar had dissipated. Taylor's voice was worryingly soft.

'I do,' Renard replied. 'I just . . . haven't thought what it is yet.'

It was the worst possible reply. The door slammed and Taylor was gone.

. . .

It hadn't surprised Aggie Posniak when she couldn't log on to work. She had fully expected Autocar to sack her and quickly.

She had skills that made her employable when she needed a job again. For now, though, there was her campaign in Wills to organise and she had additional assignments for the Luddites nationally that would take up time. After nine years, now that the moment had arrived for the Luddites to campaign, it wasn't clear to Aggie what her next move should be.

The doorbell rang. The next move, it seemed, would be to answer the door.

Two women were on her doorstep. 'Aggie? Aggie Posniak?' one asked.

'Yes.'

'Or should we say Ned Ludd?' One of them beamed. 'We're from Bicyclism Australia.'

Aggie blinked. Bicyclism Australia, the fake organisation that Autocar had created solely to get Aggie on to the Royal Commission into Road Safety. Aggie was its president. She had also created its website and was e-newsletter editor under the pen name of Will Drury. These two were obviously members of the cycling public who had joined the organisation presuming it to be legitimate. 'What can I do for you?' she asked.

'It's more what can we do for you,' they replied excitedly. They let her know they were prepared to throw the full force of the imaginary organisation behind her campaign.

Aggie considered the offer. She could certainly use the help. 'Let me check something,' she said. She went to her computer to log in. Aggie Posniak could not access Autocar's server anymore but Will Drury, it turned out, could still log on to the Bicyclism Australia website. When she had created Will Drury, she had given him all the same computer access privileges as she had. Aggie smiled. Through Will Drury, Autocar's vast computing power and control of the Bicyclism website was still at her disposal. 'This could be the start of a beautiful relationship,' she told her two would-be supporters.

• • •

Amy Zhao set the last of what had seemed an interminable number of coffee cups in the rack to dry. The dishwasher at Compink Australia was broken, but had it been working, she would have been the one filling it, emptying it and putting up signs in the kitchen asking staff not to leave their dirty mugs in the sink. She went about this work uncomplainingly. Those of her fellow employees who paid her any attention presumed she did this strategically. No place of work was ever quick to lay off the one person who voluntarily cleaned up the staff kitchen. It was the way a lowly data entry clerk could keep her job—or so she wanted them to think. They would have been astonished to know Amy Zhao was actually the undercover deputy CEO of Compink Australia.

After the signing of the Tri-Ocean Free Trade Agreement, the Communist Party of China had recognised the enormous commercial advantages of turning itself into a corporation. The rest of the world might still resent the growing economic power of China, but Compink would from then on be protected by the might of corporate law. Any government that moved against Compink would end up in court and lose. Chinese embassies still reissued lost passports, but all the real work went on at Communist Party of China Incorporated, or Compink, as it had rebranded itself. 'The K is here to stay,' their English language rebranding guru had assured them to account for the aberrant spelling of 'Inc.' She had predicted (correctly) that the letter K would occupy the same role in the 2020s as the stray letter Z had in brand names earlier this century. 'And when pronouncing the brand,' she explained, 'the "pink" softens the image of our Maoist, less business-friendly past.'

Compink China next broke up its international operations and had the component parts reregister as separate national entities where still greater corporate protections were to be had. Compink Australia, Compink Italy, Compink Brazil listed on the stock markets of their respective countries and were now legally considered to be Australian, Italian and Brazilian companies. If Compink Australia wanted to buy up some sensitive facility or vital infrastructure, the Australian government could no longer object. Not only that, but Compink Australia could issue stock and get Australian investors to front up with the money for it. Even ASIO was supposed to leave them alone, though Amy knew they didn't.

What Compink China had not realised was that in creating these separate national corporations, they would create separate interests. What was good for Compink China was not necessarily good for Compink Australia. Amy's CEO, Wilson Huang, ran Compink Australia fiercely independently of Beijing. They shouted him down at hologram meetings, they threatened—but with repeated share floats, they owned only 12 per cent of Compink Australia. Huang had the support of the board, which included the CEOs of Deutsch Compink and the formidable Compink Cayman Islands. Beijing could do little other than ungraciously accept the annual dividends he sent their way.

With Compink China antagonistic and ASIO ever snooping, Wilson Huang knew that all Compink Australia electronic communication would be monitored, all its data minable. Both agencies would attempt to infiltrate the ranks of his staff with spies. Yet somehow, Wilson had to find a way to run the business. It was to overcome these challenges he had recruited Amy Zhao as undercover deputy CEO.

Amy inserted herself as a data entry clerk. Her self-appointed role as dishwasher put her in the kitchen to overhear a lot. The initial task of discerning who was working for whom proved not terribly difficult. In their recruitment of spies, ASIO put too much focus on language. Their plants, usually second- or third-generation Australians, spoke excellent Mandarin and Cantonese. But they were Australian-educated and what they weren't good at—and it was easy for Amy to find this out—was maths. They also too readily understood the rules of cricket when it was on the TV in the staff kitchen.

The spies from Compink China took longer to flush out. There would be a few months of diligent work, but with each passing pay period, the employee's lunchtime conversation would show unusual levels of interest in the workings of long-service leave, leave loading, personal leave and all the other seductive aspects of Australian labour practices.

She left them in place. She'd rather Wilson supervised a nest of known vipers than have new ones trying to wriggle in. Through intermediaries, Amy established Paradox Consultants, an off-site office where all the real work of Compink Australia would take place. She employed no business people there, hiring graduates in gender studies, English literature and history, GPs, astronomers—highly educated people but largely unemployable. She wanted people who were both quick learners and grateful that anyone had hired them.

For electronic security reasons, Amy had them work exclusively on old manual typewriters. No one could hack into a manual typewriter. Amy quickly discovered to her surprise that this move proved to have unexpected productivity payoffs. On a typewriter, you actually needed to think about what you were going to write before you wrote it. It made the staff at Paradox Consultants not just analytical but succinct, whereas back at the infested head office, the ingratiating Compink China or ASIO agents could churn out forty-five pages updating the fire evacuation procedure and still not know the location of the nearest emergency exit.

Amy was officially paid only a data entry clerk's wages and lived in a shared Sydney flat to keep up the guise. Wilson paid her deputy CEO salary directly into an offshore account. She met in secret with him only once a week, often for just a few minutes.

The dishes all done, she was eager to meet with her CEO that evening, but didn't look forward to the security precautions.

She understood that secrecy was necessary; Compink China had the head office completely bugged. It was why Wilson had originally set up the black holes, small businesses that existed completely off the grid where he could meet with reliable employees in confidence. That had been nine years ago and most of the black holes had been shut down as either too costly or unnecessary.

Amy would have predicted that CalliNail, the last of Wilson's black holes, would have been the first to go bankrupt. Who, in a sensible world, needed calligraphy done on their fingernails and toenails? Yet here it was, still thriving, more popular than ever. Nowadays, Amy had to book ahead for an appointment.

Amy disliked having calligraphy on her nails but, of course, she had to leave it there for days afterwards as it was one of the few luxuries that Amy Zhao, data entry clerk, allowed herself. Sometimes, Amy felt annoyed with Amy Zhao, data entry clerk, who really should assert herself more . . . a process that could start with not doing everybody's dishes for them.

She had long tired of explaining the miniature Confucian aphorisms on her nails to everyone she met. 'Just give me something that won't take long,' she told the calligrapher at CalliNail. 'Roman numerals will do.'

'Do you want eleven to twenty on the toes?' the calligrapher asked. 'Or would you rather repeat one to ten on both fingers and toes?'

'It doesn't matter,' Amy muttered. She never let anyone see her toes. She would wear socks with sandals if necessary to hide her ludicrous nails.

The calligraphy nail paint required twenty minutes to dry. The calligrapher, when she had finished the final tiny XX on Amy's little toe, murmured, 'Number seven'. Amy proceeded to the numbered drying booth and entered. Wilson Huang was already there.

'The Luddites?' Wilson asked.

'Fitzwilliams damaged—only slightly,' Amy assessed.

'Network Nine.'

Amy paused. Over their years together, they had trimmed their conversations back to a bare scaffolding on which each knew how to hang the other's meaning. Even if their conversation was somehow recorded, it would be hard for others to understand what was being discussed, let alone decided.

Compink Australia had a significant but complicated stake in Network Nine. The parent company of Network Nine was controlled by a French entertainment giant. Through a Liechtenstein shell company, the French corporation was mostly owned by Compink Uruguay. Compink Australia had a 40 per cent stake in Compink Uruguay.

'The debate.' Amy let the argument sink in.

Wilson nodded. 'Three-way.'

Network Nine had bought exclusive rights to the election debate broadcast. In the old and bad days, the ABC would have covered it as well. However, according to the Tri-Ocean Free Trade Agreement, that would now constitute unfair government-subsidised competition against a free enterprise.

What Amy had proposed was that Nine invite the Luddites to participate in the leaders' debate with the Liberals and Labor. It would bring enormous viewing numbers. Everyone was interested in the Luddites. More importantly, Nine itself would be central to the story for insisting the Luddites be allowed to take part. The best way to cover the news, after all, was to be the news.

Labor would agree. Their leader, Roslyn Stanfield, needed every bit of exposure she could get. 'Fitzwilliams,' Amy pointed out. Fitzwilliams would certainly boycott if the Luddites were included in the debate. He was ahead. He didn't need to come to Nine's debate party.

Wilson considered the matter only briefly. 'Loki,' he suggested.

When she'd first recruited the mole Loki, he'd chosen his own code name. Wilson had liked it so much he'd named all his subsequent moles and spies after Norse gods.

'Loki,' she agreed. Loki was incredibly well placed. If anyone could arrange it, he could.

. . .

Renard sank into the chair. 'Gruel,' he called out to the owner. He had hidden five bags of fifty-dollar notes in his flat, reserving one to go out that night. It seemed appropriate to start this stint in the cash economy at Low Expectations. 'Weak tea as well,' he added to the order.

No job . . . or no job officially, he corrected himself. No girlfriend . . . well, no girlfriend that was speaking to him. No official job, no girlfriend that was speaking to him and he was waiting for gruel. This sort of thing just didn't happen to James Bond.

The place was crowded. Three kids were working noisily on their looms. There were diners at several tables. Why did people keep coming here?

Kate rose from her loom when she saw him and slipped out the back of the shop. Renard did a double take. Kate had a Genie phone in her hand. A phone in Low Expectations? Kate returned a short while later and more customers came in. They were showing an old BBC version of *Bleak House* upstairs, it being Thursday Telly and Tea night. Renard couldn't face *Bleak House* tonight. Another man entered and headed upstairs, this one coughing badly, his tubercular wheeze suiting the ambience of Low Expectations.

He hadn't finished his gruel when Kate approached his table. 'Come upstairs,' she said.

'I'm not in the mood for *Bleak House*,' he answered. Normally, no one at Low Expectations cared whether you watched their dreary Dickens movies, but Kate's eyes were both imploring and demanding at the same time. 'All right,' he agreed, curious as to why it should matter to her.

Upstairs, Kate brushed past the four people watching the movie and pulled open the door of a small office Renard had never noticed before. Inside there was no furniture save for three wooden chairs. A man, the man with the cough, was slumped on one.

He tried to speak, but that set off a bout of coughing. The man waved his arm to indicate he would speak as soon as he could. 'Lad,' the man managed at last, 'I don't have long to live.'

'I'm sorry,' Renard said. 'Which novel is this? I don't recognise it.'

'What do you mean which novel is this?'

'Which Dickens novel is this from?' Renard hesitated, suddenly unsure. 'This is a role play, isn't it?'

'It's not,' the man rasped, making it clear that he would be shouting at Renard if he could, 'a role play of some damned Dickens novel.'

'Oh,' Renard said quietly.

'Not long to live and yesterday you told the nation that I was a woman.'

'What are you talking about?'

'I'm Ned Ludd, the Luddite candidate for Sydney.' Another wave of coughing ensued.

'He's not well,' Kate pointed out, as if the detail could have escaped Renard.

'Dying people often aren't. I've waited for years for this election and now I'm not well enough to campaign.' Outside the room, someone in the movie bellowed, 'Shake me up, Judy!'

'You're laying it on a bit thick, Ned,' Kate said with the casual callousness of a seventeen year old. 'You might have another two, three years in you yet.'

Ned let out a Dickensian grunt. 'What I do know is that I can't campaign. I can't speak—' another round of coughing engulfed him '—and I don't have the energy.' He stared straight into Renard's eyes. 'Ned,' he said, 'I want you to run in my place. I can show you what to do, and I have all the forms for nominating with the Electoral Commission.'

Kate pulled Renard around to face her. 'I want you to run.' Her forcefulness surprised him.

'Why?'

'For my parents. They . . .' She stopped herself. Her eyes sought Ned Ludd's.

'You can tell him,' Old Ned wheezed. 'He's a Nineteener—one of the original Neds. He's not some government spy.'

Renard deduced that the term 'Nineteener' must refer to someone who'd changed their name to Ned Ludd in 2019. Renard *had* changed his name to Ned Ludd in 2019, but a few months after

90

the great mass renaming in April of that year. Old Ned did not appear to know that. Either the Luddites' intelligence-gathering was weak or this Ned Ludd didn't have access to it.

'My parents were . . . they *are*—' Kate sounded defiant '—GPs.'

'I'm sorry,' was all Renard could say.

'You know what they do nowadays? They work out the back of homeopathy clinics and crystal shops, still seeing patients. Crystals and quackery! It's like something out of the nineteenth century,' she spat, her indignation somehow all the more impressive given her Dickensian rags.

Renard inhaled carefully. Fiona Brennan had told him to find out what he could about the Luddites, though why he should take her interests into consideration on the very day she'd sacked him and ruined his relationship with Taylor was beyond him. For some reason, it was Kate standing there—all fury and determination and Dickens—that decided him. He knew nothing much about the new Virtual GPs now entrenched in the Medicare system. 'I'll run,' he told them both, 'even if it means taking on the Dr Ottos.'

CHAPTER FIVE

Prime Minister Fitzwilliams always spent the time in make-up deciding what needed to be said, even if it was to be said reluctantly, to the awaiting cameras. Tonight's video link-up to the global reality TV show *GOOMS* required the same focus he'd put in to the moments before a national debate. Possibly greater focus: *GOOMS* would have a far larger audience.

Network Ten had not been surprised when he agreed to the link-up over a month ago. But they had been when he'd asked that Labor leader Roslyn Stanfield also be invited. 'Supporting the Australian entry in *GOOMS* is a bipartisan matter,' he told the Network Ten people in his nation-united tone. The network mob had lapped it up. Roslyn Stanfield too had been delighted by the invitation.

Fitzwilliams' generosity in including his struggling rival had self-interest behind it. Network Ten scheduled their live *GOOMS* broadcast for 27 March. This had fitted conveniently into

Fitzwilliams' plan to dissolve parliament and call the election on 21 March. It committed Stanfield to a wholesome bipartisan event a week into the campaign. It meant whatever attack ads were waiting in Labor's arsenal, they'd need to hold back until this lovey-dovey event was over. Labor had a lot of ground to make up and this little interlude ate into the time they had in which to do it. Toss in Easter and two weeks of school holidays to distract the electorate's attention and Labor had a very narrow window of opportunity.

Get Out of My Space, or *GOOMS*, was sponsored by the international sporting goods giant, Fortuna Corporation. It was a global phenomenon, hailed as the ultimate reality TV show. One hundred and fifty countries (including two rogue states) had competed in the contestant selection. The world had watched the hopefuls go through the physical travails of training, the rigour of scientific study, and the unrelenting and sometimes brutal talent contests. Ten contestants, the best of the best of reality TV, had blasted off to join the International Space Station. Australia's Paula Perkins—'Our Perky Paula' as the media dubbed her—was among the final five still on board. On Sunday, the world would vote on which of the crew would be the next to be evicted. The ratings would be astronomical.

Everything to do with *GOOMS* was mega. The affable Scott and Yuri, the two actual astronauts tasked with running a space station with a crew of novices on board, were now celebrities themselves. They had received over two hundred thousand offers of marriage, the dark-haired Russian leading his American colleague slightly in both heterosexual and homosexual proposals. Australia's Paula Perkins had produced the winning effort in Week Three's Space

Music Video challenge, adapting the old *Star Wars* opening caption 'A long time ago in a galaxy far, far away' into a catchy pop tune with choreography from her spacewalk (the Week Two challenge). The Zero-G Super Chef contest (Week Six) had been viewed live by four billion people. Fortuna Corporation paid for everything. The scarcely funded International Space Station could not believe its luck.

From their separate rooms, Fitzwilliams and Stanfield were ushered into the studio. 'Fortuna Station in three minutes,' the floor director announced. 'You'll have forty-seven seconds.' Network Ten, though a *GOOMS* broadcast partner, was a lowly one. They had won those forty-seven seconds only through exhaustive negotiations.

'Let's speak together,' Fitzwilliams proposed. 'We'll both start with, "Hello, Paula!", then I'll do a "The nation is behind you" bit and you can say a sentence. After that, we let Paula say whatever she wants. We'll finish off with a few words of encouragement.'

'How about a joint "Good luck. We love you, Paula!"?' Stanfield suggested.

'Perhaps, "Australia loves you, Paula."' Fitzwilliams felt the weight of his years. He shouldn't tell twenty-seven-year-old astronauts he loves them on world television.

Roslyn Stanfield had often struck Fitzwilliams as ill at ease in her newish role as leader, but today she seemed composed. Fitzwilliams faced a predicament with this election. In the world of attack ads, Roslyn Stanfield was simply too soft a target. People didn't seem to hold strong opinions about her, and if you went cut-and-thrust at someone like that, it might appear to be mean-spirited, vicious. A badly judged attack ad could easily create sympathy for her. Fitzwilliams had a carefully graduated line-up of attack ads prepared. They were mild by industry standards, with the harshest one being of Stanfield sitting on a fence at some agricultural show. They had overlaid the voice of the Labor leader making contradictory statements about the GP reforms, the crisis in Tajikistan and the use of Go-bots in day-care centres. No matter how tired you got at one of those interminable agricultural shows, Fitzwilliams knew you never took a moment's rest by sitting on a fence. Stanfield was a leader on her L-plates.

'Twenty seconds,' the floor director called.

Onto the screen came Scott the astronaut. To Fortuna Corporation's delight, he and Yuri played to perfection their roles of the relentlessly good-natured veterans, sometimes pulling their hair out at the antics of the crew contestants. And it helped that they looked very, very good outfitted in Fortuna sportswear with the famous winged running shoe logo of the corporation prominently displayed.

'You want Paula?' Scott asked. 'I don't know where that crazy Aussie's got to.' An elbow caught him in the ribs. 'Oh, she's sitting right here.' He floated offscreen, making it look as though Paula's elbow had propelled him. Paula moved to centre camera.

'Hello, Paula!' the two party leaders chimed. 'All Australia is barracking for you this weekend,' Fitzwilliams enthused.

'You're Australia's brilliant battler. You'll be amazing in the Science Challenge Sunday!' Stanfield predicted.

That had been two sentences, Fitzwilliams noted. 'Brilliant' was an odd adjective to pair with the campaign-weary term of 'battler'. Fitzwilliams detected something in it.

Paula smiled back. 'It's a great honour to meet you both. It's a pity we don't have time for a proper debate.'

Knowing the cameras were on him, Fitzwilliams suppressed any reaction, his eyebrows displaying only the slightest twitch of alarm. The word 'debate' lay out there, blaring a Do Not Touch warning. Fitzwilliams affected not to have heard it.

These instincts were not transferable to his rival beside him. 'Debate?' Stanfield asked.

The astronaut swept back her amazing zero-g hair. 'Before blasting off three months ago, I gave my parents the paperwork to change my name by deed poll.'

Fitzwilliams braced himself. He couldn't help but let his eyelids close at what was coming.

'My new name is Ned Ludd, and I'm proud to say that I'm the Luddite candidate in the Tasmanian seat of Bass.'

The studio director gave the hand signal counting off the five seconds of broadcast remaining.

'Goodbye, good luck,' Stanfield said numbly, her hollow voice on its own. 'Australia loves you . . .'

'Ned,' Fitzwilliams finished for her.

•••

Aggie Posniak, Luddite candidate in the Melbourne electorate of Wills, rose stiffly from the couch to answer the door. She had been willing enough to become the bicyclist candidate. The two enthusiasts from Bicyclism Australia who had come to campaign for her were very organised and, through the still-operating Bicyclism Australia website, had mobilised a network of like-minded supporters. Day after day, even in the rain, they were pedalling all over Melbourne to muster votes. What Aggie had not fully appreciated was that she would have to pedal everywhere too. A week and a half into the campaign and her legs were aching.

At times, Aggie almost forgot that she had invented Bicyclism Australia and initially peopled its website with a fictitious membership with the sole purpose of being appointed to the Royal Commission into Road Safety. Bicyclism Australia had since morphed into what had to be considered a legitimate movement. There were thousands of members and they were ready for the call to action. It might not help her cause in Wills much but her campaign could persuade cyclists from across the country to swing to the Luddites in the Senate.

The two Veronicas (they had the same name, which made it difficult for Aggie to recall which one she had told what) on her doorstep bustled into the flat and bustled out their campaign maps for the day. The pair never seemed to tire.

Aggie glanced at the map of the day's itinerary. 'How many hills?' she asked. Aggie thought of herself as fit, but the Veronicas were pedalling machines compared to her.

The Veronicas were indispensable. Aggie had been chosen to be the Ned Ludd to represent the Luddites in the leaders' debate. She hadn't taken that assignment seriously at first, presuming the two main parties would refuse to debate the Luddites. Suddenly, however, Network Nine was trumpeting the Triangular Battle of the Century and now Aggie had to spend considerable time preparing for the showdown. Fitzwilliams was a skilled debater and Stanfield knew how to dodge out of corners. Aggie would need something to throw them off their game plans. Her performance in the debate could conceivably win the Luddites a Senate seat or two. And just this day, she'd received an additional assignment for the Luddite campaign, a complicated programming task. Leaving the Wills campaign to the two Veronicas eased her workload.

'Ready to go?' one of the Veronicas asked.

Aggie put on her helmet and smiled. The programming task was challenging, but through the Bicyclism Australia site Aggie still had access to the computing power of the whole Autocar server. That made the task much more feasible and, if it worked, the Prime Minister would be in for a major surprise late in the campaign.

• • •

When Alan Chandos had first proposed the GP reforms to cabinet, even Prime Minister Fitzwilliams' first inclination was to say, 'Are you sure this is a good idea?'

The government had long considered the tantalising cost savings of automating some medical positions in the Medicare system. No one but Chandos had considered starting with general practitioners. The government was used to antagonising parts of the working population. Skilled labourers could be lumped together as corrupt trade unionists holding the country to ransom. The government could attack its own bureaucracy, calling it bloated and inefficient. Even those who not only minded the nation's children but tried to teach them at the same time could be belittled by the government. The populace might consider public education important, but the government also knew every voter had childhood memories of intense dislike for certain teachers. The government could beat up on teachers whenever it felt the need.

Doctors were a different case, though, and one that needed to be handled with care. When Fitzwilliams had idly dreamed of automating parts of the medical profession, he'd thought to target specialists. Specialists wouldn't give you an appointment for five months and then kept you waiting for hours on the day they did finally deign to see you. They scarpered off to conferences in suspiciously pleasant overseas locations and made enormous amounts of money. The voting public could feasibly be steered towards resenting specialists. GPs, on the other hand, those frontline heroes of medicine, were loved. Going against them could set off a political firestorm.

Chandos had first laid out the intoxicating level of savings to be made by automating GP services. This brought most of cabinet— those for whom slashing and burning was an economic goal in itself—rallying to his standard. For Fitzwilliams and the sensible rump of the cabinet that needed convincing, Chandos articulated a bold vision. It took a while to get their minds around the concept. He wasn't just *saying* that what he was proposing was going to improve health outcomes, it *actually would* improve health outcomes.

The Automated General Practitioners, or Dr Ottos as they came to be called, could be accessed by any Medicare card holder from anywhere in the country at any time of day. All that was needed was a computer or Genie phone—or anything clever with a webcam. There was a luxury coffee maker that could connect to the Dr Otto system. Linked to Dr Otto, the patient would describe their symptoms and respond to the doctor's questions. They could hold their suddenly spotty two year old in front of the webcam at 3.45 am and Dr Otto would evaluate whether to pack the child off to the hospital or back to bed. Dr Otto was instantly available. Dr Otto did not have a waiting room full of sickly patients coughing over you. Dr Otto didn't nervously glance at the time if the consult dragged on. Dr Otto could send a prescription straight to your phone or local pharmacy. Dr Otto could display cultural sensitivity to over four hundred cultures. Dr Otto was there for you.

On the screen, the patient saw an image of a GP asking the probing questions. You could have the avuncular elderly practitioner, creaking with experience; the sharp-as-a-tack recent graduate with a trim-fitting lab coat; the middle-aged hard-working GP dedicated to public health and her two children—for the Dr Ottos came with both personalities and backstories. These developed according to a patient's responses, evolving around the patient's needs both medically and socially. Dr Otto was not averse to chitchat. During a consult, you could complain about your upcoming family Christmas or your daughter's infatuation with the boy band Wrong Side or share your somewhat guilty pleasure in following stories on the royal family. Dr Otto could not only converse throughout, but also remember it all at your next appointment.

'And all these Dr Ottos are linked,' Chandos had told cabinet. 'If we tell the program that there's only eighty million dollars in the Pharmaceutical Benefits Scheme for a particular drug, the Dr Ottos only spend eighty million dollars. There will be no rogue GP out there prepared to blow the whole lot on his or her own patients.'

Chandos even foresaw the role for celebrity Dr Ottos, the government paying Paramount an undisclosed amount for the rights to use Dr McCoy from the old *Star Trek* movies. The public went flocking to their screens to meet the Dr Ottos for themselves.

Renard Prendergast, Luddite candidate for Sydney, always chose the Recent-Graduate-With-Trim-Lab-Coat Dr Otto. He knew the

Dr Ottos worked well. They were instantly accessible from virtually anywhere and yet Renard had impulsively agreed to run on
championing human GPs. It seemed a hopeless issue on which
to campaign. For a local candidate, Renard had very little idea of
what regular people wanted of a government. From his role as an
ASIO surveillance data analyst, Renard had gleaned a good idea
of what some people wanted politically. The trouble was, those
people were mostly sociopaths, fanatics or terrorists.

Given Renard's limited knowledge on the issue of automated
GPs, the logical starting point was to meet with Kate's parents to
discuss their grievances. Obviously they had lost their jobs, but—
less obviously—what did they think Renard should do about it?

He met Kate for a bowl of gruel at Low Expectations first. Her
parents were a same-sex couple, Kate having been born by IVF.
Either because they wanted to introduce genetic diversity into
their future child or because they had not been impressed with
Australian men, they'd chosen the country of the sperm donor by
throwing a dart at a map of the world while blindfolded. Their
first attempt was too aquatic (three hundred kilometres south of
Iceland), but the second had cleanly pierced Estonia. Contacting a
donor clinic in Tallinn, they had selected Kate's sperm donor from
the short profiles of men whose frozen sperm was available. They
had chosen the one who had mentioned his love for the music
of Leonard Cohen—with the exception of 'Hallelujah', which he
thought had been covered to death. Kate told Renard (she had
heard the story ten thousand times and couldn't believe she was
now repeating it herself) that it was the most seductive thing the
Estonian could have possibly written for her parents. A Leonard
Cohen concert had been a very early date for them, a date that had

moved their relationship up several significant notches of intensity. Kate didn't like Leonard Cohen's music much, though, oddly, she thought 'Hallelujah' was probably her favourite. Embarrassingly, her mothers still had a poster of Leonard Cohen up in their kitchen. She would occasionally find one of them gazing at the poster of this old, old man in black and be perplexed at what she detected to be a tiny flutter of heterosexuality in that look. Parents were, she recognised, inherently creepy.

After their gruel, Kate took him directly to her place and sat him awkwardly in her living room before her parents. How was he to be the saviour of these two pleasant-seeming professionals so unfortunately rendered redundant? He wasn't even good at representing his own interests half the time. How could he represent theirs? Looking at them now, Renard couldn't determine which woman was the biological mother of Kate. Kate introduced him as the candidate who was ready to fight for the cause of the GPs against the machines.

Neither of the ex-GPs said anything at first. Finally, one of them spoke up. 'That's very sweet of you, Kate, but we aren't opposed to the Dr Ottos.'

The other mother (Kate had introduced both of them to Renard only as her 'mums') explained, 'They're doing good work. They can speak forty-two languages. They can spend hours with each patient. Every month they load the entire contents of *The New England Journal of Medicine* and *The Lancet* into the Dr Otto program. They are more up-to-date than the date. We were good doctors, but we can't match all that.'

'Kate,' the first one added sympathetically, 'we're happy you've found this politician—' Renard blinked, having never been called that before '—and are politically active, but don't do it for us and our old jobs; do it for what matters to you and the future of your generation.'

Kate remained silent, a scowl fixed on her face. The two ex-GPs pretended not to notice and described to Renard their current employment. They spent their post-GP years infiltrating the alternative medicine sector. Under invented New Age-sounding titles, they set up in clinics alongside homeopathy practitioners, crystologists and psychic healers. There they subtly went about introducing sound medical practices, nudging their co-workers into putting doses of proven medicines into their concoctions. The astrology charts they 'professionally' consulted tended to recommend a balanced diet, more exercise and a better sleep regimen. One homeopathy clinic, Mum Two told him proudly, was now conducting a properly randomised trial. It was their new mission in life to medicise (their word) the mystics.

Renard was glad they were so evidently content, but there went issue number one of his campaign. Ned Ludd, the Ned Ludd with the terrible cough who had originally planned to run, wanted him to have his program platform sorted by the end of the week. Kate, still scowling, took him to the door. 'Walk with me,' she muttered tersely.

They went several blocks in silence. 'That is just so fucking typical of them!' Kate finally blurted. 'They never think of themselves. If it's good for the patient, it doesn't matter if it stabs them in the heart.'

There were real tears flowing now. The odd combination of seething and filial devotion made Renard's own eyes well up. 'I think,' he attempted, clearing the choke from his throat (he had

a weak threshold for sentimentality), 'your parents are proud of what you tried to do there. And I—'

She held up a hand to cut him off. 'This isn't over!'

'Kate, I can't campaign against the Dr Ottos if the doctors approve of them.'

'They want me to be active. They want me to campaign for the kind of better world my generation wants.' Her eyes bored straight into his. 'I can do that!' she nearly spat.

'Can you?' Renard couldn't imagine saying the same. 'What kind of better world are we after?' he asked tentatively.

'I don't know!' she nearly shouted at him. She took a few breaths and then said very evenly, 'give me a week and I'll come back to you with what we're going to campaign on.'

Leaving the campaign up to an angry seventeen year old was not much of a political plan, Renard conceded, but it was, at least, a plan.

. . .

Compink Australia was a perennial worry for Fiona Brennan. The ASIO director had planted several operatives into the ranks of the suspect corporation. Collectively, however, they'd learned next to nothing of the corporation's plans. Wilson Huang, the Compink Australia CEO, worked closely with them all, played with them on the corporation volleyball team, but confided nothing to them. One of her agents had downloaded everything, literally everything, from Huang's office computer and still found nothing. Only one file on his computer was password-protected and encrypted. When ASIO cracked that open and decoded it, it contained only one sentence: *I hope you aren't reading this on company time.* Wilson Huang was playing with her head.

Fiona Brennan travelled to Sydney from Canberra that morning to see for herself the discovery security analyst Geraldine Nesbitt had unearthed. A drone image on the screen showed an Asian woman moving past some shops. Security data analysts at ASIO routinely used drone surveillance. They no doubt presumed ASIO operated a fleet of sophisticated drone surveillance cameras merely designed to look as if they were part of the regular Australia Post parcel delivery service. The reality was far simpler; they were actual Australia Post drones. Fiona had personally negotiated the contract whereby Australia Post agreed to put its fleet at ASIO's disposal. ASIO could have rogue packages delivered to a location to suss out who was frequenting a place. Australia Post could tail along unnoticed high above any suspicious character. Importantly, it did so at a fraction of the cost of ASIO maintaining such a system itself.

The woman on the screen pushed open a shop door and disappeared from view. 'That shop is CalliNail,' Geraldine said. 'It's a black hole.' She advanced the image. 'Fourteen minutes from that point . . .' She stopped the film again. 'There. Wilson Huang goes into the gymnasium next door to CalliNail. CCTV cameras from inside the gym show Huang working out only briefly and then he disappears from sight for ten minutes. There's a blind spot between the gym's cameras. Deliberate, I suspect. I also suspect there's an unmarked passage connecting the two buildings. The woman at CalliNail has been identified as Amy Zhao, a data entry clerk at Compink Australia. She leaves CalliNail a few minutes after Wilson Huang returns to view in the gymnasium.'

Geraldine froze the image of Amy. 'There's something here,' she insisted. 'Amy Zhao goes to CalliNail every week and yet . . . she never wears sandals. At work, no one has ever seen the calligraphy on those toenails.' Geraldine considered this a telling point.

'Have Amy Zhao kept under electronic surveillance,' Fiona instructed, despite sensing it would somehow prove fruitless.

Election campaigns were high terrorism-alert periods during which ASIO was always stretched. Fiona Brennan didn't really have time for Compink Australia. Then there was the problem of the Luddites. The Prime Minister was furious that the reality show astronaut Paula Perkins had changed her name to Ned Ludd and no one had told him about it—though the states ran the registries of births, deaths and marriages, not ASIO. So far the Luddites were all stunts and secrecy, but their success disquieted Fiona at a time when she couldn't spare the resources to have the Luddites closely watched.

Still, she had Renard. He'd elevated his assignment from working for the Luddite candidate to *being* the Luddite candidate in Sydney. Nevertheless, the Luddite political structure was proving elusive even to one of its candidates. Renard was certainly not yet privy to the inner workings of the organisation. As an undercover agent, Renard was dutiful but somewhat surly, complaining about having to find shops that would change his endless fifty-dollar notes and blaming ASIO (more than once in the reports) for breaking up his relationship. Fiona had never met Taylor, but the ex-girlfriend's unsupportive attitude irritated the ASIO director. She'd rather Renard was happy in his assignment. 'I think . . .' Fiona stopped, realising she had let her thoughts stray vastly off topic.

'What?' Geraldine asked.

'Do you know Renard's girlfriend, Taylor?'

'I've met her a few times . . .' Geraldine hesitated, surprised at the question. 'Why?'

The trouble with being ASIO director was that no one really felt comfortable gossiping with you. Ask a person something and they'd think national security was somehow involved. Fiona sometimes longed for a good old-fashioned catty bit of gossiping. 'I don't know,' she replied. 'This Taylor doesn't seem right for Renard.'

'Never thought much of Taylor,' Geraldine offered. 'Jealous sort. Possessive.'

'Doesn't surprise me,' Fiona remarked. Geraldine had gossiping potential.

• • •

The *Get Out of My Space* embarrassment normally would have caused the government to take a hit in the polls. When the election had been called, the polls had stood at 42–35 per cent for the Liberal–National Coalition over Labor with 9 per cent for minor parties and 14 per cent undecided. The two-party preferred vote stood at 53–47 per cent in their favour. The Luddites' call to confuse pollsters by encouraging everyone to claim they were voting for the Liberal–National Coalition had caused an immediate blip upwards for the Coalition. Fitzwilliams expected that blip would dissipate once the novelty wore off and people resumed declaring their actual voting intentions to pollsters. Instead, the movement in the polls was showing a disconcerting persistence. The Coalition had shot up further, and was now at 62 per cent of the primary vote with Labor at 27 per cent.

The 'Luddite Lie', as the media called it, had shifted 20 per cent of the electorate into claiming they were intending to vote Liberal–National when they might not be.

'The Luddite Lie has an insidious effect, Prime Minister, one I didn't grasp at first,' Langdon pointed out to him. 'We think there's a blurry twenty per cent in the Liberal–National column of the poll—people who could be planning to vote any which way and can't be relied on. It could even be worse than that. It could be twenty-five per cent. There's no way of knowing. With people lying to the pollsters, we can't tell for sure whether our forty-two per cent primary vote the pre-election polls predicted has gone up, stayed the same or is plunging dangerously.' Langdon was grim. 'To be frank, Prime Minister, our campaign has been a mess so far. It's impossible we have gone up, unlikely we've held our ground. We've sunk below forty-two per cent of the primary vote but, because of the Luddite Lie, we can't tell by how much.' The maths was making Fitzwilliams' head hurt. For the first time in his political life, the polls couldn't be relied on to say anything useful.

A new strategy was needed. Fitzwilliams had summoned his key cabinet colleagues, bringing them scuttling back from the campaign trail. Senator Olga O'Rourke, Treasurer Alan Chandos, Minister for Health and Ageing Donna Hargreaves and . . . Russ Langdon. It had never been a conscious decision by Fitzwilliams to include Langdon in his inner circle, but nevertheless he had summoned him. Langdon's left wrist was in a cast. His colleagues were sporting their Relief Kerchiefs, a boy scout-type scarf around the neck to fundraise for . . . was it bushfire disaster relief?

Their new campaign manager, Georgia Lambert, rounded out the group. Unlike her predecessor, Lister St John, Georgia listened to what they decided to do and then helped them to do it. She didn't give him orders. These were admirable qualities in a campaign manager, Fitzwilliams thought.

The media might be without reliable polls, but the Prime Minister had the PR research firm of Baxter Lockwood at his disposal. Whatever muffins Baxter Lockwood were passing out to their focus groups, they must be good. Their Behavioural Insights Unit was somehow providing clear information at a time when no one else could. The only trouble was, what they had to say was not what he wanted to hear.

Network Nine had invited the Luddites to the leaders' debate. There'd been no consultation with the two major parties, just a broadcast declaration by the network CEO that it was in the public interest. Public interest? Ratings grubbing, Fitzwilliams snorted to himself.

'The word from Baxter Lockwood,' Georgia Lambert told his colleagues, 'is that the public overwhelmingly wants the Luddites at the debate.' The group considered this in silence. 'If we refuse to debate them, Baxter Lockwood predicts it'll cost us severely. The electorate would perceive it as cowardliness. They predict—' there was no way for Georgia to sugar-coat it '—we'd lose ten to thirteen seats on that alone.'

'Then we debate them,' Alan Chandos said cheerfully. Did the man have any other setting? the Prime Minister sometimes wondered. 'You'll be more than a match for them.'

'Take them on,' Donna Hargreaves agreed. 'We've been on the back foot with this lot for too long. We need to do something bold, something striking, something to stop everybody talking about that damned astronaut.' Fitzwilliams wasn't sure whether to hope that Paula Perkins (aka Ned Ludd) be voted off the space station next Sunday or not. On Earth, she might be more of a problem.

'I might have a little something to fit the bill,' Alan Chandos piped up.

A little something. Fitzwilliams was ready to listen. Chandos's last little something had led to the GP reforms. That idea could have blown up spectacularly and shattered political careers, but Chandos had delivered it so palatably that people actually wanted it by the time it came into effect. 'Give me a week,' Chandos promised, 'and I'll have it ready.'

Olga spoke for the first time. 'Network Nine cares only for the leaders' debate. That's the only one that rates. We could undermine that. Hold a series of small debates where cabinet ministers debate Labor's shadow ministers. Invite the Luddites to each of those. Get the Luddites talking dry policy or commenting on things they don't understand. Get the media bored with them. Right now, the media are infatuated with the Luddites because they have made the news interesting, unpredictable.'

Fitzwilliams hesitated. He saw the tactical worth of her proposal—but his cabinet? Did he want them loose in potentially off-script situations? For God's sake, his Minister for Multiculturalism sometimes used the word 'wog' if he'd had a few drinks. 'I'm not sure all the cabinet ministers are . . .'

'Competent?' Langdon suggested.

Fitzwilliams diplomatically left it at not contradicting Langdon.

'I understand your caution,' Donna said. 'What if I challenged the shadow health minister to a debate and invited the Luddites to send a spokesperson?'

The Prime Minister didn't need to give that much thought. Donna Hargreaves was formidable. Her command of statistics could bewilder even the most astute opponents and leave them in a confused muddle. She would mop the floor with the Luddite.

The agreed debate strategy would be to sideline Labor first and then go for the Luddite. If Labor went after the Luddite, Hargreaves wasn't to join in. They couldn't let it look as if the main parties were ganging up on the minnow. Donna Hargreaves would give the Luddites a good mauling in formal debate, but was that enough? The Luddites had been extremely disruptive in the campaign so far.

'We should employ a broad range of strategies to neutralise the Luddites,' Georgia Lambert advised. 'My team will develop an anti-Luddite strategy and advertising campaign for you within the week.'

There was another problem. The Prime Minister produced a copy of an email from Lister St John. Though his ex-campaign manager had resigned, the letter demanded full payment of his contract. 'The threat behind this extraordinary request,' Fitzwilliams told the room, 'is that if we don't pay up, Lister is going to make the rounds of the talk shows telling tales. He also threatens legal action about workplace bullying and being physically assaulted.'

Everyone looked at Olga.

'I know,' Fitzwilliams told her, 'he insulted your favourite chess grandmaster. It's not an extenuating circumstance.'

Lister's email gave them three weeks to pay up. Of course, three weeks took them to just days before the leaders' debate. There was no coincidence in that.

Olga arched an eyebrow as she read the email. 'A full three weeks,' she commented. 'A serious mistake on his part.' Her eyes locked on to Fitzwilliams'. 'You needn't worry about Lister St John, Prime Minister. I shall take care of him.'

Olga's accent gave her promise a sinister, Stalinist tone. Fitzwilliams felt a brief pleasure at the mental image of Lister St John that conjured, but his more cautious side asked, 'He won't . . . come to any harm?'

'No *physical* harm,' Olga replied delicately.

There was a clatter in the hallway and one of the communications staffers appeared at the door. 'A Labor attack ad, Prime Minister,' the staffer panted. 'I thought you'd better see it. It's . . .'

. . . clearly bad, Fitzwilliams deduced. The staffer opened the wall screen and onto it came the image of the Prime Minister on the tennis court. Olga's voice was overlaid as the Prime Minister was scrambling back and forth after each successive shot. Olga's ominous Russian accent intoned: '*You're no longer young, Prime Minister. You're not fast anymore.*'

'This again.' Fitzwilliams waved a hand dismissively. 'Everyone's already seen this. Is that the best Labor can do?'

'They're using slow motion!' Langdon complained. 'Or is that your actual speed, Prime Minister?' he asked, uncertain.

Fitzwilliams' leg twitched in annoyance and caught Langdon's chair under the table. He saw Langdon wince and realised he hadn't connected with the chair leg.

The image of the Prime Minister's tennis struggles dissolved. In its place was Roslyn Stanfield wearing shorts and a generic AFL-type striped jersey, a ball tucked under her arm. '*It's time, Australia, to change the game,*' she said straight to camera with a smile. Stanfield pivoted to camera two, took several steps and kicked towards the distant poles. An AFL umpire rushed between the poles and gave the always dramatic two-handed goal signal. *'Our goal for a better future! Vote Labor,'* came Roslyn Stanfield's voice. The standard announcement at the end was less hasty than usual. 'Voiced by Liberal Senator Olga O'Rourke,' it drawled, 'and sponsored by G. Gregory, Australian Labor Party, Canberra.'

Langdon inhaled audibly during the clip. 'That kick must have been thirty-five metres!' he marvelled.

Who would have guessed Roslyn Stanfield could kick like that? Perhaps it was why Labor had chosen her as leader.

Alan Chandos gave a fatalistic grin. 'Well, there goes Victoria.'

'Is that all you have to say?' Fitzwilliams snapped.

The Treasurer shrugged. 'South Australia too.'

Fitzwilliams sighed. The campaign had just got nasty.

$$\cdots$$

The two employees of the Behavioural Insights Unit of the PR research firm Baxter Lockwood took a closer look at the numbers. 'Fifty-one,' Sam Turcot verified. 'Leaves . . .' he paused to calculate. 'Double sixteen to finish.' He pulled the last dart from the triple-seventeen slot and handed them to Jiang Luu.

Jiang let out a breath, needing an odd number above seven to set up closing. How would Harry the Needle, current darts world champion, approach the situation? Harry would go nineteen, double fifteen, game closed! There would be no element of randomness. Jiang squinted at the board, focusing on the nineteen, zoning out all the other numbers.

'Where is everyone?' came a startled voice.

Jiang and Sam turned in unison, Jiang's dart still poised for the nineteen. Before them was their CEO, Olivia Alcott. Olivia Alcott's offices were on the twenty-second floor of the prestigious Central Park complex on Broadway. She hadn't visited their office in Tempe in two years.

'Where is everyone?' she asked again.

Both men looked around them as if the absence of co-workers was a surprise to them as well.

'Where is everyone,' Olivia asked, alarm rising in her voice, 'and what's been going on here?'

The Behavioural Insights Unit was the elite team of Baxter Lockwood. Most of Baxter Lockwood's work was in advertising design. The BIU's work fed Olivia and the rest of Baxter Lockwood the data they needed to do that work. They were also the team that provided the Liberal Party with its firm feel on the pulse of the nation. They ran the focus groups, the statistical analyses of behavioural trends, the detailed studies of cultural and political developments. They gave the Prime Minister the information on which policies to choose and how to package them and flagged the policies of Labor to abuse and how to unpackage them. They'd given Fitzwilliams the means to win his three elections.

For all the prestige this brought, the BIU was ill-suited to the swank offices of Central Park. The BIU needed focus groups for their work and that meant Olivia and other senior managers could not entertain Baxter Lockwood's sophisticated clients without encountering people padding about in thongs and wearing t-shirts inscribed with dubious sentiments. The BIU inevitably attracted— it simply couldn't help it—the Australian people. Olivia had hit on the idea of shipping the whole unit out to the industrial zone of Tempe, rendering them out of sight in a place where office rental space was charmingly less expensive. No one at the swank head office was ever going to set eyes on another focus group straggler in daggy clothes beyond any possible claim to retro-hood.

Olivia looked about the office, dumbfounded. 'There's an election on,' she squeaked. 'This place should be as busy as . . .' A simile failed to come to her lips. 'Where's . . .' She tried to think of BIU staff names. 'Tina? Where's Mrs Giardino?'

'Mrs Giardino is on Christmas break,' Sam offered. It being late March, this was an expansive use of the word Christmas.

'What's happened here? What's all that stuff in the focus-meeting pods?' Olivia's voice seemed to implore them to give her a reassuring answer. The glass-walled rooms she asked about were filled with bric-a-brac.

'Tina's parents had to downsize,' Jiang explained, indicating the first room. 'We're just storing some of their stuff temporarily.'

'And what's that?' Olivia pointed to the next room.

'Erica set up hydroponics in there. Tomatoes mostly.' Jiang tried smiling at her. 'Would you like some?'

Olivia sank into a chair at one of the desks in the open-plan office. 'I came here to announce that the Liberal Party has offered to double their contract with Baxter Lockwood until the election is over. Doubling the contract also means doubling the KIs.'

'KIs?' Sam queried.

'Key impacts. For God's sake, Sam, the term has been around for a year at least! You ought to know it.' She hadn't meant to raise her voice with him. As a CEO, she prided herself on how she treated her staff.

'Don't worry,' Jiang assured her, 'we'll be able to deliver the KIs, even CGS's if they need any.' This was a reference to the output measures of the early 2020s. 'We'll be able to tell the Liberal Party whatever they want to know.'

'How?' Olivia gestured around her. 'By asking a roomful of tomatoes?!'

Sam and Jiang exchanged glances. 'Let us introduce you to Nostradamus,' Sam said.

. . .

Twenty minutes later—or rather twenty-five minutes later, as they'd had to make her a good cup of tea afterwards—Olivia staggered to the street and summoned an available Auto Pilot. Auto Pilot was the driverless taxi service that had crushed the manned market, taking out both Taxis Combined and the once-mighty Uber. She clambered into the front seat and stated her destination.

'Do you want Cabbie mode?' the screen asked. The vehicle was capable of banter for those nostalgic for it.

She hit *No*. She needed time to think.

She'd learned that the Behavioural Insights Unit hadn't seen a single focus group for almost the entire two years they had been in Tempe, not since Jiang had completed the design and testing of his Nostradamus program. Instead of actually surveying people and finding out how they reacted to various nuances of policy, Jiang had simply loaded thirty years' worth of focus group data into Nostradamus. Much like the chess computers that could beat any human grandmaster because they could remember and analyse every move of every grandmaster game ever played, Nostradamus could tell you how the Australian people would react to even the subtlest shifts of policy. Ask it whether voters would react better to the term 'tax break' or 'tax rebate' and it could give you the postcodes of where each term would work best. Ask whether they wanted more boots on the ground in the Caucasus republics and it would tell you not only the answer (yes), but also when they would change their minds if the situation did not improve (fourteen months). It could tell you how many people would prefer to see the Prime Minister wear a striped tie. (37.4 per cent).

Olivia felt numb. 'We've been telling our client that we've been intensely surveying voters,' she lectured her two employees. 'I mean human voters, those voters voting in five weeks,' she emphasised. 'This is fraud! We've been taking their money and we haven't been doing any of the work they contracted us to do.'

Sam put on his soothing voice. 'They've contracted us to give them answers, Olivia, and we've been giving them answers. Accurate answers. There'll be plenty of KLs to go around.'

'KIs!'

'What's a KL then?'

'I think KL is Superman's name on Krypton,' Jiang chirped.

The team had used their free time to develop other interests. Erica was planning to market her low-cost, high-yield hydroponic kits. Tina was writing a fantasy novel. Mrs Giardino's knitting group met there on Thursdays.

What wounded Olivia most was their reason for developing Nostradamus. At first, Sam claimed, they'd done it because holding all those inane focus group meetings was driving them slowly mad. 'You don't know what it was like listening to all that *opinion* all day!' he told her. However, there was another reason underlying that one. If Jiang could invent Nostradamus, they reasoned, then somebody else could as well. They'd developed the program because they presumed Olivia already had someone working along those lines and would sack them all once it was served up to her.

She wasn't like that. She wasn't one of those CEOs who schemed to have all other jobs in the company automated. She liked having co-workers. Granted she hadn't visited their Tempe office since the official opening party, but she *valued* people. Perhaps, it occurred to her for the first time, she wasn't cut out to be a modern CEO. She'd never once thought to automate their jobs and sack the lot of them.

Sam tried to point out a silver lining. Nostradamus had successfully delivered KIs for two years now, and while it did subsidise the BIU workforce to go on extended holidays and play beach volleyball in the workplace (they had actually laid sand in one of the focus pods), it had also saved the company a packet. Over the two years, the absence of the focus groups had saved the company $60,000 in muffins, coffee, tea, milk and sugar. 'I always hated that,' Sam told her. 'We'd drag in the public to ask their opinion on whether to increase our military commitment in Nagorno-Karabakh, but all they cared about was their next tea break, and they'd fret if we didn't have any boysenberry vanilla muffins.'

Olivia held up her hand. 'You saved the company sixty thousand dollars? Where is it?' She may not have visited their office, but she knew their accounts. 'You've been filing the standard muffins and coffee expenses every fortnight for the last two years.' A sudden thought jolted her. 'Hang on. We aren't just talking about muffins and tea expenses. You paid—or pretended to pay—a stipend to each of those phantom focus group members you never interviewed. That's—' the calculations whirled in her head '—over two hundred thousand dollars.' The magnitude of the sum wrenched her stomach. 'Where's that money?' she demanded.

'Don't worry,' Jiang intoned.

'You keep telling me not to worry and yet you keep telling me alarming things.'

'We were going to embezzle it,' he explained, 'but only when you had brought in a rival Nostradamus and fired us. It was our own redundancy payment fund. Since you say you weren't planning to fire us, you can have the money back. It's in our phantom account.'

'Two hundred and ninety-seven thousand dollars,' Sam told her, seemingly proud. 'No, wait,' he corrected himself. 'Two hundred and eighty-five thousand. I forgot about the Christmas party.'

She ignored the fact that they had spent $12,000 on a staff Christmas party for seven people (part of that sum had been used to fly Mrs Giardino back from Hamilton Island). 'After this,' Olivia shot at them, 'how can I possibly trust you?'

'You don't have to trust us,' Jiang replied. 'You only have to trust Nostradamus.'

CHAPTER SIX

Amy Zhao waited impatiently for the calligrapher to finish her nails. Symbols of the planets this time, apparently. She hadn't known the planets had symbols. CalliNail might be squiggling any old nonsense on her nails, she realised cynically.

She had much to tell CEO Wilson Huang. Her special agent Loki had pulled it off. The Prime Minister had agreed to allow the Luddites to participate in the leaders' debate. Amy had not risked communicating her request directly to Loki, instead engaging her slovenly underemployed flatmate, an ex-postie. He still delivered flyers door-to-door on a casual basis. She hand-wrote the coded request to Loki and asked her flatmate to slip it under the door at Loki's home address the next time he delivered Special Carpet Cleaning Offer flyers in Newtown. Amy would have gladly given the flatmate a hundred dollars to do this small task, but Amy Zhao the data entry clerk was supposed to be hard up. She'd offered instead to do the dishes for the whole month.

2028

It was, Amy sighed to herself, a case of bringing your work home with you.

When she entered the fingernail-drying room, a young girl, no more than seven or eight years old, was sitting there. 'Niece,' the girl said.

Wilson had sent his niece?

The girl admired her own fingernails a moment and then looked up at Amy. 'Odin,' she informed her.

Amy let out a breath. Odin was Wilson Huang's agent inside ASIO. All Amy knew of Odin was that he or she worked in the surveillance section, not in operations. Odin could tell you what ASIO had discovered, not what they were planning. Odin must have alerted Wilson that ASIO now knew of his clandestine CalliNail meetings with Amy.

'Pokémon,' the girl grinned, showing Amy the tiny figures on her nails.

'They're very nice,' Amy replied, realising she could speak normally in this room for a change. Her uncle's message about ASIO delivered, Wilson's niece left the room.

ASIO would certainly be asking themselves why Wilson Huang was going out of his way to rendezvous secretly with one of his data entry clerks. If ASIO was on to them, obviously Amy could no longer meet directly with Wilson. Was she sad about that? She did occasionally wonder whether she might be in love with Wilson. The answer, she always acknowledged, was no. She didn't love Wilson Huang. What she loved was their peculiar relationship, their meeting of minds in a state of utter secrecy. She wanted nothing else from him. She couldn't imagine sitting across a dinner table from him. She certainly couldn't imagine waking up next to him in bed. More fundamentally, she couldn't imagine a conversation with him where they used verbs.

On leaving CalliNail a few minutes later, she noted the Australia Post drone trailing her. She smiled. In intelligence, when the other side thought they had the upper hand on you, there was almost no limit to what you could make them believe. She could fill her ASIO watchers with disinformation. And pleasingly, Amy realised, glancing at the absurd planet symbols adorning her nails, ASIO having discovered their meeting spot meant she no longer was obliged to go to CalliNail!

That observation didn't last until the next block. Having calligraphy done on her nails was the one indulgence the downtrodden data entry clerk Amy Zhao allowed herself. Amy examined the absurd planet symbols adorning her nails. She would have to keep up the pretence, she sighed in resignation.

• • •

It was still called the National Press Club, although none of the media giants had pressed anything onto paper for several years. The only newspaper Donna Hargreaves ever saw in print these days was the *Green Left Weekly*, the irony that it was the last of the newspapers still hacking down trees to pulp evidently lost on the old geezer flogging it outside her grocery shop. As Minister for Health and Ageing, Donna recognised she really ought to delete the word 'geezer' from her vocabulary.

From behind her lectern on the National Press Club stage, Hargreaves sized up her opponents. Labor's Jessica Underhill, smiling and clearly nervous, was reviewing a bundle of note cards.

Note cards—right out of the twentieth century—which, Hargreaves mused, was roughly where Labor policy was. Anyone who relied on note cards wasn't ready for debate.

Donna Hargreaves had made it clear to Fitzwilliams that she wanted to be Minister for Health and Ageing. She wanted it because, unlike many of her cabinet colleagues, she was committed to the concept of an effective, free healthcare system. Others might run Medicare simply because it was something the government had to do—the political consequences of scrapping it altogether being catastrophic—however, they'd have gladly let it run down, wean as many voters as possible into private health care and blame the state governments for all the healthcare system's problems. She, instead, had fought for the last six years to maintain funding and kept the ailing system from haemorrhaging too badly. Instead of blaming the state government for failures, she badgered them to meet their obligations. She made sure funding reached preventative programs and under-resourced hospitals. And she was also a master of illusion. Part of keeping the whole thing running was pretending it was running along just fine. She could say with total honesty that the healthcare system was working better now than it had been six years earlier.

Her eyes shifted to her other opponent. The Luddites had sent a woman who looked eighty years old. She was small in a shrunken way. It could be inadvisable to be aggressive in debating someone so frail-looking. The Luddite was plainly dressed—frumpy, even. Hargreaves eyes lit on the long brooch on the Luddite's lapel and did a double-take. It wasn't a brooch at all, but a stick of celery pinned there. Was it a joke? For a person of this Luddite's age, it was sometimes a fine line between eccentricity and dementia.

Hargreaves' mind, in debating mode, quickly reviewed some statistics on the provision of dementia services.

The moderator began the introductions. Hargreaves reminded herself of her strategy for the triangular debate. Sideline Labor and then go after the Luddite. If Labor went for the Luddite, rise above it. 'And representing the Luddite Party of Australia,' the moderator finished, 'Ned Ludd.'

'The Australian people,' Jessica Underhill said, launching into it and pointing at the elderly Luddite, 'have a right to know your real name. Why do you and the rest of your party hide behind a false name?'

'It is my real name,' the Luddite replied gently. 'I changed it to Ned Ludd nine years ago.'

'But it's not your *real* name,' Labor's shadow health minister insisted. 'Tell the Australian people your real name!'

'Well, dear . . .' the Luddite twinkled at Jessica Underhill. The word 'dear' had been so intricately laced with condescension that Hargreaves was instantly on her guard. 'You've changed your name too, haven't you?'

'What do you mean?' Underhill was nonplussed.

'You changed your name when you married, didn't you? I suppose it was your choice to take the man's surname—though,' the Luddite editorialised briefly, 'many women of my generation thought it was important not to do so. What was your real name again, dear?'

Jessica Underhill wanted to snap back that it wasn't 'dear', but realised she shouldn't respond petulantly to the old bat. 'Braithwaite,' she muttered. 'Braithwaite,' she repeated more loudly to indicate she wasn't ashamed of it.

'But you also changed your first name,' the Luddite prompted.

'My name has always been Jessica,' Underhill replied evenly.

Hargreaves could tell Underhill was disconcerted, but she couldn't fathom why.

'Ah, but was it always spelled that way?' Ned Ludd probed.

'I don't think that's important,' Underhill said. 'We're here to discuss health and ageing.'

'You're the one who raised the names. Tell the Australian people how you used to spell your name.'

Jessica Underhill nee Braithwaite knew her parents would be watching. She had never told them about officially changing her name. She'd always insisted to them that it was just the media that couldn't get it right. 'J-E-S-S-' Underhill began conventionally enough, before pausing. 'Y,' she soldiered on. There was a titter in the audience. 'K.' A few guffaws broke out. (Poor thing, thought Hargreaves. She would have changed her name too. What kind of parents did that to a child?) 'A . . . H,' Underhill finished bleakly.

Jessykah? Donna Hargreaves had to suppress a snort and was only partially successful. She took the opportunity to move in decisively. 'I think we should talk about health and ageing and the challenges that face the next government in maintaining quality, free, efficient, accessible and fair health services.' She always liked to rattle off a smorgasbord of descriptors.

The next fifteen minutes were fought out more traditionally. Labor insisted that emergency room wait times had increased, Hargreaves countering that they had reduced. The ageing population was either suffering, neglected and abandoned or they were the recipients of a comprehensive range of community and residential services that was world-class. The Liberal–National Coalition was either leading Medicare into an abyss or a golden age.

Ned Ludd mostly stayed out of this, which worried the moderator. Having a Luddite in the debate had been the prime drawcard for the media. He directed a general question to Ned Ludd on Luddite healthcare policy.

'I'd like to raise an idea,' Ned Ludd started, 'that I hope we can get tri-partisan agreement on.'

Donna Hargreaves' eyes narrowed. She always smelled a rat when people started talking of bipartisan agreement. Tripartisan sounded triply suspect.

What followed was a startling proposal that began with the Pharmaceutical Benefits Scheme but, by the time it was finished, planned to globalise drug research, bypass the multinational pharmaceutical companies and remove all patents on drugs. All pharmaceuticals were to be sold at generic prices plus 3 per cent, saving the government an enormous amount of money. The 3 per cent was to be spent on medical research. All research results were to be made public so that researchers around the world could build on each other's work. The results of clinical trials were to be globalised so as to keep all nations at the same high standard. It eliminated the market distortion caused by multinational pharmaceutical companies needing a return for heavy investment.

It also, Hargreaves realised instantly, eliminated the need for multinational pharmaceutical companies. It would be suicide.

Donna Hargreaves was a nuts-and-bolts fighter. You had to be to keep the Department of Health and Ageing limping along. She was not used to dealing with grand utopian ideas in the midst of trench fighting. 'Ned,' she said, conceding the Luddite name—it would

make her look more gracious than the unfortunate Jessykah—
'Australia cannot act unilaterally on an idea like that. You're
talking about the whole of international pharmaceutical research,
production, distribution, patents, pricing.'

'Yes,' the Luddite agreed.

'I'm glad you realise that,' Hargreaves noted.

'Can you both read over this?' the Luddite asked them, pulling
out a hefty document to show to the camera. 'Then we can
work out the details to take before the rest of the world.'

Was the woman mad? The big pharmaceuticals—Pfizer, Bayer,
GlaxoSmithKline—would squash them like flies.

'Your idea is simply not practical,' Hargreaves replied carefully.

'Are you saying you won't read it?' Ned Ludd asked.

'I didn't say I wouldn't read it,' Hargreaves fired back in a tangle
of negatives.

'I'll read it,' piped up Jessykah Underhill, sensing an opening.

'Good.' Ned beamed. 'We can revise it together and take it to the
General Agreement on Tariff and Trade negotiations in November.'

The other two candidates clamoured that they had made no such
commitment. Who did Ned Ludd think she was, setting such an
agenda? Hargreaves was almost relieved when Jessykah Underhill
moved the debate on to the recent fiasco at Royal Adelaide Hospital.

They were nearing the end. Jessykah Underhill had come off
the worst but Hargreaves herself had not demolished the Luddite
as she had promised.

'I must say,' Ned Ludd now interjected, 'I'm surprised neither
of you saw fit to wear a stick of celery today. The stick of celery—'
she pointed to her own lapel for the benefit of the cameras
'—is to raise awareness of Sikorsky syndrome, a debilitating spinal

condition that affects one in every nine hundred and forty-three children born in this country.'

Keeping her features pleasant, Hargreaves merely imagined gritting her teeth. She had a suitcase full of damned ribbons and armbands to wear throughout the campaign. No one had told her about the celery sticks—and it was related to a medical issue!

'Labor stands for first-class paediatric health,' Jessykah Underhill asserted firmly, 'and is fully committed to more funding for further research into . . .' she hesitated at the term, 'the disease.'

When Hargreaves had first started as Minister for Health and was anxious about mastering all she had to master, her senior bureaucrats told her that if ever cornered, she could always rely on the Seven Per Cent Solution. 'Whatever you are talking about, say it is seven per cent better than it is.' 'You mean make it up?' she queried. 'No,' they replied, 'Say it is seven per cent better and rest assured, we can torture our statistics until we get a confession that it is—but,' she was warned, 'don't go above seven per cent.'

Hargreaves wasn't going to apologise for being celery stick-less tonight. 'In the last two years, federal funding for Sikorsky syndrome has been increased by seven per cent—and that is seven per cent above inflation. That is the commitment of this government.'

'Really?' Ned Ludd raised her pale eyebrows. 'I find that quite remarkable—because I made up the disease. There is no Sikorsky syndrome.'

Hargreaves shot a glance at Jessykah Underhill. The shadow minister's mouth was hanging open. She appeared dumbfounded. Hargreaves sensed that her own face might be presenting the cameras with a very similar expression.

• • •

Knowing ASIO was following her, Amy Zhao had decided to lead them somewhere they'd find absolutely perplexing. She had joined the local Luddite campaign in her Sydney electorate.

A Compink Australia agent working inside the Luddite Party would certainly keep ASIO and Fiona Brennan awake at night—which served them right for snooping on her. The drawback for Amy, however, was it meant more work. She'd already had a long day at Compink Australia that had finished with an inordinate amount of dishes. Had there been a party there in the afternoon? If so, she hadn't been invited.

She had joined the Luddite Party as her put-upon-data-entry-clerk persona. The Luddites had done no checks to verify anything about her. Their lack of suspicion seemed almost suspicious. There was definitely something going on within the Luddites. Their political candidate in Sydney, the local Ned Ludd, didn't seem to have any clear political platform and fished around for ideas from his supporters. He always paid for everything in cash, crisp fifty-dollar notes. Somebody had given money to this Luddite in cash; somebody who didn't want that campaign funding traced.

Tonight's meeting was at Low Expectations. Normally the shop was closed on Monday nights, but Kate, a young Luddite activist, worked there. Amy entered and took a seat while Kate was explaining the house rules. People could help themselves to tea, but they had to clean up afterwards. Amy sighed. She could guess where this evening was heading.

Ned Ludd did the rounds, serving tea. He might not have many political ideas, but he had a friendly smile, Amy thought, and he was good-looking, even smelled nice. Kate, only seventeen years old but the group's political strategist, did a presentation on her chosen core issue for the Sydney campaign, the national wage, a proposed base income for all Australians. It was an idea that had been around for a while, but no one had ever taken seriously; it was more of a pub conversation than a political platform in Amy's view. Kate's proposal was a far-reaching one, completely at odds with political orthodoxy. It had qualities that were—Amy searched her memory—almost communist. But it was a weirdly individualised, entrepreneurial communism. Were they really intending to campaign on that?

Ned Ludd's leadership was mild to say the least. He told the rest of the Luddites that he and Kate would campaign on this national wage idea, but they could choose other issues. The man with the Jamaican accent said he liked Kate's national wage idea, as did the two sisters from Pyrmont. Some Surry Hills post-hipster went off on a tangent about forming an artists' collective.

Ned looked over at Amy. 'What do you want to campaign on?' he asked.

What did she want? The questioned flummoxed her. Create headaches for ASIO? Keep Compink Australia running? Get the dishwasher repaired in the staff kitchen? Have a beer with Ned-of-the-nice-smile after the meeting? None of these seemed appropriate. She smiled but said nothing. It was a response typical of her data-entry self.

'You've come here in your own time to help with the Luddite campaign,' Ned prompted her. 'It is only fair you get to have a say in what we do.'

She was unused to this kind of attention. 'Greenhouse gas reduction,' she managed. Compink Australia had vast interests in renewables.

A man with a tubercular cough, who was also called Ned Ludd, began dividing up campaign areas and times for people. Amy found herself partnered with Kate, Old Ned and Candidate Ned to work Glebe—giving up both Saturday and Sunday of the coming weekend, she noted wearily.

The meeting broke up and several Luddites headed off to the pub. Kate, with sudden teenage urgency, remembered she had to meet friends. She tossed the keys to Candidate Ned and asked him to do the locking up and was out the door before he even said he would. Amy started gathering up the mugs.

'Don't do that,' Candidate Ned told her. He was the only Luddite left. 'I'll wash up.'

Amy stood stock still. She couldn't recall the last time someone had made that offer. Had anyone *ever* made that offer to her?

She felt the gentle brush of his hand as he took the mugs from her. Her skin tingled, and she felt her cheeks go hot. She realised to her dismay that Amy Zhao, data entry clerk, was considering falling in love with this man.

Whatever was happening, it showed on her face. 'Are you all right?' Ned asked, leaning closer to her.

She raised her face to look up into his. Seizing her chance, she threw her arms around his neck and kissed him passionately on the lips. Amy Zhao, Compink Australia deputy CEO, couldn't believe what was going on. Who gave that order? she demanded of herself.

She realised she was being kissed back. Finally, the deputy CEO seized control. She pulled her face away from Ned and stepped back. 'Ah,' she said, raising both hands in front of her, 'please, just forget that I did that.'

'That's a rather memorable thing to forget,' Ned observed. It was a sweet, almost gallant reply, she thought . . . or was that the data entry clerk's opinion again?

'I—I have to go,' Amy stuttered and, true to her stammered statement, she fled.

• • •

She could still feel his kiss on her lips—or, rather, she could still feel the pressure of her lips having kissed him. The hunger in her actions had astonished her. Amy opened the door to her apartment and scurried past her flatmate without saying hello, noticing only that he had used three different teacups while watching something on the internet. She rushed down the corridor to the bathroom.

The sink had toothpaste on it again. How could someone miss when loading up a toothbrush? Her flatmate must be doing it deliberately. She splashed water on her face, cupping her hands to her nose. Pulling her hands away slowly, she raised her eyes to the mirror.

The face she saw was an imploring one. While the deputy CEO was satisfied with the intrigue-filled life she led, the data entry clerk staring back at her clearly wanted something more. She held the gaze of the mirror. 'All right,' she heaved at last, speaking out aloud as if to confirm the resolution. 'If we want Ned Ludd . . .' she paused to nod at herself, 'we'll have him.'

She got a warm smile in reply.

• • •

132

If it ever got out, it would be the end of Baxter Lockwood. For two years, the work of Baxter Lockwood's Behavioural Insights Unit had been utterly fraudulent, with the BIU only pretending to survey the Australian people on thousands of issues while giving all their customers, *including the government of the country*, reports based entirely on the predictions of a computer program. Since finding out, Olivia Alcott had decided on only two things. First, this lot (the BIU staff) needed an eye kept on them. Second, no matter how uncomfortable she was with the idea, she needed to keep Nostradamus going until the election was over. Incredibly, during the two years the BIU had been using Nostradamus, Baxter Lockwood's reputation for PR research excellence had, if anything, risen. This team of hers, packing hydroponic kits, playing indoor beach volleyball and writing fantasy novels, was doing the job better than when they'd actually done the job.

They'd been surprised when she'd arrived with her takeaway coffee mug, Gargantuan holder and photo of her daughter and dramatically swept a partially completed jigsaw puzzle off a spare BIU desk to claim it as hers. The boss was back!

Her staff still worked, she discovered, the major difference being it only took them a couple of hours. They interviewed clients to find out what questions they wanted answered, which ranged from how students were responding to the introduction of Work for the Dole TAFE training courses to whether consumers would accept Dental Bomb, a prototype fizzy fluoride pellet for flossing-averse kids. They'd feed those questions into Nostradamus then write up a final report based on Nostradamus's instant answer. (They'd hold on to the report for two months before sending it off, so that the customer believed the BIU had conducted thorough market surveys.) The rest of the work day was theirs.

Olivia had the impression that the team regretted not the fraud or their planned embezzlement, but the fact that they'd deceived her. 'We would've told you,' kindly Mrs Giardino explained, 'only we thought you'd worry about it.'

Olivia gazed across at Jiang, sitting in front of his computer. 'Sam, there's something I don't understand. What does Jiang enter into Nostradamus every morning when he arrives?'

'He just keeps Nostradamus current with what's going on.' Sam looked up from his Sudoku. 'The thirty years of survey data we originally entered gave Nostradamus an understanding of how people behave. What Jiang enters each morning lets Nostradamus process any new developments in society. That maintains the program's predictive abilities.'

'But where's he getting his data from?' Olivia asked. 'And how can Nostradamus deal with anything new—like the Luddite Party, for instance? There is no relevant data for Nostradamus to draw on.'

'Why not ask the man himself?' Sam said with an indulgent smile. Olivia felt the team had a growing tendency to treat her as though she was the person at a very enjoyable party who was spending her time fretting that there was no healthy food available.

Jiang looked puzzled when she put the question to him. 'I just tell Nostradamus what's been going on.' Though standards had slipped at the BIU in the two-year interregnum between Olivia's visits, Jiang's workstation was immaculate. A tiny, curious-looking figurine stood blue-tacked atop his computer screen.

'How do you know what to enter each morning? How do you judge what developments are significant?'

'I just put in what I think needs putting in,' he said with a shrug.

Olivia paled. Subjective data. No one in PR had worked with subjective data for forty years. 'You mean your *hunch*?' she squeaked as quietly as she could.

Jiang appeared to contemplate something. 'Nostradamus is more . . . complicated than we described it. It has purposes that go beyond predicting consumer or voter response.'

Olivia could tell Jiang was concerned that further explanation would distress her. He was obviously about to tell her something quite appalling. In a nineteenth-century novel, Olivia would have been able to faint her way out of the scene. They would have carried her off to the nearest sofa and plied her with smelling salts and fussed over her until all was well. But that Austenesque escape was not available to a CEO in the twenty-first century. 'What other purposes?' she ground out reluctantly.

'You may not want to hear it,' Jiang cautioned.

'I'm certain I don't want to hear it!' she snapped. 'Tell me anyway.'

'In certain circumstances, Nostradamus can work as a kind of . . .' he searched for a term, 'lobbyist. It can persuade the government to do certain things.'

'How's that possible?'

'It's a different type of lobbying,' Jiang admitted. 'In traditional lobbying, the lobbyist promises something to the politicians. It may be jobs in the electorate. It may be money for the party. They wine and dine—'

'I know how lobbying works!' Olivia hissed. 'What does Nostradamus do?'

Jiang thought a moment. 'Remember that pro bono job you sent us? The citizens group, the environmental anti-coal activists who wanted the lignite power plant in Victoria shut down?'

Olivia certainly remembered it. It had been an example of Baxter Lockwood giving back to the community.

'We interviewed them,' Jiang explained, 'found out what they had in mind, and wrote up a recommended action plan for them to win over public support.' What he was describing was all routine. 'Then,' Jiang continued—he was clearly getting to the crux of it—'we sent the government a report saying that the anti-lignite movement had significant public support, that the replacement of the power plant with renewables would be hugely popular and would make people think the government was on top of things.'

'How did Nostradamus know that?'

'Well . . .' Jiang seemed to hedge. 'It didn't. We write that part up ourselves. We tell the government something bad will happen if they do this and something good will happen if they do that. They almost always choose "that". It's lobbying, but without having to bribe them.'

He actually expected her to think this was clever, she realised. Jiang was calling it 'lobbying', but it was outright deception. He might seem totally amiable, but Olivia was increasingly aware he was completely unscrupulously amiable. If he was deceiving the government that paid Baxter Lockwood so handsomely, it was likely he was deceiving her as well. 'That figurine,' she said, indicating the tiny figure atop Jiang's computer screen.

'What about it?' Jiang asked, surprised by the change of topic.

'That's Loki, isn't it?'

Sam scoffed. 'That's not Loki,' he said, chuckling. 'It doesn't look anything like Taron Egerton!'

'What are you talking about?' Olivia asked.

'Taron Egerton. The actor who played Loki in the *Avengers* 2024 reboot.'

'I'm not talking about Taron bloody Egerton!'

'Well, it's not Tom Hiddleston from the original *Thor*.'

'Sam,' she queried, 'do you have any other setting besides perma-nerd?' She turned back to Jiang. 'That figurine is Loki—the trickster.' Olivia shot a glance at Sam. 'From Norse mythology, not from some children's comic book made into a billion-dollar movie,' she clarified. Olivia levelled a finger at Jiang. 'You're not telling me the whole story.'

Jiang held up an index finger. 'We are in a position to be . . .' again he appeared to be searching for the right way to present the next idea, 'a force for good.'

'A force for good?'

'PR research firms are in a unique position with the government. We can suggest to them good things to do and it becomes just the nudge the government needs to go out and do them—like shutting down that lignite power plant, for instance.'

'So you're what—a band of do-gooder superheroes making sure the government serves the people?' Olivia couldn't believe the gall of them. 'How do you decide which good works you'll dupe the government into doing?'

'The whole unit votes. It has to be unanimous.' Sam put in. He seemed proud of the unit's democratic principles. 'We don't do it that often,' he added, reading Olivia's disapproval correctly for once. 'Besides, it's a nice little money spinner for the company. That one made eighty thousand dollars.'

'How could it be a money spinner? The anti-lignite mob had no money. We did everything for them pro bono.'

Sam realised he had blundered. 'There was a paying customer as well,' he responded quietly.

Olivia trembled. A paying customer? 'You mean, there are companies out there that know you're manipulating the government?' This was potentially catastrophic. It meant more than the ruin of the company; this might be flee-the-country-level corruption.

'No, no, no,' Jiang replied. 'Almost always, the customer thinks they've done it. We give them an analysis that says "Do this campaign, take out these sorts of ads, organise this kind of lobbying"—any old nonsense. They do all that and they think they've won over the government. They've no idea we were the ones who spurred the government into action.'

'Where's the money?' Olivia queried. 'You said you have paying customers. Where's the money been going?'

Sam cleared his throat. 'We keep it in a special account . . .' he began.

'In case I sacked the lot of you!' she yelled, cutting him off. Heads turned from the other desks and focus pods. Olivia lowered her voice. 'Just how many different slush funds do you have around here?' she asked sarcastically.

Sam's eyes looked upwards as if he was tallying something.

She spun back to Jiang. 'You said "almost always".'

'I did?'

'You said, "Almost always, the customer thinks they've done it." That means there are some customers who do know you are manipulating the government.'

'Just one,' Jiang said soothingly. 'In fairness, it was their idea. We hadn't thought to manipulate the government this way until they suggested it.'

'And they gave us the eighty thousand dollars to shut down the lignite power plant,' Sam added. 'They're big in renewable energy.' He decided it was not the time to mention the $15,000 Compink Australia had recently paid them to ensure the Luddites were invited to the leaders' debate.

Just one company, Olivia thought. One might be manageable. How many in that company would know? Possibly only a few people . . . but those few could threaten to tell, blackmail Baxter Lockwood. 'Who is it?' she asked.

Jiang gave her his you-don't-want-to-know look.

'Just tell me,' she pleaded wearily, her head spinning.

'We sort of . . . do work for . . . Compink Australia.'

'Only occasional jobs, special jobs when they ask us,' Sam put in.

Olivia's visual field seemed to close in on her and her head was swimming. She wobbled on her feet. Sam's arms shot out to steady her but he found himself catching her instead. 'My God!' he cried. 'She's fainted!'

Mrs Giardino rushed across the office. 'What did you boys do to her? Carry her over to that sofa,' she ordered. 'Tina, get wet towels to put on her head. Erica, make her a strong cup of tea with sugar.'

When Olivia came to, they were all fussing over her. Tears welled in her eyes as she savoured the brief comforting moments before reality intruded again.

CHAPTER SEVEN

The blitz was on. Labor had started saturation advertising, a preliminary softening up of the electorate on the party's chosen issues, the ones Roslyn Stanfield intended to hammer home during the leaders' debate. Labor was bombarding all high-rating media targets: the reality shows and cooking competitions—everything except Fortuna Corporation's *Get Out of My Space*. *GOOMS* was building up the hype for the program's pinnacle moment, the much-anticipated Fortuna Friday. Though no details had yet been revealed, it was being modestly billed as 'the greatest event ever to take place in space'. With an unpredictable Luddite astronaut/candidate still on board the space station, any association with the show was fraught with political danger for both major parties.

Labor's catchphrases—hardly even catchphrases, Fitzwilliams snorted, being only two words long—constituted an endless supply of alliterative adjectives to pair with the word 'battler'. Telephone poles around the country were affixed with images of Beleaguered Battlers (Liberal Party housing policy), Buoyant Battlers (Labor's Opportunity-Based Employment policy), Brilliant Battlers (Labor's Advancement-through-Education policy), Bruised Battlers (Liberal health policy) and so on. Negative adjectives were framed in Liberal blue, positive ones in Labor red. In the TV ad, the Beleaguered Battlers were a photogenic white family being told by the hated figure of a banker that the bank was foreclosing on their mortgage. '*What are we to do?*' asks the father, directing the question not to his wife or, more pertinently, to the banker, but to the camera. Cut to Roslyn Stanfield, standing on yet another AFL pitch. '*First thing to do,*' Stanfield says, '*is kick this lot out,*' concluding the ad with a perfectly placed kick between the posts (forty metres, Russ Langdon estimated), the goal umpire giving his two-handed endorsement to the Labor Party.

'This battler business is tiresome,' campaign manager Georgia Lambert declared. 'Another week of saturating the media with this and they'll be hit by serious Ridichet.' Fitzwilliams was familiar with the term. Ridichet (Ridicule Ricochet) was the term for policies or, more often, politicians pilloried mercilessly by political satire shows.

'Do we know of any comedians working along those lines?' Donna Hargreaves asked.

'Careful,' Fitzwilliams cautioned. 'We can't be seen to encourage anyone in that direction.'

Everyone had played that game to some extent, offering choice material about political opponents for comedians to feed upon. It was their unlamented former Minister for Industry who had embellished this pastime by also offering a tidy $5000 to a certain comedian to take the satirical axe first to his shadow minister opposite and later, utterly disloyally, to his own foreign minister, whose job and travel perks he desired. The ensuing Cash for Comics scandal had rolled more than that one head.

'What do you think of their ad, Quentin?' Fitzwilliams asked.

Russ Langdon, as Minister for Security and Freedom, had insisted that bodyguards be attached to all party leaders at all times, including at confidential meetings. Given what had happened to Langdon in the last election, Fitzwilliams could hardly overrule him. If the bodyguards had to sit in on meetings, Fitzwilliams decided he might as well use them as a portable vox populi to consult whenever the opinion of the 'general public' was needed. Quentin seemed a name ill-suited to a bodyguard, Fitzwilliams thought. It didn't sound protective. The other bodyguard was Leon. Quentin and Leon. It sounded more like a comedy duo than the people charged with guarding the life of the nation's prime minister.

'Stanfield can kick, Prime Minister,' Quentin conceded, 'but I've never been a fan of that aerial ping pong stuff.' He thumped his chest. 'Rugby league's my game.'

Perhaps the intolerance followers of different football codes had for each other's sports might limit the appeal of Stanfield's kicking prowess—unless (Fitzwilliams grimaced at the thought) Stanfield proved able to master NRL dropkicks as well. The Prime Minister checked his watch. Where was Olga? Lister St John, his former campaign manager, had teed up two prime interview spots, both just before the leaders' debate. St John was making good on his threat to give tell-all interviews to the media unless he was paid out his full contract. Olga had promised to deal with him.

'The campaign song,' Georgia Lambert announced. 'One of your staffers discovered this gem.'

Onto the screen came a conventional four-piece rock band, a bit scruffy, but not hard-edged. The lead singer, half swallowing the microphone, cut into a lively opening riff, singing about a bush town pulling itself up and making a go of it. By the chorus, all four band members were singing:

> We are Aussie, it's what we are about.
> We are Aussie, let me hear you sing and shout
> Here you know you'll get a fair go
> You have your say, it's the Aussie way
> We are Aussie, it's what we are about.

'It's catchy,' Fitzwilliams agreed. The lyrics had reassuringly expressed nothing but utter clichés.

Alan Chandos spoke up. 'Georgia, this band . . .'

'The Jaggernauts.'

'The Jaggernauts don't look like the sort of people who vote Liberal.' Chandos looked around the room. 'No offence, but they look, well, cool. Would they agree to let us—the Liberal Party—use their song?'

Georgia Lambert chuckled. 'That song is five years old. The Jaggernauts never made it big. The lead singer is now really fat. The drummer offered to join the Young Liberals if it would help seal the deal.' Georgia paused. 'Only she's no longer young enough to qualify. They'll take any money we offer and consider it cream.'

'Subsequent verses?' Hargreaves asked. It was a pertinent question. Even the second verse of the Australian national anthem sometimes sounded like seditious anti-government propaganda.

'Harmless. All Aussie spirit stuff. There's even self-mocking humour in verse four about our annual thumpings at the hands of the All Blacks.'

'Pay the band for the rights,' Fitzwilliams decided, 'and we'll test it out. Use it as closing music at events.'

Georgia next summarised the polling data. The Luddite Lie had transformed misleading pollsters into a national sport; 81 per cent of the people were claiming they intended to vote for the Liberal–National Coalition and 19 per cent for Labor. Everyone had thought it impossible for Labor to drop below 20 per cent. Normally, 20 per cent of the population were rusted-on Labor voters, people who'd vote Labor if they were running a block of granite for prime minister. Incredibly, some of that Labor core were now lying to pollsters as to their voting intentions. If the Luddite Lie was even being taken up by some of these Labor stalwarts, you might as well give up polling altogether.

'Which brings us to the problem of countering the Luddites,' Georgia Lambert pressed on. 'The Luddite candidates are using no social media platforms. They are simply going around meeting people face-to-face. The Luddite candidates for the House of Representatives could be described as a hundred and fifty-eight loose cannons, each proposing policy positions independently of the rest of their party. For instance,' Georgia pointed out, 'only the Ned Ludd at the debate with Donna has advocated that radical overhaul of the pharmaceutical industry.'

Donna Hargreaves ducked her head at the memory. Fitzwilliams had been kind to her afterwards. 'At least we found out how dangerous they can be. It would've been worse if that celery stick trick had happened in the leaders' debate,' he'd said. She still felt humiliated. Anywhere Hargreaves spoke now, some jokers in the crowd were wearing celery sticks on their hats.

Fitzwilliams had dealt with populist parties before. Luddite policies, however, were not so much populist as complex. They required lengthier explanations, and during those lengthier explanations the cameras were focused on the Luddites. It was hard to counter them with catchphrases. Being committed to 'building innovation capacity for Australia's future' would sound like a vapid reply after some Luddite had droned on about a fascinating new way to fund scientific research.

'We have identified over three hundred of these … *ideas*,' Lambert said, choosing a word that seemed distasteful to her. 'The Luddites just throw them out on everything from child care to defence policy.'

She presented the Prime Minister and his colleagues with a sheet marked *Confidential*. 'This comes from our PR research unit at Baxter Lockwood. They've identified four of these Luddite ideas that the public will find highly objectionable. Corner the Luddite spokesperson at the debate on these. You'll either get her to disavow her fellow candidate—not a good look—or, preferably, defend a policy that the public will hate.

'Then we hit the anonymity issue,' Georgia continued. 'So far it has all been a bit of fun, a party with a hundred and fifty-eight candidates all named Ned Ludd. But we're getting close to the election now. The Luddites have no leader. Who's really in charge of the party? It will start to spook the electorate. We won't attack the Luddites directly. Instead, we market our reassuring personalities. Here's a cabinet full of familiar faces. Here's a prime minister you know, his steady hand on the tiller. Here's his family. Here's his dog.'

Fitzwilliams could see Donna Hargreaves giving tiny shakes of her head at the new campaign manager. Beatrice, Fitzwilliams' wife of thirty-five years, didn't do publicity. An IT professional, she didn't understand or like politics. Hers was a simpler world of designing things well and fixing them immediately if they weren't designed well. 'If something is a bad idea,' she would tell him when he was weighing up his political options, 'don't do it. Who cares if some MP will lose a seat because of it?' It was worst whenever she caught a bit of question time on the news. 'You all act like a bunch of schoolboys when the teacher is out of the room,' she would exclaim. 'Is that any way to discuss the nation's business?' She had famously left the platform on the night of his first victory as prime minister; she'd been on call that night and her beeper had gone off. He'd made a virtue of it. 'Her work is important,' he told the media after she hustled off the stage during the part of his victory speech where he thanked his family for their fantastic support. 'Gone are the days when a woman is defined by her husband's job even when that husband's job is prime minister.' Still, he sometimes sighed when other politicians trotted out their adoring partners to gaze at them with misty-eyed pride.

Meanwhile, his daughters had been raised so thoroughly imbued with the independent Aussie spirit that they'd both scarpered off to Europe at the first available opportunity. One was studying archaeology in Berlin and the other was a part-time pub waitress in Manchester and bass player in a band prophetically named The Unemployables. As for the dog—clueless. Hyperactive years beyond its puppyhood. Good only if you wanted to be bowled over or slobbered on. It was like living with a backbencher.

He was about to explain this to Georgia Lambert when Olga O'Rourke appeared in the doorway. 'I've brought someone for you to meet.' She smiled as she ushered in a tall, casually dressed man.

'My God!' Langdon cried, lurching to his feet.

'Quentin, Leon—grab him!' Fitzwilliams shouted at the bodyguards.

Langdon tried to step in front of Fitzwilliams, but caught his good leg on something and sprawled into Fitzwilliams, knocking him aside.

'What's going on?' Hargreaves demanded. 'Who is this?'

The bodyguards had the man by each arm. He was unresisting and smiling. 'I'm ex-Senator Bolen of Arkansas,' he announced with a pronounced American drawl. 'You won't find a piece on me, boys,' he informed the bodyguards proudly. 'It's been two years and three months since I last carried a gun. I've taken the pledge.'

• • •

The Luddite Party had given Aggie Posniak this specific task because of her reputation as a computer programmer. Programming had its specialities, though, and this current assignment was entirely different from her former work at Autocar. She'd been presented with an already completed program that involved a laser projection. Her task was to alter the shape of that projection.

The two Veronicas, the Bicyclism militants running her local campaign, had practically moved into her flat, which had become the headquarters for her campaign for the electorate of Wills. They were organising the day's itinerary now, mapping out the route. On some days this involved upwards of eighty kilometres of cycling, pedalling their message beyond Wills to the whole of the greater Melbourne area. Aggie's thighs had finally stopped aching and she was fitter than she'd been in years, but she was physically tired. It was a relief to spend some familiar, sedentary, bad-posture time slumped in front of a computer screen.

This week had seen the unexpected arrival of a bodyguard sent around by the Department for Security and Freedom. Aggie was the only Ned Ludd to have received one. The department clearly presumed she was the leader of the Luddite Party, having been designated the Ned to take on Fitzwilliams and Stanfield at the leaders' debate.

Both the bodyguards sent so far by the department had run afoul of the Veronicas. The first had thought to protect Aggie by driving a car alongside her bicycle. The Veronicas, annoyed at this motoring presence on the campaign team, chose an itinerary that crisscrossed public parks and scooted down narrow laneways and gave the poor, earnest fellow the slip a dozen times. A different bodyguard arrived the next day with a department-issued bicycle. However, he was a sports car owner who let the Veronicas know he believed bicycles were for ten year olds and had no place on public roads. The Veronicas had deliberately sprinted on the hills to punish him. 'No cardiovascular,' they'd observed derisively as he puffed up a hill behind them. Tensions spilled into outright argument by the end of the day and he'd told them the department would need to send some other chump tomorrow. 'Go. Go crawl back into your car, you . . . *motorist*,' one Veronica had shouted at him in disgust. It was possibly their vilest term of abuse.

This programming task she had been sent to work on for the Luddites, Aggie realised, was a bit like sculpting. She knew the shape of what she had and knew the shape of what she wanted. It was the old adage about how to work like Michelangelo: you take a block of marble and just chip away everything that doesn't look like a statue of David.

Fortunately, this job wasn't entirely up to her. The Luddites had another programmer on it. He wasn't an official Ned Ludd, but went by a codename. She had never met him, but she could contact him. Although the Luddite system of communication was cumbersome, it did work. You just had to plan ahead. She would have a crack at this Michelangelo approach and see what he thought of it.

'Before you go,' Aggie called to the Veronicas, who were readying to leave, 'the debate is on April twenty-third. I have to meet with several Luddites in Canberra beforehand so I'll need to be there by the twenty-second.'

'We can leave on the twentieth,' one of the Veronicas suggested.

Aggie looked at her, puzzled.

'Or the nineteenth if you want to do it more leisurely,' Veronica offered.

Aggie's facial expression switched from puzzled to aghast as she took in the meaning of what was being proposed. 'I'm not cycling to Canberra!' she told them flatly. Melbourne to Canberra would be more than six hundred kilometres. 'There are buses, you know.' She had to lay down the rules to these two. More leisurely! Was that their idea of more leisurely? A hundred and fifty kilometres a day!

'Ned,' Veronica said, adopting the tone one uses to reason with a recalcitrant child, 'you haven't thought it through. Listen to what Veronica and I have planned. With the debate just days away, we announce the great "On to Canberra" cycle event. Hundreds of cyclists will join us along the way. Think of it. By the time you enter

Canberra, you're not just the candidate for Wills, you'll be leading a cavalcade of cyclists into the city! It'll be amazing media!'

'I'm not Julius Caesar,' Aggie protested. 'I don't need to enter Canberra at the head of some pedalling cavalry!' Aggie drew in a breath. She could tell she'd just set off a major double sulk.

'Ned,' one Veronica said quietly after a protracted silence, 'I don't think you appreciate the effort we've put into this.'

They looked so hurt, so pathetic to Aggie. 'We'll compromise,' she said, exhaling. 'I don't have time to bicycle all the way. We'll take the train to . . . Wagga. We'll kick off your "On to Canberra" cycle from there. How far is that? A hundred and fifty kilometres? Two days,' she stressed, flashing the V sign at them. 'I can't exhaust myself before the debate. We'll overnight somewhere along the way.'

The Veronicas perked up a little. Wagga Wagga to Canberra was more like two hundred and fifty kilometres, but neither of them opted to point this out.

There was a knock. When Aggie opened the door, there stood what looked like a lycra-clad Greek god.

'I am your new bodyguard from the Department for Security and Freedom,' the man said. He hadn't removed his bicycle helmet to introduce himself. He was close to two metres tall, Aggie estimated, with the physique of a sprint cyclist. 'My name is Timothy Sakic, Ms Ludd, but you can call me . . .'

'Thunder thighs,' she heard one of the Veronicas whisper behind her.

'Tim,' he finished.

The department had sent them a real cyclist.

• • •

'He's telling the truth. He doesn't have a gun on him, sir.'

'Let him go.' Fitzwilliams waved to the two bodyguards. They released each arm of the American ex-senator.

A groan came from the floor. Russ Langdon was struggling to his feet, a hand clutched to his forehead. 'What in blazes were you doing?' Fitzwilliams asked.

Langdon was groggy. 'When I saw who it was I went to step in front of you. I tripped. Hit my head on the table.'

Fitzwilliams had not recognised the act, having only ever seen it done in slow motion in movies. Langdon had been throwing himself in front of his prime minister to protect him. That Langdon would do that for him briefly overwhelmed Fitzwilliams. God, if Langdon had taken a bullet for him, Fitzwilliams might have had to make him deputy leader or governor-general. If he kept it up, Langdon could well wound his way to the secretary-generalship of the United Nations.

Quentin produced a first-aid kit and pressed a bandage to Langdon's forehead. Fortunately, there wasn't much blood.

The Prime Minister turned towards Senator Bolen. No one had heard anything of him for years. His sensational trial and acquittal after shooting and wounding two hecklers at one of his rallies had been all over the news and then he'd disappeared. It had only been the most generous interpretation of the Stand Your Ground legislation that had enabled him to get off. The pledge. Fitzwilliams had heard of it. It was for American politicians who had literally gone mad over guns. It was sometimes called the 'de Milo pledge', referring to the disarming it entailed.

'Yes, sirs and ma'am,' ex-Senator Bolen said, acknowledging Donna Hargreaves' presence, 'I've got my life back thanks to the pledge. I did some terrible things with guns and I . . . chhlkk . . .' Something seemed to catch in his throat. 'It's very fortunate,' he managed, 'that I did not hurt those people worse than I did.' He seemed to choke again on something. 'I brought a lot of strange and, I'd say now, dangerous ideas to the Senate and I . . . chhlllk . . . have moved beyond those narrow ideas I once held.'

Hargreaves' health-minister eyes appraised the former senator. 'I don't mean to be rude, but do you have Tourette syndrome?'

'No, ma'am, I do not have Tourette syndrome,' Bolen answered proudly. 'I have taken a double pledge. I will not carry a gun anymore and I will not—' the Senator switched into a quoting tone '—ascribe any of my political beliefs as being directly linked to the intervention of God, nor declare that ideas or actions I may disagree with are caused by satanic forces in any form.' Bolen stopped. Fitzwilliams supposed he was expecting to be applauded; that was probably what they did for each other at the De Milo Clinic. The verbal tics in Bolen's speech, the Prime Minister realised, covered pauses where he would have previously inserted *praise God* or *thank God* or any other godly utterance.

Fitzwilliams turned away from the mesmerising man. 'Olga, what's the plan here?'

Olga chuckled. 'I've arranged for Senator Bolen to be interviewed on the very same shows where Lister St John plans to tell his campaign tales. You know the format of those shows. One guest is interviewed and then sits there when the next guest is brought out. When Lister St John comes out, he'll be greeted by the smiling face of the former senator.'

'And I can reminisce about how Lister helped with my campaign in 2020,' Bolen declared. 'Lister was the one who wrote the "I Have a Nightmare" speech. He had an instinctive feel for what prejudices to feed to which audiences.' The senator stopped his reminiscing. 'I'm terribly ashamed of that speech,' he reminded himself. 'When I gave voice to those words, they were the thoughts of a very ignorant and narrow man. I . . . chhkllk . . . am grateful I've moved on from there. I'm not sure Lister has made the same journey.'

'You could ask him on national television,' Olga suggested.

Fitzwilliams' eyes rested on Olga in utter admiration. If Lister St John was a mosquito annoying him, Olga had arranged to hit it with a sledgehammer. He could hardly wait to watch the show.

One of Olga's staffers led Bolen away.

'He's using Australia as a warm-up ground to see how well his new persona plays,' Olga explained. 'It may be just to go on the book and lecture circuit or, who knows, perhaps his new personality is electable over there.'

'The bleeding has stopped, Prime Minister,' Quentin reported. 'Minister Langdon won't need stitches. I can bandage him properly now.'

'Ahem!' Alan Chandos cleared his throat grandly. 'If we can move on from goal-kicking opposition leaders and no-longer-gun-toting American senators, you may recall I promised you an election-winning policy.'

'What is it?' Fitzwilliams asked eagerly. His mood had lifted. Comedians would savage Labor's Battler ads, Olga was going to smash Lister St John, Chandos was promising to produce a gem. *We are Aussie, it's what we are about*, his brain hummed.

'Tax reform,' Chandos answered.

The humming in Fitzwilliams' head ceased. Tax reform? Tax breaks the electorate could comprehend in an election, but tax reform was always complicated. 'There're always some losers in any tax reform,' Fitzwilliams cautioned. 'They won't take it well during an election.'

'Ah,' Chandos replied, savouring his PM's comment. 'There're no losers in this tax reform, only winners!' He clicked on the screen immediately behind him and turned to it almost affectionately to begin his presentation. 'The trouble with income tax,' he explained, 'is that the benefits of paying it are too indirect. People want the things the government provides—schools, hospitals, bitumen on the runway when your plane is landing—but no one really likes paying taxes. My reform—' he paused as if waiting for a trumpet fanfare to finish '—will make paying income tax *popular*. Let me introduce to you . . . "Play as You Go" taxation!'

It was unlike any tax reform ever proposed. There was no change to tax rates or deductions whatsoever. Instead, for every one hundred dollars paid in income tax, a taxpayer received one Tax Lotto ticket. Each week, the tax office would draw one ticket to win a million dollars. If you paid $5200 in taxes one year, you got a ticket in each of the weekly draws for the following year. If you paid $10,400 in taxes, you got two tickets. The more income tax you paid, the better your chances of winning. It would cost virtually nothing to run. Taxpayers would receive their Tax Lotto numbers each week by email. All that would have to be paid for was the five-minute Lotto razzamatazz broadcast to reveal the week's winning number. It would be a windfall for the government.

'Maybe it's because I was just hit on the head,' the bandaged Langdon said, 'but I don't get it. How's it a windfall for government? It'll cost us fifty-two million dollars per year. Nice for the fifty-two winners, but it doesn't help our coffers.'

'Thank you for asking.' Chandos beamed. 'There has never before been such a clear incentive to pay income tax. Think of the grumbling taxpayer sitting down to do their tax return. Now when they look over all the petty things they write off as deductions—the depreciation on a home computer they allege they use seventy-five per cent of the time for work purposes, the work-related travel expenses, education deductions—they'll pause and think: why bother with this receipt for the Effective Communication training course they took last February, a course they can't even remember? If they don't claim it, they'll get more chances to win. Eat that receipt instead of filing it and you might win a million dollars! Our modelling predicts that the average taxpayer will reduce their deduction claims by two hundred and eighty-three dollars per year!'

Russell Langdon, doing some rough calculations in his head, whistled appreciatively.

'More significantly, after Play as You Go starts, we can abolish just about any tax deduction in the Tax Act we want. If some special interest group starts moaning about it, the rest of the populace will just think, "What are they complaining about? They'll get more Tax Lotto tickets, the whingers." Play as You Go will be a weekly celebration of paying income tax where one Aussie income tax payer gets thanked with a million dollars!'

There was an almost Pavlovian salivation in response to the proposal.

'I take it we only announce this as a weekly celebration of income tax payers,' Langdon said. 'I mean, we announce the prize, but not the two hundred and eighty-three dollars of deductions modelling. We're just thanking our taxpayers.'

Chandos nodded at him contentedly.

'It's brilliant.' Fitzwilliams was awestruck. 'It's a perfect last-week-of-the-campaign announcement. Into the home stretch. Our government has achieved such fabulous financial management that we'll reward our taxpayers each week with the chance to win a million dollars. Let Roslyn Stanfield try to kick that between the goalposts.'

'What do you think, Leon?' Chandos asked the bodyguard.

'The chance to win a million dollars for paying my taxes? I'm in, if government employees are allowed to play.'

We are Aussie, it's what we are about, the Prime Minister's brain chirped happily.

• • •

The four stumbled into the flat, laughing. Old Ned Ludd, the one with the appalling cough, clapped both young Kate and Candidate Ned on the back and gave Amy a hug. 'We're going to win!' he declared.

Amy couldn't recall having had so much fun in recent years: meeting people, laughing, talking, debating—mostly laughing. She'd spent the Saturday as part of this Luddite gang of four campaigning throughout Glebe and Ultimo. The reception the Luddites were getting was amazing. And Kate, only seventeen years old, had impressed. The national wage concept of hers and how it would work was a difficult idea to get across, and yet she'd seen people question the young woman on it all day and come away if not converted, at least considering it. 'It sounds a bit utopian,' one man had told her. 'You got a problem with living in utopia?' Kate had retorted.

Candidate Ned put the pizzas on his coffee table and disappeared into the kitchen for drinks and plates. He had the opposite campaigning style to Kate. He spent the time discussing with voters what was important to them. He was a perceptive listener and he came across well. He was—Amy paused on the words even in her thoughts—very attractive.

Kate took off her hat and, with a flourish, pulled off the celery stick affixed to it and took a chomp out of it. It didn't give the satisfying crunching sound she had hoped for as it had been gradually wilting in the sun all day. The celery stick had become the de facto Luddite campaign symbol. Nobody had organised it, but people everywhere were wearing them. 'Michael at the fruit-and-veg told me yesterday that he sold out of celery by eleven am. Today, he was selling them as individual sticks,' Kate informed them. 'How brilliant is it to have a party's symbol distributed nationwide by fruit-and-veg shops!'

The momentum was incredible. Amy had seen people sporting celery sticks on their hats, their bags, their lapels. Younger voters seemed to like two half celery sticks worn as epaulettes.

'Who wants a beer?' Candidate Ned called from the other room.

A chorus of 'I do' answered him. Ned stuck his head out of the kitchen. 'Kate, you're seventeen. I'm not giving you a beer.'

'For Christ's sake, Ned! My mothers let me have beer occasionally.'

'Then go home and have a beer with your mothers,' Ned replied bluntly.

'I've worked all day on your campaign,' Kate pleaded.

'Kate, as an MP, I can't be giving beers to underage kids.'

Kate stood up. Amy assumed she was offended at being called a kid, but she raised her hand in a high five gesture. Candidate Ned slapped it reflexively. 'What was that for?' he asked.

Kate was grinning broadly. 'You said "as an MP". We're going to win, aren't we!'

Candidate Ned seemed to stiffen. 'There's still a long way to go in the campaign,' he replied cautiously, but Amy could tell that cautiousness was tinged with excitement.

Old Ned gave a few hacking coughs. 'All the stars have aligned,' he said. Sydney was traditionally a safe Labor seat, but the much-loved Labor MP had retired. Their new candidate was supposed to be an up-and-coming bright light of the party, but on the campaign trail, he seemed to have only the light part down pat.

'I had never realised,' Old Ned wheezed, 'what an asset the Ned Ludd name was going to be during an election.' He paused for breath. 'Normally, if you run as an independent, ninety-nine per cent of the electorate has never heard of you and you don't stand a chance, but every voter in the country—' he coughed for emphasis '—knows the name Ned Ludd!'

Candidate Ned re-appeared with plates, beers and a glass of ginger beer, which Kate took grudgingly. 'On October fourteenth,' she muttered, 'you owe me a beer.'

'What's October fourteenth?' Ned asked.

'My eighteenth birthday, obviously!'

'Won't that be the middle of your Higher School Certificate exams?'

'God, Ned,' Kate despaired, 'you're worse than my parents!'

They sat down around the pizzas. Amy took a seat on the couch next to Candidate Ned, her leg gently touching his. He didn't pull his away. Kate noticed it and smirked at Amy, as if privately amused. Amy looked away and attacked the pizza hungrily.

'There's news,' Candidate Ned announced. 'I've been contacted by the Luddite … high command.' Nobody had a proper term for it. There was a degree of communication taking place between Luddite candidates, but no one knew who was coordinating it. 'I was handed this surreptitiously,' Candidate Ned showed them a folded piece of paper, 'by someone who shook hands with me in Ultimo.' He unfolded the paper carefully and handed it around. 'Kate and I are to go to Canberra next weekend. We're to meet with Ned Ludd to help her prepare for the debate next Sunday.'

'How did this come about?' Old Ned demanded.

'I suggested it to her,' Candidate Ned answered. 'I sent the message to the Ned Ludd in the leaders' debate. I met her on the march in Canberra.'

'The nude one?' Old Ned asked. 'I mean you were all nude that day, but she was rather …' he coughed, 'wonderfully nude.'

'It's not as though we're nudist pals,' Candidate Ned answered mildly peevishly. 'I have seen her with her clothes on.'

'That is rather an odd thing to boast about, lad,' Old Ned wheezed.

Amy felt herself flush, the conversation reminding her that she had seen this Ned nude on the news reports that day. Was she imagining it, or had his leg pressed against hers more firmly during this discussion?

'I put the paperwork through,' Kate told Candidate Ned.

'Kate has changed her name to Ned Ludd,' he informed them. 'Your parents were okay with it?' he asked her.

'Yeah, they're just happy I am taking "an interest in something",' she said, quoting them directly. 'As if toppling the government were no different from collecting Pixar movie memorabilia. If you do anything at all at my age that doesn't involve taking drugs,' she explained, 'parents are thrilled.'

'Why change your name to Ned Ludd now?' Amy asked. 'You're not a candidate.'

Kate went to answer but Candidate Ned held up a hand to stop the conversation. 'I'll tell you, but not here. There's a good chance this flat might be bugged.'

Amy blinked. Might be bugged? She gazed at Ned. Was there intrigue to him beneath his friendly exterior? Her hand fiddled with the top button of her blouse and idly unbuttoned it. She caught herself at it and quickly rebuttoned it.

Old Ned was worried about Candidate Ned being away next weekend. 'Don't spend too long hobnobbing with the Canberra crowd. Keep your eye on the local game. We've got an electorate to win over.'

Amy assured him the local volunteers could handle the Sydney campaign for one weekend. The Pyrmont sisters alone had recruited forty of their friends to work for the team. 'The thing about campaigning for the Luddites,' she told Old Ned, 'is you don't need Ned Ludd to do it.'

The conversation, which had started so upbeat, now dragged on. Old Ned seemed to want to belabour a number of points. Fortunately, he was so short of breath, he couldn't go on for long. With the pizzas finished, Amy decided that the meeting really should be over—or, more to the point, Old Ned and Kate should leave. She picked up the plates.

Kate chuckled. 'Save your file and close it,' she said with the affectionate derision she often used with Old Ned. The phrase, even Old Ned knew, meant 'shut up' in under-twenties speak. 'Come on, up you get. I think they'd rather we headed off.'

Old Ned glanced between Amy and Candidate Ned. 'What, them?' he asked.

'Ye-es,' she drawled. 'Haven't you noticed? She's been goggling at him all evening as if he was Leonard bloody Cohen.'

Old Ned chortled as Kate ushered him to the door. Kate turned at the doorway. 'I don't care what you two get up to tonight,' she lectured them, 'but you just make sure you're ready to campaign tomorrow morning. We start bright and early.'

When the door was shut, Candidate Ned took Amy's hand. 'It seems the campaign team has decided rather a lot for us tonight,' he observed.

Amy smiled. 'Who's Leonard Cohen?'

'A singer. A romantic one. I don't know his songs. Kate's parents fell in love at one of his concerts, or so they tell her.' He let go of her hand and went over to his voice-activated sound system. 'All-Tunes. Leonard Cohen. Random Selection,' he told it. 'This one is called "Everybody Knows",' he said, reading the name from the screen of the music player. A pulsing intro came over the speakers. Returning to Amy, he put his arms around her waist. A deep voice filled the room. Far from being romantic, the opening lines of the song were perturbing: about dice being loaded, good guys losing and everybody knowing it.

'It's a bit menacing,' Amy observed.

'If I were to kiss you,' Ned asked, 'would you run out the door again, like you did last time?'

She raised her face and kissed him gently. There was no desperation to it this time. 'I think I'll linger,' she whispered, kissing him again.

Leonard Cohen continued to serenade them. Now he was singing of boats leaking, captains lying and everyone feeling broken as though their father or their dog had just died.

Amy broke off the kiss. 'You ever met Kate's parents?' she asked, suddenly concerned.

. . .

Renard lay on his back in bed, Amy curled snugly into him, his arm under her. It was unbelievable. When he had first met Amy, she'd seemed so reserved, painfully shy. Now she had transformed into this passionate, savvy, humorous and . . . wonderful person. How, he had no idea. Renard knew he didn't have that sort of effect on people. Something had happened with Amy, something splendid, as if she had decided to release her real self from hiding. And, he sensed with relief, Amy was uncomplicated. Taylor had been controlling and jealous. Belinda had been flighty and irascible. There was depth to Amy, he could tell, but there was also fun and excitement. They were only—he glanced at the clock radio— some two and a quarter hours into this relationship, depending on when you declared it to have started. He liked the initial kiss during the Leonard Cohen song. They had repeated that strangely ominous song three times, kissing and partially undressing each other before they headed off to his bed. Looking at Amy now, he realised it was a bit early to be asking himself if she was the one, but he sensed he already had.

'Ned,' Amy murmured, 'I hope you don't mind me asking this, but why are you running for parliament?'

'Old Ned was too ill.'

'Yes, but why are *you* running?' Her lips were resting on his chest. 'I don't mean this as an insult, but you don't have any political ideas. You just listen to other people and process their ideas. I mean, listening to people is good . . .'

'I suppose it comes from being a data analyst. You spend a lot of time working out how other people think, what they're after. Maybe it makes you think less about what you want.'

She ran her hand delicately up his leg. 'You said you think this flat might be bugged. Who'd be bugging your flat?'

'ASIO,' he whispered. It wasn't that he owed her an explanation, he just wasn't going to keep secrets from her. Amy became very still against him. 'Don't tell the others,' he said, 'but I work for . . . I mean, I *worked for*—' he wasn't really sure which tense was appropriate '—ASIO. I was sent by ASIO to find out what the Luddites were up to. Now I find I'm running for parliament. Now I find . . .' He stopped, trying to decide what exactly he was these days. 'Now I find that I am a Luddite. I want the Luddites to win.' He stayed silent a moment. 'I stopped sending reports to ASIO two weeks ago. They will wonder why. I wouldn't be surprised if I'm now being monitored and my data analysed.' He thought of his co-worker Geraldine; Geraldine at her desk looking over information on him and his movements. He shivered.

Amy was unmoving by his side. Panic suddenly gripped Renard. It's over, he thought, the idea sending a jolt through him. She would hate him. Amy was committed to the Luddites. She would loathe him. A spy sent to infiltrate the party? He was contemptible.

Though she hadn't moved, he had felt her tense. She felt like a coiled spring. His fingers resting on her tingled as a ripple of goosebumps rose on her back.

Suddenly, in a flash of movement, Amy was on top of him. Her mouth went straight to his ear. 'We're going to make love again,' she whispered urgently, 'and while we're making love, I'm going to tell you something and you must stay calm and not be alarmed. This is going to work out. We're going to make this work.'

To Renard's astonishment, his penis had snapped to attention at this abrupt foreplay.

Amy reached for a condom, the last one in the packet, the one Renard had been saving for the morning. She lifted one leg so he could slip it on then straddled him again, bringing her mouth to his ear, her breasts resting on his chest.

'I am,' she began, slipping his penis easily into her as Renard gave a short gasp, 'a spy for Compink Australia.' She moved her pelvis slowly as she spoke. 'I've been sending reports back to Wilson about your campaign.'

Wilson? Renard's mind roved wildly. Wilson Huang, the CEO of Compink Australia! He tried to think, but the only comment he could manage was an inhaled-exhaled 'uhhh-haa' as he moved gently in sync with Amy.

She pulled away from his ear, straightened her back upright, rocking up and down, appearing to be in deep contemplation. Renard could contemplate either her words or her seemingly perfect breasts and could not decide on which to focus.

She came down to his ear again, sliding a hand under his back. 'We discovered a few weeks ago that ASIO is monitoring my movements. I decided to join the Luddites then.'

Renard tried to ask why. It came out as a soft cry.

'Why?' Amy asked. Her mouth was so close to his ear he could feel her smile against his cheek. 'If your Fiona Brennan wants to conduct surveillance on me, I'll give her some disinformation to think about.' Her voice was barely audible she was speaking so softly.

Fiona Brennan. Wilson Huang. Amy was moving in the highest ranks of . . . The thought stopped as he let out a groan. When he took the next breath in, he couldn't recall what he'd been thinking.

'I've been undercover for years. Everyone thinks I am a data entry clerk. I'm the deputy CEO of Compink Australia,' Amy continued, her words coming in the pulse of their rhythm. 'No one . . . in the world . . . knows that . . . except . . . Wilson and me . . . and now you.' She rose up again as if collecting her thoughts, rocking more forcefully. After only a moment, she swooped back down on him, pressing her breasts firmly against him and her mouth once more to his ear.

'Then I met you.' Amy's faint voice acquired more urgency and her movements grew in pace. 'I want you, Ned.'

'I want you too,' he answered, proud he'd managed a whole sentence, 'I want you more than . . .' He groaned again, scattering whatever words were to follow.

'Like you . . . I'm a Luddite now,' Amy rasped faintly in his ear. 'We're Luddites . . . and we're together!'

Her movements became rapid and Renard was thrusting almost desperately along with her, clasping her to his chest as she spoke. He was nearing climax, but she was still speaking. He had to restrain himself until she had finished.

'We'll make this work,' she declared sotto voce. 'You're my . . . Ned Ludd!'

Renard could hold back no longer. He let out a gasp. A surge of exhilaration coursed through him. He felt his body shudder three or four more times and sputter to an exhausted halt.

Amy rocked slowly on top of him a few seconds longer, her eyes closed. She let out the softest of sighs and rolled off him. He could feel the beating of her heart. Amy raised her face to his ear. 'Openness...disclosure...honesty—they're such exciting concepts for me,' she whispered. 'The possibilities are so . . . intriguing!'

Amy spoke again, this time at a normal volume. 'Now we better get some sleep. I don't want to hear Kate's comments if we aren't energetic and ready to campaign in the morning.'

Sleep? Renard could only wonder at the word. What could he possibly dream after that? His mind was whirling, flitting from fret to fret, but always returning to Amy's whispered declaration: 'We'll make this work.' Amy's breathing had slowed. If she could sleep contentedly, surely he could sleep contentedly beside her.

Just as he was fading away, however, that eerie Leonard Cohen song came back to him. As he drifted off, he could hear the deep voice warning him: *Everybody knows.*

CHAPTER EIGHT

The Easter Monday public holiday was business as usual in the analyst room of the ASIO Sydney office. The world of security (or insecurity, Geraldine sometimes thought) never took a day off.

Less than a week ago, she had reported to ASIO director Fiona Brennan that the Compink agent Amy Zhao had attached herself to the Luddite campaign in Sydney, the campaign her former co-worker Renard was in the thick of. Geraldine was never told why Renard left ASIO, but the abruptness of his departure spoke of its seriousness. They'd been instructed to say Renard left ASIO months earlier than he actually had. Now, he was running for parliament—and meeting with a Compink Australia agent?

Fiona Brennan had instructed Geraldine to report to her directly on the surveillance of Amy Zhao and to mention it to no one else at ASIO. Geraldine must have appeared puzzled at this, because Brennan explained, 'There are occasions, Geraldine, when Wilson Huang at Compink Australia does things that make me believe he knows exactly what we know over here at ASIO.' She said this in that grandmotherly voice of hers, as if she were passing on a pavlova recipe, but she'd as good as told Geraldine outright that there was a Compink Australia mole within the Sydney ASIO surveillance section.

And now Geraldine had this incriminating footage. On Saturday, a drone followed Amy Zhao, Renard and two other Luddites to Renard's flat. Geraldine then picked up the feed from a nearby parking meter that commanded a view of Renard's front door. Around 10.15 pm, the two Luddites left the building. Geraldine fast-forwarded through hours of Parkie footage before Amy Zhao emerged at 8.17 the next morning. When she did, she was with Renard. He was holding her hand and they were both laughing. You didn't have to be much of an analyst to figure this one out, Geraldine thought.

Geraldine went to a secure room. Fiona Brennan always worked public holidays, an example of vigilance to her staff. Geraldine connected the security scrambler and sent a request for a video link to her director.

Fiona Brennan's face appeared on the screen. 'Yes, dear?'

'I'm sorry to inform you, Director, that the Compink Australia agent, Amy Zhao, has . . .' Geraldine searched for the right way to put it. 'She and Renard are sleeping together!' she blurted. 'I mean . . . holy shit, Ms Brennan!'

Fiona sucked in a breath. 'That's bad.'

'I'm sorry, Ms Brennan. It just came out.'

'I wasn't concerned about your excremental reference, dear. I mean that I fear Renard may be involved in something over his head.'

Geraldine felt she should defend her former co-worker. She had worked with him for several years. She knew him. She trusted him. 'Renard's not a Compink Australia spy.'

'I didn't say he was, dear. Let's have a look at your footage.'

Amy Zhao and Renard Prendergast appeared on Fiona's screen. They were leaving Renard's flat. A drone picked them up as they descended the steps to the street. After a block, Australia Post switched to a different drone moving obliquely above their path. Fiona had to admire their work. They did nothing so tell-tale as have a single drone trailing a suspect.

Renard and Amy Zhao were walking hand in hand, laughing, bumping their shoulders as they walked along. Was Amy Zhao playing Renard? If so, what was she after? What was there to be gained from seducing Renard?

She watched that video feed twice and then moved it back to an earlier section. She let it play for a few seconds then froze the image. It caught a moment when Amy Zhao was gazing at Renard, the softest of smiles on her lips. Fiona Brennan scrutinised the image carefully. 'It's possible that . . .'

'What's possible, Director?'

'That she may be in love with him,' Fiona murmured.

'Ms Brennan?'

'Maintain surveillance of Amy Zhao. I'm not certain, after all, but keep your mind open to the possibility. This could simply be a Romeo and Juliet scenario.'

'Romeo and Juliet?' Geraldine asked uncertainly. 'With ASIO and Compink Australia being the Montagues and the Capulets?'

'Yes.'

'What does that make me?' she asked. She was a friend of Renard's. 'Mercutio?' she wondered.

'You're being too literal, dear,' Fiona Brennan told her. 'But don't get into any sword fights.'

• • •

Aggie had her head down to keep the slashing rain out of her eyes. A gust of wind almost stopped her bike in its tracks. Only two hours into it. Binalong, their overnight stop on the way to Canberra, was God knew how many kilometres away.

They'd met the Wagga Wagga Ned Ludd at the train station and he took the small party from Melbourne to a cafe before they set off. Several people in the cafe were sporting celery sticks, including the barista. Wagga Ned had mustered a small contingent of cyclists to set off with them. It plumped up the numbers for the first photos of the 'On to Canberra' trek. None of the Wagga Wagga cycling honour guard was available to go all the way to Canberra. They accompanied Aggie, her government-assigned bodyguard Tim and her two fanatic cyclist campaign directors for the first ten kilometres but fled back to Wagga Wagga when the rain set in.

Four forlorn figures cycling along the A41 in the driving rain was hardly the inspiring image the Veronicas had originally painted. Aggie crouched over the handlebars as another gust whipped into her. It galled her that the Veronicas weren't even apologetic for getting her into this. 'The "On to Canberra" ride has got folklore written all over it!' one of them insisted. 'We four alone! Overcoming adversity! A triumphant entry into Canberra tomorrow!'

'Folklore?' Aggie grumbled aloud to herself. 'Four idiots cycling in the middle of nowhere in the driving rain?'

Tim pulled alongside her, looking at her with concern. 'Ms Ludd,' he said. (This Tim was very formal with her. Wouldn't even call her Ned.) 'As your bodyguard, it's my professional opinion that there's no terrorist daft enough to lay in wait for us along the road in this weather.'

'I agree with that,' Aggie muttered.

'Since I don't need to protect you from the likes of them, the least I could do is protect you from the wind and rain.' He nodded at her. 'Get into my slipstream.'

He pulled in front of her and sat upright to shield her as much as possible from the wind. 'Hey you, Veronicae!' he shouted, using a Latin plural Aggie wasn't sure was correct, 'Get back here and start protecting your leader. What kind of supporters are you? Get on each wing!'

The Veronicas moved into position without protest, seemingly deferring to the cycling authority in Tim's voice. Aggie raised her head. A fond memory came of her father letting Aggie and her sister stay up to watch the Tour de France with him during school holidays. It dawned on her that she wasn't just part of a campaign anymore. For the first time in her life, she was part of a peloton!

• • •

At Compink Australia, Wilson Huang stopped the video at almost exactly the same point that Fiona Brennan had. Amy was sleeping with the Luddite candidate. It was an unanticipated development.

Wilson Huang didn't like using moles. This was for practical rather than ethical reasons. Moles were just regular workers, after all. They chucked sickies, their children got conjunctivitis or they dozed away at their desks because they'd been up all night watching Wimbledon. Half the time they weren't there and the other half they weren't alert. With the exception of Loki, moles weren't good value for money.

Wilson had always let Amy think Odin was his mole within ASIO, but Odin was much better than that. Odin was a straightforward business arrangement Wilson had negotiated with Australia Post. He'd deduced that ASIO must be using the postal service's drones to carry out national surveillance. His contract with Australia Post was simple. Wilson didn't need to know everything ASIO knew. He just needed to know what they knew about Compink Australia. He supplied Australia Post with an electronic photo profile of each of his employees. They then provided him with a duplicate of any material they gave ASIO in which one of his own employees featured. It was a totally confidential relationship he had fostered with Australia Post and he was very satisfied with it.

Amy Zhao was his right hand at work. He knew her. If she was sleeping with the Luddite candidate it would only be because . . . well, if she wanted information from the Luddites, she would have simply found it out. No, if she was sleeping with him, she must have fallen for him. 'Lucky fellow,' he said aloud. Wilson chuckled. ASIO would see only a Compink Agent sleeping with a Luddite candidate and would be having who knew what sort of anxiety attacks about it. Wilson pictured Fiona Brennan running her fingers through her perfectly coiffed hair till it resembled an Einstein-like mess. He laughed again.

• • •

Lister St John sat in the dressing room of the *Ken Kendall Kenetics Show* ('the show where sparks fly!') at Network Seven. 'Bastard,' Lister St John thought. He'd won three elections for Fitzwilliams. The Prime Minister owed him big, yet he had refused to pay out his contract. For that, Lister snorted, Fitzwilliams would pay dearly.

Ken Kendall was one of those photogenic, lightweight hosts current affairs shows like. The Ken Doll, as Lister sometimes called him, thought of himself as the one who asked the tough questions. Lister would have no trouble controlling the interview.

He would disclose his revelations reluctantly for Kendall. Yes, the Prime Minister can be a petty man, he would admit. He'd reveal how shocked he'd been when Fitzwilliams said Russ Langdon getting his leg blown off was the best thing Langdon had ever done for the Liberal Party. Fitzwilliams hadn't actually said that; Lister had—but Fitzwilliams hadn't told him he was out of line for making the comment. Lister would speak of the chaos in the PM's team and how Fitzwilliams had let that psycho Russian bitch, Olga O'Rourke, assault him.

Bitch. Lister stopped at the word. Shows like Kendall's liked a bit of foul language—it made them think they were edgy—but they didn't like the language to be too uncouth. He could say, 'At times, I thought Fitzwilliams was off with the fucking fairies,' but he couldn't say, 'Fitzwilliams is a fucking fuckhead who should get fucked,' even though that was certainly true. Lister recalled his 'fucking Garry Kasparov' quip followed by that psycho Olga launching herself at his throat. Fitzwilliams had watched approvingly, he seethed. 'I resigned from the Liberal campaign team, Ken,' he tried saying aloud, testing a few light-hearted descriptors, 'because Fitzwilliams' team were fucking off the wall . . . fucking loose cannons . . . a fucking battery of loose fucking cannons.' Was that last one perhaps a bit too much? A knock at the dressing room door interrupted further deliberation.

He opened the door and immediately took a defensive step backwards. 'What do you want?' he snarled, holding back the 'you Russian bitch'.

Senator Olga O'Rourke smiled. 'I understand you're disappointed that we didn't pay out what remained of your contract, Lister, but—' she raised her eyebrows at him '—you were the one who resigned. You can't really expect to be paid for deserting your post.'

Lister laughed derisively. 'Is that the best you can do? Plead? You should've paid up, Olga.' He couldn't be bothered to add an insulting elaboration. 'In a few minutes, I'm going out there to tell all those tales you and Fitzwilliams would rather not have told.'

Olga gave him a school teacher-like look of disappointment. 'Lister, when you tell tales, it's difficult to predict where they'll end, but also difficult to know where they'll begin.'

Lister furrowed his brow. 'What's that? Some kind of threat? Who are you to advise me on what stories to tell?' His mind searched for something she might find offensive. 'Fee-a-door Dostoy-bloody-ev-ski?' he mocked, banging on a heavy ocker accent to mutilate the name. 'I bet you'd like me to forget the time you tried to strangle me,' he sneered.

Olga shook her head. 'I came to remind you that being reasonable might be your best option in the circumstances.'

'Yeah,' he drawled, 'I'll bear it in mind. Now if you don't mind, could you fuck off?' He shut the door in her face.

God, she made him mad. That composed cunning she always affected. She was just Fitzwilliams' trained rat, doing his dirty work, and yet she always treated Lister as if he was a lowlife. He stopped himself. She'd wanted to distract him, rattle him. He had to stay focused. He'd promised Kendall an exclusive, the insider's story, and he would deliver. 'A fucking battery of loose cannons,' he said aloud.

The show's runner came to take him to the edge of the studio set where guests wait to be introduced. He could hear the voice of the previous guest being interviewed.

'Yes, I have met your prime minister,' he heard an American accent say. 'I told him I thank . . . chhlkk . . . was appreciative that the Australian government was kind enough to let me visit this fine country of yours given my, er, chequered past.'

Lister St John froze.

'And no, we did not discuss the election, but while I don't wish to intrude on Australian politics, I do wish him well. Prime Minister Fitzwilliams has been a good friend of America.'

There was no mistaking that voice. Lister St John's mind was racing but, unfortunately, only around in circles. How the fuck had psycho Senator Bolen got into the country and how the fuck was it that he was going to be sitting right next to him on the fucking *Ken Kendall fucking Kenetics Show*? There was no time to think. Fuck!

'You're on,' the runner said. 'He introduced you.'

Lister St John didn't move.

'Get on!' the runner hissed. He gave Lister a shove.

Lister made his way to the designated seat. Ken Kendall asked Lister his first question but Lister didn't catch it. Senator Bolen gave Lister a wink.

• • •

Prime Minister Fitzwilliams finished watching the clip. The look of stark terror on Lister St John's face every time Senator Bolen spoke was hilarious. His ex-campaign manager had sussed the situation instantly. If Lister told tales, Fitzwilliams had Senator Bolen on the spot ready to do a bit of reminiscing—career-ending reminiscing in Lister's case. Whatever stories Lister had planned to tell, he shelved them all, deciding, as his emergency fallback position, to opt for the folksy, ex-campaign-manager, long-years-together-with-the-Prime-Minister, amusing-stories-to-tell schtick. He was hopeless at such a style.

The self-important Ken Kendall was almost as amusing to watch. Kendall had been promised meat by Lister and was being served pap. You could see his anger as the probes he made for the promised revelations disappeared in the goop of Lister's tepid anecdotes. Olga had reported to Fitzwilliams that the furious producer of the show had vowed afterwards that Lister would never appear on Network Seven again. The Lister St Johns of the world often had a lucrative sideline in being 'pundits' for the networks when they couldn't find any proper work to do. It looked like Lister might have derailed that future gravy train as well.

For the first time in the campaign, Fitzwilliams tasted triumph. Granted it was against his own ex-campaign manager, not Labor or the Luddites. It was a splendid triumph though and, of all his opponents, against the one who deserved it most.

He would have watched it again had Russ Langdon and Georgia Lambert not entered the room along with the bodyguard duo of Quentin and Leon. Did he really need bodyguards in his office? Who were they protecting him from? Langdon?

Georgia Lambert turned on the big screen in the room. 'An interesting development, Prime Minister.'

On the screen appeared Roslyn Stanfield in her AFL outfit on an oval somewhere. Stanfield really put her boot into the kick that followed, the upward thrust of her leg lifting her completely into the air. The kick was not well aimed though, drifting off to the left. The goal umpire tapped the post several times and reluctantly signalled 'behind'.

'Definitely a behind,' Langdon observed.

'Whether it was a goal or a behind isn't what's important,' Georgia cut in. 'Look at Roslyn Stanfield,' she instructed. The Labor leader gave a good-natured you-can't-kick-them-all shrug. Her smile was tight—very tight, more like a grimace. Georgia moved the clip back to just before the kick. 'Don't follow the ball this time,' she instructed. 'Watch her face.'

Stanfield did her run-up and put her full force into the kick. As the camera left her to follow the ball, her face was momentarily a mask of pain.

'She's done her hamstring,' Leon diagnosed.

Olga O'Rourke entered the room quietly. Fitzwilliams' bodyguards were occupied with the leg injury of the Labor leader on the screen and appeared not to have noticed her arrival. It was fortunate that Olga wasn't a heavily armed terrorist, Fitzwilliams thought.

'That was three days ago,' Georgia informed them. 'Since then, Stanfield has tried seven more of her Campaign Kicks, as she calls them.' Georgia chuckled, slightly gruesomely Fitzwilliams thought. 'One goal, five behinds and one boundary. You should have seen the face of the umpire who had to wave the boundary call.'

'She's playing injured!' Langdon cackled, but quickly collected himself. Playing injured was the sort of thing you did in the AFL code. Respect should be shown.

'Five behinds and a boundary. Labor will be pulling Stanfield off that field pretty quick smart,' Georgia predicted. 'With two weeks until the election, she won't be putting that particular boot into us again.'

Georgia's tone turned grim. 'To less happy news: eighty-three per cent of voters are now claiming to be supporting us, up five per cent from before Easter. The situation is so confused. Baxter Lockwood reports that some of our most loyal voters are now telling pollsters they're voting Labor.'

'Why on Earth would they do that?' Fitzwilliams asked.

'Because telling a pollster you're voting Liberal has become tan-tamount to supporting the Luddite Lie. We're flying blind, Prime Minister,' Georgia told him bluntly. 'I now believe everything rests on the leaders' debate. I'm confident that you can handle Roslyn Stanfield on Sunday. However, I'm increasingly concerned the Luddite is the greater danger.'

Liberal candidates had already tangled with Luddites at local Meet the Candidate nights and the Luddites had been getting the better of them. Luddite candidates tended to be smart and well-informed—qualities, Fitzwilliams admitted, that left half his caucus badly outgunned. He'd asked (ordered, actually) certain of his less-gifted candidates to avoid Meet the Candidate nights altogether. They were getting clobbered out there.

The Luddites were unpredictable opponents. In the middle of a debate, Luddite candidates could spring some complex major reform to the business-as-usual structures of government. Put on the spot, it was hard for a government MP to find the necessary holes in Luddite proposals. And because the Luddite candidates were independent of each other and didn't campaign on the same things, the central campaign team couldn't pass on clear instructions to their MPs on how best to counterattack Luddite ideas.

Georgia Lambert levelled her eyes on the Prime Minister. 'The Ned Ludd you're up against in the debate is the candidate we first saw, the one who called the election and told people to lie to pollsters.'

Fitzwilliams closed his eyes at the memory of the day: the off-script scrambling, the impromptu tennis match, the storm, Langdon's fall off the stage, being sealed inside the Stadlet. That had been the opening salvo of the Luddites, and in the weeks since, Fitzwilliams hadn't managed a single decent shot back at them. In military terms—and elections lent themselves to such terms— Luddite skirmishers had been harassing his troops relentlessly and Fitzwilliams had let those troops down.

'This Ned Ludd has campaigned locally on bicycle rights,' Georgia reported. 'She's the head of an organisation called Bicyclism Australia.'

That, at least, Fitzwilliams found reassuring. A cycling activist was probably just a greenie campaigning for the Luddites because the Australian Greens were in receivership. Fitzwilliams knew he could handle Greens. For all their irritating carping, Fitzwilliams missed having the Greens around this time. The Greens were always easily ridiculed, while their pedantic, 'principled' stances made Labor's core constituency uneasy. Besides that, when you were tired—and you did get really tired during a campaign— you could drop all the issues and just have a go at the Australian Greens as 'leftie latte drinkers', 'chardonnay socialists'. When you were so fatigued you couldn't think straight, let alone recall your party's policy on tree-plantation subsidies, you could simply dismiss the whole braying lot of the Australian Greens for eating mung beans.

'I would caution against presuming that Ned Ludd will debate you on cycling issues, Prime Minister,' his campaign manager warned as if reading his thoughts. 'The only thing I predict with certainty is that she's going to hit you with something we can't predict.' Georgia Lambert was no longer even making a pretence of hiding her disquiet.

'What do you recommend then?'

'Normally, before a leaders' debate, I'd recommend using Saturday and Sunday to prepare. Rehearse your policy explanations, do practice drills.' She folded her arms. 'I'd do none of that this weekend.' Georgia sighed. 'Stick with the strategy of hitting them in the four areas we discussed before.' These were positions advocated by four different Luddite candidates that the firm of Baxter Lockwood indicated would be most unpopular with the electorate. 'Other than that . . .' Georgia was clearly thinking it out as she went along, 'you're going to have to improvise against them. Let's get you some improv theatre coaching.'

Fitzwilliams groaned softly, having once sat through a whole evening of puerile improv theatre. His government could sponsor some pretty damn stupid things through the Arts Council, and the Improv Theatre National Championships had been a painful three-hour example.

'As you'll need to be in Canberra this weekend for the debate,' Russ Langdon piped up, 'why not campaign in Eden-Monaro? Eden-Monaro is the bellwether electorate. Since 1972, it has unfailingly elected an MP from the party that wins the election.'

'No, it hasn't,' Fitzwilliams corrected him. 'It went to the opposition in the 2016 election.'

'That one doesn't count,' Langdon replied. 'The point is everyone still thinks of Eden-Monaro as the bellwether seat.'

'Campaign in Eden-Monaro because everyone thinks it's a bellwether seat even though it isn't?' Fitzwilliams asked.

'You're missing the point, Prime Minister,' Langdon replied. Fitzwilliams remarked yet again the degree to which Langdon had changed during this election. Two months ago, he couldn't have imagined Langdon telling him he misunderstood anything. 'We stage a huge rally in Eden-Monaro this weekend,' Langdon proposed. 'Bus in supporters if needed. Make the nation believe we're strong in Eden-Monaro. For years voters have been told that Eden-Monaro will elect the party that wins the election and it does . . . usually. Look strong in Eden-Monaro and we will look like the party on the road to victory.'

Early in the election, Fitzwilliams had hoped to claim underdog status, traditionally a favoured campaign position. After all the setbacks of the campaign, he'd become alarmed that the Liberal–National Coalition might actually have become the underdog. He agreed they needed to do something. 'How are we travelling in Eden-Monaro?' he asked Georgia.

She consulted her Gargantuan. 'Worse than the national average, Prime Minister. Eighty-eight per cent say they intend to vote for us. Baxter Lockwood had an interesting finding a few years back as to Eden-Monaro, a throwaway question at the end of a survey that asked Australians to define the word "bellwether". Sixty-two per cent of respondents said, "Errrr," but the other thirty-eight per cent replied, "Eden-Monaro." The only time people hear the word is during federal election campaigns and always in association with that electorate. No one knows where the word comes from.'

'Medieval English,' Olga spoke up. 'A bell tied to a ram to lead a flock. Wether was a word for ram.' As everyone in the room stared at her, she presumed they wanted her opinion. 'I agree with Russell: campaign in Eden-Monaro,' she recommended.

'Book the largest hall in Eden-Monaro,' Fitzwilliams ordered. 'Round up the usual suspects,' he told Georgia, meaning the party faithful, the kind of people who would applaud even if he read the text of *Finnegans Wake* at them—so long as there were free sandwiches afterwards. 'We'll win Eden-Monaro this weekend or, if nothing else, make the nation think we're going to win Eden-Monaro.' He savoured his sudden return to decisiveness.

'I have some good news,' Olga announced. 'Lister St John cancelled his interview for tonight and boarded a plane to London this morning. So long as former Senator Bolen remains with us in Australia, we're unlikely to see Lister back.'

Fitzwilliams clenched a fist with satisfaction. One enemy fled. Another hamstrung. It was time—time long overdue, Fitzwilliams determined—to take on the Luddites.

• • •

Aggie felt a hand shaking her shoulder. 'What time is it?' she rumbled. 'It's still dark.'

'It's six am,' one of the Veronicas said. 'Get up, we have to be in Yass by nine.'

Aggie sat up and put her feet on the ground. She stood up slowly. There were aches, but not nearly as many as she'd expected. Her back mostly. She flinched.

The rain had not let up at all yesterday. Eight hours of hard push into a driving wind, but they had made Binalong at last. Aggie had had a shower, a handful of trail mix, half a glass of red wine—that glass was still on the bedside table—and collapsed into bed. 'I need a coffee,' she told them now.

'There's no cafe open yet,' a Veronica informed her.

'We'll get one in Yass. We kept a piece of pizza for you in case you were hungry,' the other Veronica said, aware of the meagreness of the offer.

Tim the bodyguard entered the room. It struck Aggie that both the Veronicas looked sheepish.

'How far is it to Yass?' Aggie asked.

'About forty. Maybe a bit less.'

'Forty!' Aggie couldn't help groaning. 'How far is it to Canberra then?' They had to get there today. Tomorrow, Sunday, was the leaders' debate.

'Sixty from Yass to Canberra. A hundred kilometres all up today,' Veronica answered.

'If it's any consolation,' Tim interjected, 'I estimate we did a hundred and sixty kilometres yesterday.'

Aggie turned her glare onto the two Veronicas, who suddenly seemed preoccupied with their Genie phones. They had let her

think Wagga Wagga to Canberra was a hundred and fifty kilometres total.

'The footage from yesterday was brilliant,' the taller Veronica
declared. Having formed their mini-peloton, the small group
had been joined by an Australia Post drone that was sidelining its
parcel delivery obligations to provide news footage for the media
networks. 'It's played well with the public overnight.'

'Everything's in place for today,' the shorter Veronica added
eagerly. 'Just wait until we get to Yass.'

The patter of rain on the roof picked up. Aggie suppressed a
scowl and took a bite of cold pizza. She shot a glance at the half-
finished glass of wine, but thought better of it. 'Right then,' she
said, 'I'll get dressed and we'll go.' There wasn't any other option.
'They better have a good cafe in Yass,' she added, making this mild
hope sound something like a threat.

Three people with bicycles were waiting for them in the dark
outside the hotel. 'We're here for the "On to Canberra" trek,' they
told her. The Veronicas had recruited local Bicyclism Australia
members to join them.

Aggie surveyed the sky but it was too dark to tell much
other than that rain was currently falling on them. 'I appreciate the support,' she said, 'but you don't have to bike in the rain
with us.'

The recruits laughed. 'We don't want to miss this,' one of them
replied. 'Today's the day!'

What did they think was going to happen? Aggie wondered. The
Binalong contingent cycled in the vanguard with the Veronicas
following. Having served as her windshield all day yesterday, Tim
now pulled alongside her.

'When I fell asleep last night, you were having an argument with the Veronicae,' she said, adopting his term. 'What was it about?'

Tim paused before replying. 'I told them they were driving you too hard, that they shouldn't have made you bike so far.' He lowered his voice. 'I told them that you weren't a cyclist, and they had no right to demand such distances from you.'

'Not a cyclist?' Aggie exclaimed, surprised at the indignation in her voice.

'You're a cyclist,' Tim conceded. 'You're just not a cyclist like them or me. You probably ride to work and all that, but in wanting you to churn off a hundred and sixty kilometres, they were being bloody-minded. They have the legs for that kind of distance, but your pedalling yesterday, it was done on guts and grit alone.' There was admiration in his voice. 'I told them they ought to appreciate that.'

Aggie said nothing for a few hundred metres. 'Two months ago, I'd never biked further than fifteen kilometres,' she admitted at last. 'Today, when I was told we had a hundred kilometres to do, but that we'd done a hundred and sixty yesterday, part of me was proud at the one-sixty and the not-really-very-sensible part of me thought, given yesterday, well, a hundred kilometres isn't much, is it?'

Tim laughed. A cry came from one of the Binalong riders up front. 'There be blue skies ahead,' he shouted as if he were up in a crow's nest. A soft cheer rippled through the group. The first drone of the day swooped alongside Aggie, some controller at Australia Post having judged there was enough light for decent footage.

'We're heading for Yass and a coffee,' Aggie told the drone, 'and then it's on to Canberra from there!'

• • •

The sight of Yass put even the thought of coffee off her immediate agenda. Aggie was gobsmacked. With other things needing her attention in the campaign, she had given control of the Bicyclism Australia website to the Veronicae. Now, with her mouth half open, she perceived the full organising scope of her two campaign assistants. Cyclists from all along the Melbourne–Sydney train line had descended on the town from Friday evening to Saturday morning. A festive atmosphere filled the streets. Someone generously handed Aggie a takeaway latte to save her queuing up for one. Aggie gave interviews to a swarm of drones. Behind her the Veronicae and a local teacher were mustering the Yass Primary School recorder band to perform a rendition of 'A Bicycle Built for Two'. One of the Veronicae then clambered onto a penny-farthing that had been produced from somewhere. She pedalled out into the gathered mass. 'Give me your answer do, Australia!' she shouted at the crowd and the drones buzzing around her.

'Ned Ludd! Ned Ludd!' the cyclists shouted back.

Aggie found the emotion of the moment almost too much. Ned Ludd was the answer? For the first time, she saw the passion of the Luddite campaign and the hope that passion contained. Did she deserve this kind of support? She'd been so busy campaigning, she hadn't considered that question before. Regardless of where her thoughts were going, her body was busily scrambling up onto a nearby wheelie bin, her legs betraying nothing of their weariness. 'On your bikes everyone!' she shouted. 'On to Canberra from here!' She jumped acrobatically to the ground. A school kid with a recorder took Aggie's empty takeaway coffee cup as if it were a prized souvenir.

'Can you sign the cup?' the girl asked, producing a pen.

Aggie scrawled *Ned Ludd* underneath the barista's L for latte. She mounted her bicycle amid more chants of 'Ned Ludd'. There were hundreds of bicycles. This time it was a full-on peloton that hit the road.

The sixty kilometres to Canberra were a blur. They had slowed to keep the pack together and not lose any stragglers. Incredibly, Veronica was able to keep pace on the penny-farthing. Was there nothing this woman couldn't do on two wheels? Aggie wondered. There was often a breakaway group running ahead, but they always came back to the pack, sensing that the peloton and its Ned were what mattered. Other cyclists joined from side roads on the Yass-to-Canberra leg. When they hit the outskirts of Canberra, newcomers pedalled in from all sides, making Tim more attentive to his body-guard duties. Still, he took a moment to turn to Aggie and blurt, 'Ms Ludd, this is amazing! I'm so glad I got to be part of this!'

The penny-farthing pulled alongside them. 'It's two kilometres to our hotel,' Veronica shouted down at her. 'We could go straight there, or we could . . .' Veronica caught Tim's glare and withheld her alternative proposal.

Aggie laughed. 'Or we could take the whole peloton on a spin around Lake Burley Griffin,' she proposed. 'What's that? Ten kilometres? That's nothing!' she scoffed.

Veronica whooped and rode ahead to lead the pack.

Partway around Burley Griffin, the Veronicae halted the entire mass and hustled Aggie up to a vantage point from where she could address the crowd.

Tim, by her side, was worried. 'Ms Ludd,' he said, 'while we were moving, we could be considered traffic, but stopped like this—' he pointed to a distant police car approaching '—we'll be considered a demonstration and we don't have a permit. Nobody has got official Demonstration Participant IDs. We don't have anything. It could be major trouble for you, trouble for the Luddites.'

'Don't you be worrying about that,' a Veronica replied. She smiled and, adopting the term herself, said, 'Your Veronicae have already taken care of that minor detail.'

'That's impossible!' Tim swept his arm across the whole range of the crowd. 'You can't have registered them for a demonstration. You don't know who most of these people are.'

Veronica pulled a tiny red item from a pocket. 'This is all we're going to need.'

'What is it?'

'A ribbon. A first-place ribbon.' She pointed at a young girl in the crowd wearing a *Ned Ludd for Eden-Monaro* t-shirt. 'Tim, get that girl up onto this hill and . . .' She turned to Aggie. 'Ned, when that police car gets here, you make a big show of pinning this ribbon onto her t-shirt and congratulating her on winning the first annual Yass-to-Canberra bike race.' She grinned at the bodyguard. 'What you see here, Tim, is not a demonstration. It's an amateur athletic event. The government might have slapped a thousand regulations on our right to demonstrate, but they never thought to restrict amateur sporting events!'

It dawned on Aggie that the Veronicae were, in their own mad way, geniuses.

Aggie delivered a rousing spontaneous speech to the faithful— the Pelotoni, as she affectionately called them, not sure whether she had just invented the word or not.

Whether it was Aggie's speech or the quiet word a Veronica had had with the police or just simple prudence on their part, the police did nothing to interfere. Candice, the twelve-year-old ribbon winner, told the crowd that cycling was fun and a good way to stay fit.

Aggie surveyed the crowd. There was still work to do. She had to meet with several Ned Ludds to prepare for the debate tomorrow. She needed a shower. She needed a hearty meal. She was going to take the amazing Veronicae and the loyal Tim out to dinner tonight for a proper feast. She was famished from her exertions. Her stomach was rumbling, but she also felt an almost equal hunger for the looming debate.

What she could really use, the indulgent part of her brain suggested, was a leg massage. That wasn't going to be possible, Aggie told herself as the chant of 'Ned Ludd' filled the air yet again. First, there was an election to be won.

CHAPTER NINE

Prime Minister Fitzwilliams had expected his improv theatre coach to be some sensitive New Age twit murmuring scientific-sounding nonsense about expressive transmission or some other current fad. Instead, Georgia Lambert had sent him a battle-hardened stage and B-movie actor with a badly broken nose and a very direct manner.

'Improv is the best weapon you'll have against the Luddite in the debate,' Paul, his coach, had declared. 'A weapon you'll have and they won't.'

Fitzwilliams looked at him, surprised.

'Yeah,' Paul said, 'everybody thinks the Luddites are skilled at improv, instinctively hitting the dramatic moment in debate, that they are making it up as they go along, but that's crap.' Fitzwilliams half expected Paul to spit for emphasis. 'They aren't improv artists, they're chess players. All those supposedly creative ideas they keep springing on you and Labor? They've worked out all that stuff beforehand and they carefully set it up during the debate and then spike it like a volleyball player.'

'I thought you said they were like chess players,' Fitzwilliams quibbled.

'Yeah, well, they're like both. When you do improv, you can mix metaphors.' Paul jabbed a finger at him. 'That trick with the celery stick the Luddite pulled on Donna Hargreaves and that Labor health person whose name I can't be bothered to remember . . .' Fitzwilliams could not believe how much he was liking this fellow. 'There was nothing improv about that. She tricked them into declaring policies on a non-existent disease. The Luddite lured them both into that trap and then sprang it. That's chess. That's what they do. Improv can counter that.'

This actor was right, Fitzwilliams saw. The Luddites followed an already-worked-out strategy, and that strategy depended on the other parties campaigning in the standard political way. If Fitzwilliams did the unexpected, if he went 'improv', it might well disrupt whatever debating plan they had.

'Let's do this, Paul,' Fitzwilliams told the actor. 'Let's go improv.'

'Okay,' Paul said, shelving the rest of his pep talk. He hadn't expected the PM to accept his analysis so readily. Paul rubbed his hands together. 'A lot of people are treating the Luddites like they're heroes. They aren't heroes. They've just thrown a spanner in the works and people are going, "Oh wow! Aren't they something?" So some no name of a Ned Ludd is going to front up against you at the debate. We're going to cut that Ned Ludd to pieces. Agreed?'

'Delighted to.'

'Right, but some people aren't going to like it if you cut their hero to pieces. They'll call you a bully. The only way to do it, therefore, is with humour. Make cutting them to pieces so funny the public will go along with it because people like to share in a joke. Nobody wants to be the one standing outside, not getting the joke or not approving of it.'

'I'm not that good with humour,' Fitzwilliams cautioned. 'I do question time kind of jokes, but that stuff isn't really funny,' he admitted. 'We have to tell the backbenchers to laugh along with it.'

'I don't want lame question time kind of humour. I want you to forget the last twenty years of your political life, where you've massaged your messages, weighed the consequences of everything, taken no chances. Humour isn't homogenised that way. With humour, you've got to take people some place their brain hasn't been before, a place that's funny.'

'I'm not sure I can do that,' Fitzwilliams confessed. He didn't want to let the actor down, but Paul should know the truth.

'Yes, you can,' Paul insisted. 'First, remember, you're not a comedian, you're a prime minister. So do all those other things, all that political shit, so the voters will recognise you're not half bad as a prime minister, but when you want to go for the knockout blow, that's when you hit the Luddites with comedy.'

Paul cracked his knuckles. 'We're going to start with an exercise: knocking down a hero. I'm Neil Armstrong a'walkin' on the moon and you're Richard Nixon.'

'Richard Nixon?' Fitzwilliams asked. Practising being Richard Nixon didn't sound like a winning idea.

'You and I are old enough to remember this. Neil Armstrong and Buzz What's-his-name were walking on the moon and Richard Nixon called them from the White House to congratulate them. Nixon probably didn't give a shit about the space program, but he wasn't going to miss a chance to claim glory on worldwide television.'

Fitzwilliams recalled it vividly. He'd been five years old, his whole family around the television. Neil Armstrong stopped moving on the surface of the moon while his president spoke to him. The young Fitzwilliams was fearful a giant meteor was going to smash the astronauts to pieces before his very eyes.

Paul now set a different scenario. 'This time, Richard Nixon isn't just seeking a bit of easy high-impact promo. The Nixon you're about to become has had a gutful of the space program. NASA's been bleeding money from your treasury and now that they've finally got someone on the moon, all the TV stations are trotting out that old tape of John Fucking Kennedy vowing to put a man on the moon before the end of the decade. You hated Kennedy and NASA's a right pain. So now, make all America recognise that Neil and NASA need to be taken down a peg or two.' He held up a cautionary hand. 'But do it with humour. You need to start now.' Paul snapped his fingers.

Fitzwilliams squared his shoulders and pretended to hold an old-style phone to his ear. 'Neil? Buzz? This is your president,' he intoned, affecting a Richard Nixonesque voice.

Paul stood stock-still. 'Yes, Mr President.'

'As your president, and on behalf of the American people, I'd like to know what you're doing up there.'

'We're collecting rocks, samples to bring back to Earth.'

Fitzwilliams felt a glimmer of an idea. 'Rocks, huh? You know, Neil, it has taken about ten billion of the taxpayers' money to get you up there . . . and you're going to bring us back some rocks?'

'Yessir, Mr President.'

Fitzwilliams paused, not because he was out of dialogue. He'd paused, he noted to himself, out of comic timing. 'Neil, I don't know how to break this to you, but we already have a lot of rocks down here. We have a lot of rocks in America,' he emphasised. 'We have so many rocks, we have a whole mountain range named after them.'

'It's for science, Mr President.'

'Science?' Fitzwilliams affected his friendliest tone in his Nixon voice. 'I guess you're keen on rocks, are you, Neil? A bit of a geologist?'

'I wouldn't say that, Mr President. I'm a test pilot. NASA did give us some geology lessons though.'

'So what do you know about rocks then?' Fitzwilliams did not wait for an answer. 'What are the three types of rocks, for instance?'

'Well, there are igneous . . . uh, metamorphic and sedimentary,' Paul/Neil replied.

'Sedimentary?' Fitzwilliams took the opening. 'Look around you, Neil. Do you see any lakes? Do you see any rivers? Do you think you're going to find any sedimentary rocks up there? I know it's called the Sea of Tranquility, Neil, but did NASA ever tell you there's no water up there?'

Paul/Neil, quietly, 'I know that, sir.'

'So you're going to be bringing us back about twenty pounds of these rocks, I understand, and the Apollo program has cost us all, who knows, maybe twenty billion dollars, I can't keep track. NASA just keeps sending us these invoices with astronomically long numbers on them. Tell me, Neil, how much do you think these moon rocks are costing us per ounce?'

'That would be . . . uh . . . I reckon a lot, Mr President.'

'So you're up there collecting rocks, Neil. Well, do bring back some pretty stones for us, maybe a nice shiny one, a good flat one for skipping on a lake.'

Fitzwilliams winked at Paul and hung up the imaginary phone to indicate he had finished.

Paul stepped out of character. 'Not bad,' he murmured, looking at Fitzwilliams with what seemed a new-found respect. 'You trivialised the whole Apollo program. You had Neil Armstrong uncomfortable up there and, more importantly, the audience amused. If you can do that to a genuine hero like Neil Armstrong,' Paul continued, 'somebody standing on the bloody moon, then you can take apart some Ned Luddite nobody.'

If Fitzwilliams needed a confidence boost, he had surely got it. Off script wasn't to be feared. It was the weapon he would use to take down the Luddites.

The other exercises were equally stimulating. Fitzwilliams played the Mayor of London in 1348 putting a positive spin on the bubonic plague. 'There has never been a better time to get into the housing market.' To practise against the known Luddite tactic of springing a policy proposal in mid-debate, Paul ran a series of exercises. Fitzwilliams was cast as the French Minister for Health tearing into Louis Pasteur and his crackpot smallpox vaccine; a publishing house executive rejecting J.K. Rowling and her bland children's series; and, to give it an Australian flavour, a patent office official kicking out the inventor of the Hills hoist. 'It doesn't matter that in each case you were wrong in the long run. All you have to do tonight at the leaders' debate is win the moment,' Paul advised. 'That's what people will remember.'

Direct from the improv training, Fitzwilliams headed full of vigour to Queanbeyan to campaign in the heartland of the Eden-Monaro electorate. Georgia Lambert had delivered everything he'd requested: an auditorium full of Liberal Party faithful, a relatively coherent local candidate, even a band to play the unofficial campaign tune, 'We Are Aussie, It's What We Are About'.

That's what he'd requested before his training sessions with Paul. Now he was eager to try some spontaneity. He and his two new bodyguards—Quentin and Leon had the day off—strolled the streets of Queanbeyan. Fitzwilliams enjoyed being out of the protective cocoon. Here were Labor voters. Here, too, were Luddites. A gaggle of celery-wearing Luddites were being led by a girl sporting a red ribbon on her *Ned Ludd for Eden-Monaro* t-shirt. The Luddites noticed Fitzwilliams and one shouted at him, 'We are the Pelotoni!'

'What's that?' Fitzwilliams shouted back. 'A type of pasta?' That got a laugh, not just from the local Liberals accompanying him but also, he noticed, from the general public. He was on form.

He'd been enjoying himself so much he let it run late, but even that could be turned to his advantage. Here was a prime minister so capable he didn't have to spend the afternoon swotting for the debate. By contrast, Roslyn Stanfield had been sequestered somewhere all weekend being drilled on her own Labor Party policies and the supposed loopholes in his.

Fitzwilliams opted to close his eyes and rest on the short ride back to Canberra. The limousine was a self-driving car. Desmond the chauffeur's only role was to key in the destination and step in should the driverless car system fail. It never did.

He must have nodded off, for the next thing he heard was a voice ordering Desmond to pull over. Fitzwilliams blinked and took in the surroundings. They were already in the outskirts of Canberra. 'Why are we stopped?' he asked.

The bodyguard in front with Desmond had the coiled look that came over bodyguards when they thought something might actually be happening. 'The TI alert light has come on, Prime Minister.' He pointed to the dashboard of the prime ministerial limousine. 'The terror incident light,' he clarified. 'It indicates there's a terror incident occurring somewhere within fifteen kilometres of here. The procedure is we stay put until we have assessed the situation.' He turned to the driver. 'Engage security lockdown,' he ordered.

'Christ!' Desmond exhaled. 'Is that what you're on about?' He gestured a hand towards the flashing red light. 'It's a malfunction. We've tried getting that light fixed, but no one can figure out what's wrong with it.'

Fitzwilliams broke in more urgently. He was behind schedule. 'I've been through this before. It's a false alarm. It pinpoints the terror incident to the middle of Lake Burley Griffin. So unless you think some terrorist group is trying to blow up the nation's flotilla of paddleboats, can we get to the studio?' Even under this unwelcome stress, Fitzwilliams recognised he was in form. Flotilla of paddleboats! Bring on the Luddite! He was ready.

'We aren't going anywhere, Prime Minister,' the bodyguard in the front seat replied sternly, 'until we've ascertained the nature of the threat.'

'There is no bloody threat!' Fitzwilliams insisted. 'Quentin and Leon ignore that light all the time.'

'It's a red light, Prime Minister! There's no point to having red alert lights if you ignore them when they go off,' the the bodyguard beside Fitzwilliams declared peevishly. 'We have a terror incident alert and we have protocols to follow! Let us get on with our job.' The bodyguard picked up his Genie phone to indicate the discussion was over.

They were starting to run seriously late now. 'If I don't make it to the debate, your bloody protocols could cost me the election!' Fitzwilliams snapped, but the bodyguards were through responding to him.

Several minutes went by, the two bodyguards on their phones double- and triple-checking whatever was on their damned emergency protocols. A city bus was approaching the bus shelter next to where they were parked. Improv, Fitzwilliams thought.

The bus slowed. Someone was getting off. Fitzwilliams waited, then clicked his seat belt with one hand, swung open the door with the other and sprang from the car. Both bodyguards were caught unaware, but their reflexes had them out of the limousine and after him in an instant. Fitzwilliams pushed past the passenger getting off the bus. The bus doors closed behind him with a delightful whoosh. The bus began to pull away, the two bodyguards running alongside it slapping on the door and demanding that the non-existent driver let them on. 'Driverless bus,' Fitzwilliams shouted back at them. 'Go finish your protocols!' He clenched his fist in triumph. On the way to Canberra now, improvising all the way!

Several of the bus passengers had already recognised him. He smiled at them and took a seat. He'd be cutting it fine now. He'd just have time to shower and change at the studio before the debate. Those bodyguards had not only aggravated him, they'd taken him out of his mental zone. He'd been so on his game.

'Please pay the fare,' a voice intruded. 'Payment can be made by tACT card or credit card.'

Fitzwilliams looked up. 'Put your Transit ACT card in the box over there,' a passenger instructed him. 'Your tACT card.' She pointed to the red box at the front door. Fitzwilliams went over to the machine. It had been years since he'd ridden public transit. 'Please pay the fare,' the automated voice intoned again.

Fitzwilliams felt for his wallet, but he never carried his wallet when campaigning. His image consultants insisted that the public like their prime ministers to have sleek, tapered lines. No bulging pockets. Besides, you were meeting with the general public and some of them could pick pockets. He'd learned that bitter lesson on his first campaign. 'I don't have my wallet with me,' he told the machine.

'Please pay the fare or the Fare Evasion Procedure will activate in twenty seconds,' the voice warned.

'I don't have my wallet!' he repeated, but got no answer. 'I'm the Prime Minister!' he shouted at it. 'I don't have my wallet!'

'Fair Evasion Shaming Procedure in ten seconds.'

'Shaming?' He turned to the other passengers, 'What do I—'

'Face Recognition Software activated!' the voice announced with just a slight undertone of menace to its automated chirpiness.

On-bus cameras swirled to face him and flashed simultaneously. Fitzwilliams reeled in the brightness, stunned. Flashes? What kind of camera used flashes these days? This was being done solely to humiliate, he thought indignantly, though fare evaders were not a group with whom he normally identified.

'Face recognition software identifies fare evader as . . .' The machine paused, it seemed dramatically. 'Adrian Fitzwilliams.'

Fitzwilliams turned to look at the passengers. It was almost as if he were their Fuhrer, he thought. Straight arms were extended towards him, but not in salute. Each held a Genie phone. The episode was probably already uploading onto YouTube.

· · ·

Georgia Lambert stared at her phone in disbelief. She couldn't raise anyone in the Prime Minister's car. The debate started in half an hour and the Prime Minister had dropped off the radar. His car was rejecting all calls.

Russ Langdon bit his lip. 'It has to be an LTI,' he said. 'During a local terror incident, the Prime Minister's car can only receive telecommunications from F-TES, the Federal Terror Emergency Services.' It prevented terror-hackers from potentially feeding false information to the Prime Minister's personal security that might lure them into an incident danger zone. Langdon was flummoxed. 'But if a terror incident was underway, as Minister for Security and Freedom, I'd have been informed,' he pointed out, mostly for his own benefit.

Though her stomach was in turmoil, Georgia Lambert's face didn't show it. The debate was scheduled for 7.30 pm. Network Nine had shelled out a fortune for its debate coverage. At this moment, their sample selected audience was being slotted into MRI machines in fifty different hospitals across the country so Nine could monitor their brain activation patterns during the debate. This high-tech version of the infamous Worm would have cost them a bomb. The debate had to go ahead on time. 'Russell,' she said, 'head to make-up.' Langdon looked back blankly. She would have to spell it out. 'We don't know where the PM is. You'll have to go on in his place.'

A staffer came belting towards them. The run alone indicated bad news.

'The PM's on a bus somewhere!' the staffer panted. 'Look!' The hand holding her phone was literally shaking.

They peered at the tiny screen. The PM was gesturing at the bus ticket machine and shouting, 'I'm the Prime Minister. I don't have my wallet.'

'It gets worse,' the staffer warned.

• • •

Fitzwilliams needed to take charge of the situation. 'Yes, I'm the Prime Minister,' he told the motley crew of bus passengers. God, public transit users! What could he possibly have in common with this lot? 'I need to get to the debate. How close does this bus get to Parliament House?'

'No bus gets close to Parliament House,' one of them replied. 'You brought in that rule.'

She was right. One of Langdon's security measures, after three buses laden with explosives were detonated outside the Algerian parliament. No buses of any kind were allowed within a kilometre of Australia's Parliament House.

'This bus can drop you at Kingston,' another told him. 'You'll have to hoof it from there.' The passenger seemed to say this with satisfaction. She was wearing a celery stick. Bloody Luddite, Fitzwilliams thought.

Kingston. About two kilometres. Seven or eight minutes' running he calculated, but it was the part of his brain that remembered being an athletic twenty-three year old that had made that calculation.

He couldn't run two kilometres! He only had about half an hour. A brisk walk with a few hundred metres of running to leave enough time to change clothes and have a hasty make-up job.

He didn't even have his phone. Georgia was fielding all his calls today. He had to remain focused. 'Can one of you call a taxi to meet me in Kingston?' he asked the public transit mob.

'How are you going to pay for it?' the Luddite inquired. 'Or are you planning to stiff the taxi for the fare too?'

'Auto Pilots won't take you anywhere without a credit card inserted into them,' a kindlier passenger informed him.

He looked at his watch again. Trot half a kilometre and then brisk walk the rest of the way to recover. Wash his face and go straight to the debate studio. It was a plan.

The bus disgorged him at Kingston. Fitzwilliams oriented himself and set off. He'd try to run as far as Brisbane Avenue.

It started to drizzle.

· · ·

Fifteen minutes from the start of the debate. Despite all the Wagga-to-Canberra pedalling of the previous days, Aggie had been happy to cycle to the parliamentary studio. It had steadied her nerves, but that had been an hour ago. Her nerves had ratcheted back up. A few other Ned Ludds were with her in the waiting room. Good for morale. She wasn't alone, but she would be when she went out there.

The stillness of the trenches before going into battle, she thought. No one was talking or doing anything except for the young girl who had accompanied the Sydney Ned Ludd, who was absorbed by something on her Genie phone. 'Ned,' the girl suddenly called to Aggie, brandishing her phone. 'Have a look at this!'

The small knot of Ned Ludds in the room gathered around the phone. Perhaps, Aggie mused as she watched the clip, she was under less stress than some other party leaders.

• • •

There was no time to sort out why it had happened. A woman walking her dog had found the Prime Minister running through the streets of Canberra and all three of them, dog included, were heading to the studio by Auto Pilot taxi. Russ Langdon was getting the finishing touches to his make-up. 'They've found the Prime Minister,' Georgia Lambert told him. 'He'll be here in five minutes.'

Langdon looked relieved, but Georgia could not let him relax. 'You'll still have to go on. The PM is soaked and in a terrible state. We'll need time to make him presentable. Don't make excuses. Say he was delayed. Many viewers will have already seen the YouTube video.' Georgia hadn't yet come up with a strategy for dealing with the bus fare evasion video; 'tACTless PM Doesn't Pay his Way!' was already trending. That damage-control task could wait until tomorrow, she decided. She put a hand on Langdon's shoulder. 'Hold the fort until we get him ready.' Langdon nodded, but not convincingly.

'You can do it, Russell. Just go out there . . .' She needed to simplify the task. This was high-stakes play beyond Langdon's comfort zone. 'And defend,' she told him. 'Stall them until the PM is ready. Don't go on the attack. Deflect any attack from Stanfield. Under no circumstances discuss the merits of anything the Luddite proposes. Just defend. Even if the Luddite looks vulnerable on something, don't go for her. It could be a trap.'

'Like at the Battle of Hastings,' Langdon agreed.

The analogy threw Georgia. 'In what way?'

'King Harold knew his Saxon army was tired,' Langdon explained, oddly pleased to be asked. 'He drew them into a tight formation and ordered them to hold their positions and let the Normans exhaust themselves attacking. After one charge, the Normans fell back in disarray. The Saxons couldn't help themselves and surged forward after them. A trap,' Langdon told her sadly. 'Norman forces, waiting on the flank, fell on the Saxon axemen.'

Georgia had long recognised that male politicians thought of elections in terms of warfare. Even the word 'campaign', they shared with Napoleon. She'd given Langdon what she thought were simple instructions, but his mnemonic for remembering them involved the detailed carnage of some battlefield from a thousand years ago. Still, if that was how his male brain operated, she would work with it. She gave his shoulder a gentle squeeze. 'I'll get the PM out there as quickly as I can. Go out there and do it. Do it, Russell,' she said, summoning a Shakespearean tone, 'for Fitzwilliams and King Harold!'

She had got the tone right. Langdon flung off the make-up bib that protected his suit and stood up, his shoulders straight.

'1066 and all that!' Georgia cried, urging him towards the studio floor.

• • •

Roslyn Stanfield had a small phalanx of her team escort her to the lectern to block the view. The cameras weren't going to see how badly she was limping.

She had been determined to carry on despite her hamstring pull, but the few more kicks she'd attempted had proved a humiliating failure and severely aggravated her injury. Labor yanked its leader from any more appearances on AFL pitches. She knew her advisers didn't fear further damage to her leg; it was damage to Labor's election chances that concerned them.

Painkillers had helped her to walk with a more normal gait but they fogged her brain. Twice she forgot her local candidates' names in the whirlwind of touring electorates. For the leaders' debate, she needed every bit of mental sharpness, so she'd gone off painkillers three days earlier. She could think clearly again but, unfortunately, foremost among those thoughts was just how much her bloody thigh hurt.

The election was hers to win tonight. She might be suffering shooting pains, but Fitzwilliams was clearly in worse condition. Minutes earlier, she'd been shown a clip of the Prime Minister freaking out at a bus ticket machine. Had Fitzwilliams—stalwart, steady, dull Fitzwilliams—finally lost it?

But Fitzwilliams wasn't her only foe. She sized up the Luddite behind her lectern. Leadership was the gaping hole in the Luddite campaign. Her Luddite debate opponent was just one in a sea of anonymous candidate Neds, but with the nation facing so many challenges, the people needed a prime minister. Tonight, she would make them realise that was her.

Liberal staffers entered the studio and Roslyn did a double take. Russ Langdon was taking the Prime Minister's place behind the lectern! Where the hell was Fitzwilliams?

Up against Langdon as a last-minute replacement and a generic Ned Ludd, Stanfield was the only actual leader there! She had to seize this opportunity. She decided she'd go at the Luddite first, make the Australian public see that the party was a farce. Then she'd run rings around Langdon.

A sudden thought made Stanfield grin in excitement. Had Fitzwilliams been arrested for bus-fare evasion?

• • •

Georgia Lambert hadn't uttered a word of reproach. She was all business when Fitzwilliams was bustled into the dressing room. 'Get those wet clothes off him,' she ordered, and staffers quickly began removing his jacket and shirt. 'Don't put a clean shirt on him yet,' she instructed, leaving the PM shirtless in front of his team. 'No time to shower. Splash cold water on him, then towel him off.'

The make-up artist touched his face and drew her hand back. 'Can't put make-up on him. He is sweating like a . . .' She tactfully left the barnyard animal unsaid. 'He's flushed. Anything we put on him will melt in two minutes.'

'Au natural, it is then,' Georgia decided.

They were working on him like a Ferrari pit crew, Fitzwilliams thought. Someone pressed an ice pack to his cheek, trying to de-flush his face. He let them get on with their work. His job was to regain his debating frame of mind. Every minute was critical. Langdon was out there doing Fitzwilliams' fighting for him. Langdon. Langdon with his peculiar fixation with prime numbers. Anything might happen. Perhaps only even numbers would come up in the debate while Langdon was out there, Fitzwilliams consoled himself.

• • •

'Anyone who votes for the Luddites has no idea who would be their prime minister,' Roslyn Stanfield told the camera. She turned to face the Luddite. 'Who's the leader of the Luddite party?' she demanded. 'Are you their leader—or just a face to put before the camera? If you are the Luddite leader, why do you hide it from the Australian people? Why don't you tell us who you actually are? Tell the Australian people who is funding the Luddite Party. Tell the baffled battler out there what your party stands for!' She let the barrage of demands buffet the Luddite. Her opponent would inevitably fail to answer one of them and then Stanfield could accuse her of refusing to answer the question.

'The Luddite Party has no official leader,' Aggie replied calmly, 'because we want Luddite ideas to be discussed on their merits alone. Party leadership has become a national distraction, an obsession, so pervasive we have a PM who shouts about being prime minister at bus ticket machines. And you've promoted your policies by showing how good you are at kicking AFL goals. What has that got to do with the merit of your ideas?' Aggie gave Stanfield a concerned look. 'By the way, give your leg a rest,' she advised. 'You need to be careful with hamstring injuries.'

Stanfield didn't answer. If she denied being injured, it would mean she'd have to kick a goal tomorrow to prove it.

'We don't pretend the Luddite Party is the only source of good ideas,' Aggie continued, 'but we do want ideas to be discussed. By having all our candidates called Ned Ludd, we avoid the party leader being the prime political fixation.'

Stanfield shot a glance at Russ Langdon. 'As the Prime Minister has not condescended to show up tonight, perhaps I'm the only one here who does think that leadership of this nation is of prime importance.'

'Leadership?' Aggie asked. 'You toppled the previous Labor leader, saying at the time it was a question of direction for the party, yet you kept all the same policies. What you wanted was not based on ideas or policy but solely on your desire to be leader.'

Stanfield scoffed. 'You're remarkably uninformed, Ned, if I may call you that. Under my leadership, Labor brought forward the Opportunity-Based Employment policy that gives the battler— whether that's a builder battler, a beautician battler, a barista battler—gives *every* battler enhanced pathways to advancement.'

'Sounds like a good idea,' Aggie admitted.

Stanfield had not expected the reply. She hesitated.

'Sounds like something I'd be willing to support,' Aggie continued. 'How does it work?'

Stanfield adopted her visionary pose. 'Labor's Opportunity-Based Employment will deliver seventy thousand new jobs, increase blending of casual jobs to full-time equivalent positions, and provide Australian workers with increased pathways in emerging employment sectors. Opportunity-Based Employment brings twenty-first-century employment opportunities to beleaguered battlers everywhere.'

Aggie shook her head. 'Those are its promises. I asked: how does it work?'

'We enhance pathways to employment,' Stanfield began again.

'But how does anyone find the pathway and take it to wherever it's leading?'

'Opportunity-Based Employment will create employment hubs centring on innovation-based industrial/managerial solutions.

Stakeholders will be part of the process to incentivise entrepreneurs and business leaders . . . to develop enhanced corridors to . . .
employment.'

'You lost me,' Aggie replied.

'You lost me too,' Russ Langdon chipped in. 'Are they corridors
or pathways—or does a pathway lead into a corridor?' he asked.
'And just how do you *incentivise* entrepreneurs? I'm not sure it's
even a word.'

• • •

'Well done, Russ!' Fitzwilliams clapped at the screen. They had
nearly finished their overhaul of his face. A staffer looped a tie
around his neck. On the screen, Stanfield looked as though she
was hurting—which, in fact, she was, her right thigh having shot a
prong of pain through her.

The make-up person touched his cheek. 'Still too hot. The surface
skin has cooled, but the underlying layers will heat it up again.
Nothing we can do. You'll look your age, Prime Minister,' she predicted bleakly.

Ten minutes into the debate and Langdon was holding his own.
Stanfield had tried to take charge, but Ned Ludd had made her look
vapid. Seeing Stanfield bested, however, was not reassuring. The
seemingly mild Luddite evoked an odd sensation in Fitzwilliams.
He suspected it might be fear.

Georgia Lambert gave him a last look-over. 'You're still red-
faced, but you have to go on anyway. This is what you've trained
for all weekend. You know how to do it. Take out Ned Ludd.'

She clapped him on the back. 'Like King Harold at the Battle of Hastings!' she encouraged.

'Surely you don't want me to be like that,' he replied, turning back to her. He clasped a hand over one eye. She looked at him, puzzled. It was not a good sign; he'd expected her to laugh.

• • •

The changeover went smoothly. He waited for Langdon to finish defending a nit-picking attack from Stanfield on transport policy and then strode out to assume his rightful place behind the lectern. Langdon held up his hand for the exchange of a jaunty high five with the Prime Minister. It might be the gesture of tag-team wrestlers, but at least it looked like tag-team wrestlers in control.

'I apologise for my lateness,' Fitzwilliams began, 'and want to thank Russ Langdon for stepping in. That's the kind of cabinet this government has: one in which everyone is able to step up, a cabinet of depth and experience,' he declared in a vast overstatement of the abilities of the motley place holders who made up most of his team.

'I thank the Prime Minister for condescending to attend,' Stanfield replied. 'A clearer case of this government's hubris . . .' she let the word hang for a moment, knowing it was a good one to pin on a long-term government, 'in taking the Australian people for granted could hardly have been better demonstrated.'

'Could we get back to discussing policies?' Aggie suggested.

'I'd be delighted to,' Fitzwilliams said, smiling at her. 'I note that the Ned Ludd candidate in the electorate of Flynn is in favour of bringing back the death penalty, an opinion opposed by the vast majority of the Australian people. I'd like to know whether you stand by this Luddite policy of restoring the death penalty.'

'No,' Aggie replied.

'No?' Fitzwilliams had at least expected her to hedge.

'No, it wouldn't be a good idea. As a bare minimum standard, a government should try to avoid killing its own citizens,' Aggie elaborated.

'Are you prepared then, right now, to disendorse him as the Luddite Party candidate for Flynn? A candidate of your own party is advocating policies that, in your own words, don't meet "a bare minimum standard" of acceptability.'

'I wouldn't worry about it,' Aggie reassured him. 'It's a minority view. If he put that up as a private member's bill, it wouldn't get up.'

'He's talking about executing people. I think you have to do a little more than tell me not to worry,' Fitzwilliams prodded.

Aggie disagreed. 'Let's say you, Roslyn and I all get elected, and the Ned Ludd in Flynn gets elected, it would be three-to-one against him already. In a general vote in parliament, it would be voted down.'

'That is not the point,' Fitzwilliams persisted. He wasn't going to let her fob him off so easily. 'A member of your party is advocating a policy that is repugnant to the people of Australia. Are you prepared to denounce the Ned Ludd of Flynn?' he demanded.

'Denounce him?' Aggie asked. 'If he's elected, I'm going to have to work with him on other issues. It's not sensible to denounce people because they disagree with you on one issue.'

'So no policy position is beyond the pale for the Luddites then? Your candidate for Solomon has very extreme views on Aboriginal Native Title. She proposes that traditional ownership means actual physical ownership of all mineral rights in this nation.

What she advocates would end the mining industry in Australia!' he thundered. 'Is that Luddite policy too?'

'It is a radical interpretation of traditional ownership,' Aggie conceded, 'but surely she has the right to propose it. Would it hurt parliament to listen to what she has to say on the subject? You, Prime Minister, are always banging on about political correctness muzzling free speech. Perhaps you could be open enough to listen to someone else's opinion in parliament. And I mean listen,' she stressed, 'not engage in catcalls and childish antics when someone else is speaking.'

'Parliament is not some coffee club for latte-drinking lefties,' Fitzwilliams declared, 'to propose ideas that would eviscerate the mining industry and the economy of this nation.'

Roslyn Stanfield had been left out of this exchange too long. 'For once, I agree with the Prime Minister,' she plunged in. 'Electing Luddites would tie up the important work of parliament in an endless stream of private members' bills on crackpot ideas.'

'You shouldn't say, "I agree with the Prime Minister," Roslyn, when I have just used the phrase "latte-drinking lefties",' Fitzwilliams pointed out. 'Half your party are latte-drinking lefties.' Comedy improv, he reminded himself. 'Think of your base, Roslyn—they like a good latte.' He chuckled towards the camera.

'Well, who doesn't like a good latte?' a male voice asked. Fitzwilliams turned to see a tall man standing where Ned Ludd had been. 'Who are you?' he demanded.

'I'm Ned Ludd, candidate in O'Connor. As we are talking about the mining industry, I want to outline potential reforms to that industry. There's a great deal of disruption done to local communities by fly-in, fly-out workforces.'

'The Luddites can't—' Fitzwilliams stopped himself in time. He'd been about to say, 'change debaters midway through'.

'This is precisely the leadership issue I was talking about,' Stanfield jumped in. 'The Luddite Party can't even manage a debate without it becoming a game of musical chairs. Who exactly is the spokesperson for your party?'

'The Luddite Party agreed to send Ned Ludd to the debate,' the new Ned pointed out. 'I am Ned Ludd and so was Ned Ludd, who preceded me. Now can we discuss fly-in, fly-out workforce policy?'

Fitzwilliams' radar signalled alert. Ludd was going to spring some complicated idea on them and then expect everyone to discuss it. He gave only very guarded responses to the Luddite, and Stanfield too, he noted, was keeping her head down. Fitzwilliams took the first opportunity to pull the rug from under new Ned by shifting the debate to foreign affairs. What would the single-issue twerp from Western Australia know about that?

It turned out he knew a fair bit. The bastard could even speak Malay. Still, Fitzwilliams had been able to assert a degree of prime ministerial-ness over both his opponents. Overall, Fitzwilliams judged the debate was going all right, but all right was not good enough. He was still looking to land a knockout blow on the Luddite and brushing away the buzzing irritant of Roslyn Stanfield was a distraction.

He got into a tangle with Stanfield on tax incentives so protracted that the moderator had yawned. Fitzwilliams needed to put some life back into the debate. He could almost hear the voice of his improv coach urging him to go for it.

When he broke off from Stanfield, however, a young woman, no more than a schoolgirl, had taken the most recent Ned's place. 'What, another one?' Fitzwilliams complained to the moderator.

'I'm a volunteer working on the campaign of Ned Ludd in Sydney,' the young Ned said by way of introduction, looking about nervously in the lights.

'You're not even a candidate,' Stanfield protested.

'But I am Ned Ludd,' the girl shot back. 'I changed my name officially.'

The moderator shrugged. 'The Luddites agreed to send Ned Ludd to the debate and they have done that—repeatedly it seems.' He held up a hand to silence any further objections.

'I'm here to propose the establishment of a national wage,' the adolescent Ned announced to the viewing audience. She went on to describe something Fitzwilliams thought ought to sound ridiculous but which this wet-behind-the-ears girl was making appear feasible. Cappuccino communists, part of his brain suggested, but he'd already discussed coffee. She was proposing that the whole adult population receive a wage from the government of $17,000 per year for doing nothing! Everyone. There was to be no means testing.

He wanted to go for the kill, but caution held him back. The Luddites sending out this naive girl with her pipedream idea for him to tear her apart—it was obviously a trap ... but what kind of trap? Was it just about how bad it would look if the Prime Minister let loose on a teenage girl? 'How old are you?' he asked.

'Seventeen. However, it's the national wage proposal we should be discussing, not my age.'

He would condescend, but not too heavily. 'You're not even old enough to vote.'

'I'm old enough to live under the consequences of government policies. They affect me.'

'Do you have any idea how much your little scheme would cost the Australian taxpayer?' he prodded gently. 'Every adult in Australia receiving seventeen thousand dollars from the govern-ment would be—' the Prime Minister swallowed, realising he had just posed himself a maths problem in front of a national audience '—beyond the ability of the government to pay,' he salvaged.

'You haven't done the maths, Prime Minister,' the young Ned shot back. 'It is not seventeen thousand dollars times the number of adults in the country. To begin with, the seventeen thousand would be taxed at the recipient's marginal rate of taxation. The richest would therefore give back a fair portion of it.'

Fitzwilliams didn't quite get her point, but thought it ill-advised to say so. She might be saying something simple and he was missing it.

'Second, we spend an awful lot of money running Centrelink, employing armies of people to verify people's entitlements, inves-tigate complaints and translate complaint forms into community languages. None of that would be necessary anymore. Everyone over eighteen gets the money deposited straight into their bank account by the tax office. You can get rid of almost all of Centrelink. Smaller government, Prime Minister! Save a packet there.'

Fitzwilliams blinked. Smaller government? That was Liberal Party mantra. How dare she try to pilfer it!

The young Ned pressed on. 'You can get rid of the Work for the Dole schemes. Think of all the workers you have employed over the years just to organise and monitor the people who are working for the dole. Think of all the pointless Work for the Dole jobs people have had to do. Think of the waste of talent. Those people could have been doing something useful instead.'

Fitzwilliams knew he needed to respond to this. He had to wedge her somehow. 'It must be very tempting to you, as a seventeen year old, to get seventeen thousand dollars next year for doing nothing. It would be a cruisy bludger's life for you and your young friends, wouldn't it? All paid for by the taxpayers, the hard-working mums and dads, the small businesses, all so you can slack off.' He would be dismissive. 'It's not going to happen. We are not going to turn the entire nation into bludgers. "Here's a handout. Don't even bother looking for work." That is not the sort of Australia I'll lead.'

'Is that what you think?' Ned asked. 'You think everyone would quit their jobs if you gave them seventeen thousand dollars per year? Is that your opinion of Australians?'

She was twisting his words. 'No. Australians are hard workers,' Fitzwilliams insisted. 'You are too young to—'

'Australians are hard workers,' Roslyn Stanfield cut across him. 'Whether you're a brawny battler or a brainy one, Labor's goal for everyone out there is a fair day's pay for a hard day's work.'

'Think of the difference it would make,' Ned Ludd persisted. 'For all your talk about innovation and enterprise, do you know what holds most people back? We have to make ends meet. We can't take risks. We don't start businesses, we don't invent new products. Instead we work in coffee shops, as security guards, take jobs in call centres. Yes, the seventeen-thousand-dollar national wage would help poorly paid people to live more comfortably, but its most important consequence would be what it does for the young entrepreneur, the young researcher, the young person with a business dream. They can unleash their ideas, put their energies towards creating something new and know they aren't going to starve to death while doing so. It'll release the locked-up creativity of the nation! Is this something you can support, Prime Minister? Is it something we can carry forth together?'

Here was the moment, Fitzwilliams realised. Here was what he practised. Throwing Louis Pasteur out of his office, rejecting J.K. Rowling. He had to smash this idea. Paul the improv coach had told him to win the moment.

'You're not saying anything, Prime Minister,' Stanfield cut in. 'I think the Australian people, the bewildered battlers out there, have a right to know where you stand.'

He turned on Stanfield. 'The bewildered battler? What's next? The bewitched battler? The bothered battler? Who else is out there for Labor? The bucolic battler? The boorish battler? You're not running a campaign, Roslyn,' he told her, 'you're running a tongue-twister.' He was on a roll. He felt the surge of improv upon him. 'Who's running your *Sesame Street* campaign, Roslyn,' he asked his opponent, 'the fucking letter B?'

The stillness, the silence was terrible. He had just sworn on national television during primetime in front of the children of all the mums and dads whose hard work he'd only shortly before been extolling. It had just come out. It had just seemed right for the sentence—for the comedy structure of the sentence, Paul would have said. Stanfield had rocked back on her heels under his verbal assault and—Fitzwilliams paled—she was wiping tears from her eyes. He'd made her cry! Even those who thought his comment funny, even they would think he'd been a bully. He wasn't even supposed to use improv on Stanfield, he remembered bleakly. He was supposed to go at the Luddites with it.

The day had been too much for him. The bodyguards, the bus ticket machine, the public transport passengers, the running, the rain, the rotating Luddites . . . He needed solace. He needed to be somewhere else, not debating policies on national media. He wanted Langdon to come out to take his place again and calculate how many billions or trillions the stupid national wage would cost, but that wasn't possible. Without even thinking how it would look on the screens of the nation, he put a consoling hand to his face, covering one eye.

'Excuse me,' came the voice of the young Ned. 'Can we get back to discussing the topic?'

CHAPTER TEN

If there was a collective term for fiascos, Fitzwilliams felt this campaign merited its use. There was already a debate t-shirt out, featuring two entwined, amorous letters B, cavorting above the words *The Fucking Letter B*. It had reportedly been available online forty-seven minutes after the debate. The makers of t-shirts had a faster response time than most emergency services.

'For today, we're in damage-control mode,' Georgia Lambert summed up succinctly. Olga O'Rourke and Russ Langdon grimaced their agreement.

Yesterday had spun out of control. His team deserved better than a prime minister who shouted at bus ticket machines and lost it during the debate. Oddly enough, Roslyn Stanfield had apologised to him afterwards. 'Sorry about the tears. I wouldn't normally . . . but my leg is killing me,' she'd confessed. She'd looked over at the teenage Luddite being congratulated by her fellow Neds. 'It was all too much. I just couldn't hold it in anymore. My leg . . .' She winced.

Fitzwilliams had felt his heart go out to her. She was making no attempt to hide her limp. 'I'm so sorry. I shouldn't have gone off like that,' he told her. 'I didn't mean to . . .' He almost gave her a consoling hug and he sensed she'd have appreciated it. But Stanfield? Hugging Roslyn Stanfield? What had the Luddites done to them?

'At least we won't take a hammering in the polls,' Langdon predicted. The most recent polls had the Liberal–National Coalition at 86 per cent. Even Buddhist monks were lying to pollsters.

'After that debate, we'll probably top ninety,' Fitzwilliams muttered glumly, giving in to inverse correlation despair.

'Prime Minister, you have to put last night behind you,' Georgia told him curtly. 'We have twelve days to turn this around. The next two days are damage control. After that, we must be ready to seize the initiative in the final stretch.'

The first order of business was the YouTube video of Fitzwilliams shouting at the bus ticket machine. Georgia had arranged a closed film shoot later that morning of Fitzwilliams buying a tACT card at Transport ACT. The media wouldn't be allowed anywhere near. They'd be sensing blood and barking questions. Fitzwilliams would buy his tACT card, hold it up proudly and say to the camera, 'Don't be caught without it.' Georgia had also pre-emptively paid the fine's Confidentiality Premium to prevent the automated tACT fining/shaming system placing the offender's name and photo on their website.

He would publicly apologise for the swearing and apologise to Stanfield personally. It was lame, but the excuse he would use would be the old 'heat of the battle' chestnut. Yes, he is passionate about his government's vision for Australia's future. Unfortunately, that passion last night spilled over into 'colourful' language that had no place in a public debate.

They would do the tACT card first to clear that issue, he decided, before he fronted the fucking jackals of the media about his language.

Georgia took a deep breath. 'The elephant in the room is the Luddite Party. Nothing we've tried has worked against them. We've had to pull our attack ad.'

Their anti-Luddite ad had featured a town out of an old Western movie. A hatted stranger clad in a Driza-Bone rides into town on a horse, past the partly askew town sign which reads ECONOMY. The town is a complete wreck. The narrow-eyed stranger surveys the devastation. No one is in the street. There's an overturned carriage. A tumbleweed blows past. A boy crawls out from underneath a porch and approaches the stranger warily. '*What happened here, son?*' the stranger asks. '*The people here, mister,*' the boy says hesitantly, '*the people here, they voted Luddite.*' Boom! Fifteen-second (hence cheap) ad. They could afford to show it across hundreds of media platforms.

It had seemed perfect until polling of public reaction revealed that 86 per cent of those polled, on a scale of Very Poor to Excellent, ranked it Excellent. It was the same 86 per cent that proclaimed their intention to vote for the government. The public was cheerfully and enthusiastically misleading pollsters about everything. To make matters worse, Labor released an anti-Luddite attack ad the very same day (only theirs featured a gutted hospital and a beleaguered nurse with abandoned, moaning patients strewn down a long corridor). There was a terrible look of collusion about the ads, of the two main parties ganging up on the newcomer. Both

221

parties subsequently, and nearly simultaneously, withdrew their ads, making it look all the more like collusion.

They had been holding in reserve Alan Chandos's 'Play as You Go' lotto for income tax payers. The commercials for it were ready. Georgia particularly liked the young mum completing her tax form and filing it online. Her husband pops his head into the doorway. *'Time for the P&C meeting, dear,'* he says. The mum smiles. *'I work hard and I give a lot to the community,'* she tells the camera. *'It's nice to know that under a Coalition government, each Thursday the government will give a million dollars to a hardworking taxpayer, someone like you or me. They recognise that we're out there doing our jobs, paying our way and making Australia the wonderful place it is. It's nice to know you're appreciated.'*

'We don't release this until Thursday,' Georgia proposed. 'Earlier and it would look as if we rushed the announcement to distract from your bus fare evasion and other problems, Prime Minister. Thursday, you and Alan Chandos make the announcement together. The PM and his able Treasurer. We saturate the media with the ads next weekend.' That matter settled, Georgia moved on to the next pressing issue. 'We've been badly damaged in this campaign. Under these conditions, we should fall back on our core voters and also align with the issues of potential allies. My top recommendation there, Prime Minister, is the Free Drivers Movement.'

Fitzwilliams couldn't help making a sour face. The Free Drivers were opposed to self-driving cars. Supporting them overtly would leave one open to accusations of wanting to bring carnage back to the roads. 'They are not a partner I would choose,' he said with a sigh.

2028

'Prime Minister, we're past the point where we can choose our allies,' Georgia informed him bluntly.

'There's another hazard awaiting, Prime Minister,' Olga warned. 'The Luddite astronaut aboard the International Space Station. The Fortuna Friday event on the space station is fast approaching. That event will command the whole nation's attention. Fortuna Corporation is advertising it as a monumental step forward. You must be seen to be associated with it in some capacity. The Luddite on board, however, makes that problematic.'

'Get yourself to Parkes or some other astronomical centre,' Langdon recommended. 'Surround yourself with scientists to witness whatever it is Fortuna is going to do. The Ned Ludd on board the space station is just a reality TV show contestant, after all. She's not Galileo. Surround yourself with white coats. Make yourself look serious, distinguished.'

Fitzwilliams resented the implication that he did not normally look distinguished, but Langdon's suggestion was sound given the unpredictable element of a Ned Ludd in space. 'Find me a suitable astrological observatory,' he instructed.

There was an awkward silence. 'That's astronomical, Prime Minister,' Langdon pointed out with barely masked concern.

Fitzwilliams gave a silent moan. He was tired. He half wished for an international crisis to deal with, something that could excuse him from the campaign trail for a few days. Instead he had to head off to the tACT office. 'Don't be caught without it,' he murmured, rehearsing his line.

• • •

'Come on, ask a question,' the station manager at 2RT implored, listening to the live feed. It was one of those callers who goes on about how much the *Jim Jarvis Show* means to her, how much she appreciates Jim Jarvis sticking up for the little guy, blah, blah, blah. Jarvis ate that sort of stuff up, but it made for boring radio. Jarvis needed to nudge her along, but he was letting her drone on. Even in death, the man's ego was out of control.

When popular shock jock Jim Jarvis had died of apoplexy in the studio in 2023, many thought Radio 2RT would shrivel without him. He was a man beloved by his listeners and despised by almost everyone else. What even his detractors would admit, however, was that he was irreplaceable. No one was going to fill those shoes.

In the end, no one had had to. Shortly after Jarvis's death, this kid had waited in the station's reception area for so long that eventually the manager had agreed to meet with him. He still remembered the conversation.

'I can give you an algorithm,' the kid had told him, as if the station manager was supposed to understand nerd mumbo-jumbo. 'I can give you an algorithm of Mr Jarvis,' the nerd reiterated.

'What is it you want, kid?' the station manager had asked. 'I'm a busy man.'

The kid made the most outlandish proposal the station manager had ever heard. Jim Jarvis had been on air for more than three decades. From the audio archive of his shows, the kid claimed he could extract approximately twenty thousand words to serve as the vocabulary database and would similarly compile an intonation registry to cover the emotional range of Jim Jarvis's vocal reactions. More amazingly, the kid promised he could provide an analysis of Jarvis's political positions over the last three decades to determine how this Virtual Jarvis (as the kid called him) would react to events taking place after his death. The kid was proposing, it had finally dawned on the station manager, that they could use this algorithm to continue running the *Jim Jarvis Show*. A posthumous radio show host! Death might not Jim Jarvis and 2RT part!

The idea was preposterous. A sarcastic response had been forming on the station manager's lips, but something held him back. The kid was dead serious—and he was Asian. Asian nerds were, the station manager knew, like the superheroes of nerd-dom. The station manager didn't really believe it was feasible, but he heard himself asking what it would entail.

Even the financial arrangements had been a sweetheart deal. The kid didn't expect any payment until he proved his product would work. He spent a week in the electronic archives and about a month somewhere else doing whatever nerds do. Then the kid returned with his laptop and, for all intents and purposes, loaded Jim Jarvis onto the 2RT server.

When they tested it, it was uncanny. There was Jim Jarvis, angry about some current event that hadn't happened in his lifetime; Jim Jarvis predicting his beloved Canterbury Bulldogs would go all the way, despite the recent injury to Troy McNaughton; Virtual Jim Jarvis, deep within the air-conditioned server at 2RT, moaning about the weather outside. It was like having Jim Jarvis alive and back behind the microphone. To be honest (something that didn't come naturally to the station manager), it was better than having the real Jim Jarvis behind the microphone. The real Jim Jarvis had been a fucking temperamental pain in the arse.

How would the audience react? Phoning in to a dead person had an inherent ick factor, particularly for 2RT's older listenership.

The first order of business was to get control of the body. Jarvis's ex-wives, squabbling over his fortune, were happy enough to spare themselves the cost of burial. The station manager arranged for an elegant rococo marble block to be hauled into the foyer of 2RT and, after an uplifting ceremony, plonked onto it a magnificent sarcophagus containing the late Jim Jarvis. He waited for the other media outlets to finish carrying on about Tasteless Fetishism and Ugly Indecency to get a free punt of publicity and then announced the bombshell that Jim Jarvis would be returning from beyond the grave to serve as host once again of the morning 2RT *Jim Jarvis Show*.

'*Good morning, Sydney. This is Jim Jarvis coming to you dead from the 2RT studio in North Sydney*' first aired in March of 2023. He'd been off the air for a mere six weeks. Initially, nobody wanted to be interviewed by a dead man. But then 2RT's morning ratings stayed up and the pollies came cap in hand, begging to be on the show.

The station manager paid the kid a one-off $25,000 and in return got perpetual rights to Virtual Jim Jarvis. Perpetual! While alive, the money-grubbing Jarvis and his agent had screwed the station for every cent they could. Now 2RT had him forever and on no salary! Jarvis's agent had come creeping around demanding a percentage of Virtual Jim Jarvis's income. 'Well, you can have twenty per cent,' the station manager had told the bastard. 'Hell, you can have forty per cent—because I don't fucking pay Virtual Jarvis anything!'

He had only seen the kid once or twice after that. Having paid him peanuts for his intellectual property rights, the station manager felt he could offer some friendly business advice. 'You do good work, kid, but you got to price yourself according to what you're worth. When it comes to selling yourself, you're too low-key.'

'Too low-key,' the kid had murmured, flicking him an enigmatic smile. 'Low-key. I rather like that.'

No wonder they ended up nerds, the station manager had thought. Conversation with them was enough to give anyone the heebie-jeebies.

That had been more than five years ago. Jim Jarvis rolled along with higher ratings than ever and better-paying advertisers.

'Jim, I don't know, Jim, what to think about the Luddites.' The caller had finally got to a topic. Virtual Jim Jarvis had struggled with the Luddites. He was antagonistic, but a bit haphazard. The station manager supposed it was the scattergun strategy of the Luddites, where they sprayed ideas around and discussed just about anything. It was hard to box them in, nail them down.

Not a single Luddite had asked to appear on the *Jim Jarvis Show*. That alone, in the station manager's thinking, meant there was something suspect, something elitist about them. Why wouldn't they talk to the people, the 2RT listeners? The station manager half wanted to call up himself and put that to Virtual Jim. Instead, he decided to invite Luddites on to the show. It would be great radio. The Luddites were all media newcomers. Jarvis would devour them. And if they refused to come on, then Jarvis could chew up the elitist bastards for refusing to face the scrutiny of 2RT and its listeners. Either way worked.

'You know, Jim, you do a terrific job.' Oh, God. The caller was back on to the praise. The station manager realised he'd missed a golden opportunity with that programmer whiz kid five years ago. He'd only got the job half done. He was fed up with listening to the old bats, the dazed, the single-issue obsessives, the stooges— the whole phone-in populace, really. He should have had the kid automate the phone-in callers as well. He'd sack all the staff and just have the computer phone itself from 6 to 9 each weekday morning. It would be paradise.

• • •

Only a week and a half to the election, Olivia Alcott consoled herself. After that, she'd deal with the fraud the Behavioural Insights Unit at Baxter Lockwood had perpetrated on the government. No, she wouldn't, she admitted to herself. The government must never know that on several occasions the BIU advised them to pursue certain actions based on not a shred of public opinion research, but because the unit thought it would be a worthwhile thing for the Fitzwilliams government to do. In two instances, the BIU had taken money from Compink Australia to alter government policy. Compink Australia! Did these naive nerds of hers think they could play this game with the likes of Wilson Huang and win?

Olivia had ordered an absolute ban on such 'special jobs', their term for deceiving the government into doing some public good. 'No one is to speak to Compink Australia,' she had nearly shrieked at them. 'If they contact here in any way—whether by email or phone call or smoke signals, I don't care—you put them through to me.' She didn't normally shriek at people.

She permitted Nostradamus to continue to do commercial work, but it was to keep its IT nose out of political analysis. Her risk management plan was for the BIU to crawl into the bunker and wait for the election to be over.

The team shared none of her anxiety and were as gallingly busy as ever. Little of it had anything to do with work. There was a new large order for the hydroponic kits and everyone but Jiang was busy helping Erica pack them for shipping. Jiang had been at his computer solidly all day. This unusual diligence—not a single game of table tennis—was beginning to unsettle Olivia.

With a heave of her shoulders, she crossed the office to his desk. 'What are you working on?' she asked.

He leaned back in his chair, but she could tell he wasn't relaxed. 'A computer program,' he replied. 'I've been working on it with another programmer for a few weeks. Nothing to do with work,' he added quickly. 'I've been doing it on my own time.'

The BIU had a peculiar idea of what constituted 'their own time' but Olivia let that slide for the moment. 'You look worried.'

Jiang sighed. 'It's not the sort of program I'm used to and we've been asked to alter it.' He cracked his knuckles. 'The final version has to go off today and I'm—' he paused '—not certain it'll work as planned.'

'Can't it be tested?'

'Oh, it's going to be tested.' Jiang gave a half-laugh. 'It's going to be tested big time.'

He might as well have rung an alarm bell for her. 'I think you'd better tell me exactly what this program is for,' she enunciated slowly.

'You may not want to hear it,' Jiang cautioned. She caught him shooting a glance at the sofa.

'I'm not going to faint this time!' she shouted at him.

Heads turned. All work stopped on the hydroponic kits. Mrs Giardino quietly moved towards the first-aid kit.

'Bear in mind, I'm doing this in my capacity as a private citizen,' Jiang pointed out, 'not as an employee of Baxter Lockwood.'

'Just tell me,' Olivia instructed. 'I don't need a preamble.'

'This job I'm doing is for the Luddites,' Jiang murmured. The now familiar blood-draining-from-her-face look came over Olivia yet again, but he pressed on. 'I do volunteer work for them. I've never changed my name to Ned Ludd, but I'm a member of the Luddite Party.'

Olivia took this in calmly, a picture of control. The important thing was to establish the immediate priority. 'Let's go sit on the sofa,' she suggested.

• • •

Olga O'Rourke appearing at his hotel door in Townsville unexpectedly had to be bad news. She was supposed to be in South Australia campaigning in marginal seats. 'Sorry to intrude, Prime Minister,' she said, interrupting a mini planning session for the next day's activities. 'A matter of some urgency. Not something I wished to discuss on the phone.' She waited for him to nod his staffers from the room.

'I regret to inform you, Prime Minister,' Olga said very formally when the others had left the room, 'that our Play as You Go tax reform policy has already been announced—and not by us.'

For once there was no YouTube clip to project. This bombshell came in the form of a radio podcast. *There are no losers in this tax reform. There are only winners!* Fitzwilliams heard the radio voice say. *In Play as You Go, for every one hundred dollars paid in income tax, a taxpayer will receive one Tax Lotto ticket. Each week, the tax office will draw one ticket to win a million dollars. The more you pay in income tax one year, the better your chances are of winning the next.*

It was word for word from Alan Chandos's proposal. 'Who the hell is this?' the Prime Minister demanded.

'Her name is Ned Ludd,' Olga almost groaned. 'Candidate in Geelong.'

'When was this broadcast?'

'Last Sunday.'

'Why wasn't I informed?'

'Because,' Olga replied calmly, 'I only just discovered it. It was broadcast on Radio National on some show called *Money Matters* that nobody in Australia listens to. It's probably on at four am.' Her eyes narrowed. 'This was an ambush, Prime Minister. They wanted Play as You Go on the record as a Luddite idea, but put it on some obscure radio show for insomniacs. Their hope was that you and Alan Chandos would announce it later this week. Then this *Money Matters* podcast would have bubbled to the surface and you'd have faced the humiliation of having been caught pilfering Luddite ideas.'

'Pilfering!'

'We have avoided that ambush, Prime Minister—though at the heavy cost of the loss of Alan's income tax reform. We cannot announce Play as You Go now. The Luddites have raided our—' she paused to find the right English word '—larder and they've stolen our best campaign announcement.'

'For them to have—'

'Yes, Prime Minister,' she cut him off. 'Someone from inside our campaign team leaked Play as You Go to the Luddites. There were not many who knew of its existence—some in the Treasurer's department, some staffers, some in cabinet, Quentin and Leon. One of us is working for the other side.' He had never heard Olga sound so cold and determined. 'Fiona Brennan at ASIO warned us at the start of this campaign that we had a mole within our ranks. Do you remember?'

Fitzwilliams did remember. The Luddites had known exactly when the election was going to be called. Brennan had warned him! What had he thought about it at the time? He couldn't recall. He likely put the blame on the indiscreet mouth of his then campaign manager, Lister St John. A mole! No wonder the Luddites were ahead of him no matter which way he turned in this election.

'At the risk of locking the barn door after the horse has . . . bolted—' the way Olga hesitated over such colloquial phrases gave Fitzwilliams the impression that she had once memorised an entire list of them '—I will search in every cranny until the mole is found.'

Fitzwilliams smiled, despite the grimness of their situation. 'You mean "every nook and cranny".'

Olga frowned at him, clearly puzzled.

'The phrase in English is "every nook and cranny",' he explained.

'I have already checked the nooks,' she replied. 'No, trust me, Prime Minister, this one will be found in a cranny.'

From the fierce look in her eyes, Fitzwilliams didn't doubt her.

CHAPTER ELEVEN

How was it that during a campaign a mall was considered an ideal place to meet and greet people? Fitzwilliams was in this dismal mall to launch the Eradicate Feral Animals Day event and trying not to appear glum. The insipid music, the visual noise, the same shops. He could be in Cairns or Hobart or Fremantle. There was a sense of nowhere-ness about malls that depressed him.

The relentless growth of the mall's role in society could potentially consume both church and state, Fitzwilliams sometimes thought. His own government had installed Dr Otto kiosks in malls, blurring the boundary between government services and the retail sector. The well-known retailer Bull's Eye now routinely had a dedicated wedding venue space on its shop floor where bridal couples could be married surrounded by the gifts from their wedding registry. The church, to his surprise, had not denounced but collaborated, having long wanted a toehold in the malls. You couldn't stroll through a mall nowadays without bumping into someone in a clerical collar.

Ultramart had been even more ambitious. There were now six Ultra-hosps in Australia, public/private maternity hospitals combining the best in natal and postnatal care with the widest retail range of infant clothes, toys and baby accessories. The lifetime 10 per cent off the recommended retail price for all Ultra-babes (children born in Ultra-hosps) was an attractive incentive 'to birth and shop at Ultra-hosp'.

Even cemeteries were to be attached to malls, seamlessly integrating burials and visiting departed family into the shopping experience. A British chain with the jaunty name of Till You Dropped was rumoured to be opening five of these 'malloseums' over the next year. It was considered the ultimate form of capturing customer loyalty. Who could shop at Market Town when Dad was buried at Broadway? The idea made Fitzwilliams shudder.

Why the Eradicate Feral Animals Day event should be held in a mall was beyond him. Those taking the fight to the cane toads, feral cats and foxes, those mixing the myxomatosis, weren't doing it in the Stockland shopping centre in Townsville. Yet here he was with some professor, several PR types, and numerous cameras and microphones. The crowd at such things, once they'd taken their selfie with Prime Minister in the background, typically had the attention span of goldfish. He could announce he was invading Poland and they'd probably all smile and clap.

'What's involved in this one?' he asked a staffer, trying not to sound weary.

'This one's a bit of fun,' she told him. She had some sort of helmet in her hand with what looked like a plunger attached to it. 'How well do you do a Dalek voice?' she asked.

• • •

'You can't go on the *Jim Jarvis Show*.' Renard tried to stare Kate down. She wasn't an easy stare-down. 'You're seventeen years old. He'll eat you alive.'

'What's my age got to do with it?' Kate answered, giving a theatrical teenage sigh. 'You're just like the Prime Minister!'

Jim Jarvis was the worst of the radio shock jocks. Renard had been less nervous about Kate facing off against the Prime Minister. 'He won't let you get a word in edgeways. You know why it's called the *Jim Jarvis Show*? Because it is about him—not his guests.'

'I can handle Jim Jarvis,' Kate declared. 'He's been dead for five years!'

'Don't let that detail mislead you,' Renard warned. Kate was the one invited on to the show, not Renard. He knew he didn't have the final say in the matter. 'It's a school day tomorrow,' he tried. 'You'll miss some of your morning classes.'

'For Christ's sake, Ned.'

'I know, I'm worse than your parents.' Renard heaved a sigh. 'It can get really nasty on that show.'

'As Luddites, we talk to everyone,' Kate lectured him. Ned's concern was somewhat sweet, she supposed, but in that exasperating, parental way that needed to be quashed. She hadn't been surprised by the invitation; she might not be a candidate, but since the debate Kate had become one of the emerging stars of Luddism.

The 2RT listenership was not a priority. Most of them were so old that Kate presumed half of them would die on their way to the polling station. Something else had motivated her to appear on the *Jim Jarvis Show*. 'What does "paraphernalia" mean?' she asked. 'I think I know, but I need to make sure.'

Renard waved a hand. 'Equipment . . . apparatus . . . stuff. Like "chemistry lab paraphernalia". Why? What's this about?'

Kate smiled. 'Because I found this in my bag when I got home from school yesterday. No idea how it got there.' She pulled the letter from her pocket and handed it to him. 'It's from head office.'

The letter instructed Kate to agree to appear on the *Jim Jarvis Show*, to speak about her national wage proposal and . . . Kate watched Ned's eyebrows arch as he read.

'Why would they want you to say that?'

The letter instructed:

. . . in your opening remarks use the two words 'Transylvania paraphernalia' in that order with no words in between. Enunciate them clearly.—Ned Ludd

'It's just chemistry,' Kate said.

'What is?'

'The class I'll miss tomorrow morning.'

. . .

The doorbell rang. Aggie grabbed her helmet. With the leaders' debate done and dusted, it had been great to get back on to the cycling campaign trail in Melbourne. Her collaborator on the programming task had rechecked their final version and sent it off. Now her campaign in Wills called to her on a glorious day for cycling.

Aggie swung open the door and her face fell. 'What's wrong?'

The Veronicae were on her doorstep, helmetless, in business attire, one wearing a skirt.

'We have a new strategy for the final week,' one of them replied. They came into her living room and sat down.

'Aren't we biking today?' Aggie asked, still by the door. It was too perfect a day to waste inside discussing strategy.

'We both think the campaign needs a broader approach,' one of them began.

Aggie didn't understand. 'We've been campaigning all over greater Melbourne. We can't feasibly go much further afield than that.' A swing to Geelong might be manageable, she thought, about eighty kilometres each way.

'Ned,' a Veronica said gently, 'your campaign is too focused on bicycle issues.'

'You need to talk about other issues—like you did at the debate,' the other added.

They were both giving her their encouraging look, the same look they'd used at the start of the campaign when she'd been struggling up a hill.

'It's just,' a Veronica continued, 'if you're going to be prime minister, we can't only be about bike lanes.'

'I'm sorry?'

'Don't be sorry,' the other broke in hastily. 'Some of that was probably our fault.'

Aggie let the enormity of that comment go by to the keeper. 'No,' she clarified, 'I meant *I'm sorry* as in *I'm sorry, did you just say prime minister?*'

'Well, yes, obviously,' a Veronica answered. 'You're the leader of the Luddites.'

Aggie looked at them dumbfounded. 'But the Luddite Party doesn't emphasise a leader.'

The two Veronicas exchanged a glance. 'And you're the Luddite leader who has been emphasising that to the Australian people,' one replied. They'd known what she was going to say, Aggie realised.

The Veronicae were now aiming for an outright Luddite victory nationally. The best way to achieve that, they insisted, was to take advantage of the national profile Aggie had created.

'I contacted Dragonbreath yesterday,' one said with a grin, 'and they've sold twenty thousand of those posters. They're up everywhere.'

It was a poster of Aggie speaking outside parliament on the day she'd called the election. Incredibly, considering she had been nude at the time, the poster was a tasteful shot of her head and shoulders with just a hint of cleavage. *Vote Luddite!* it urged, the V being two celery sticks. The poster's distribution had nothing to do with the Luddite Party; two freelance photo journalists had sold the image to Dragonbreath Posters, which was now selling them across the country.

The Veronicae outlined their revised campaign strategy. Aggie was to appear in key electorates alongside local Luddite candidates. The campaigning would be similar to what they had done so far: meet with people, listen to what they said, raise a few ideas. The difference was no bicycles. Aggie must be seen to be more than a single-issue candidate.

They handed her an itinerary from an automated travel agency. It had her crisscrossing the country. Adelaide, Brisbane, Launceston, Cairns, Perth, Brisbane again, returning to Melbourne on the eve of the election. It made no geographic sense.

The Veronicae read the look in her eyes. 'We know you're financing your campaign entirely yourself.' Aggie had given them control of her $3000 campaign budget. Their only expenses so far had been the hotel along the Canberra trek and getting Aggie's bicycle tuned up. 'Sorry about the two red-eye-special flights.'

They were going to make her prime minister on the cheap, it seemed. 'We don't know which electorates are winnable,' they explained, 'so we just went with whatever seat sales Jetstar and Virgin had on offer and some new airline called Howzat!' The airline actually had an exclamation mark in its company name, Aggie noted.

Aggie was to be greeted by Bicyclism Australia members in each city she was scheduled to visit. They weren't to saddle up though. She was to meet with P&C committees, public sector workers, local business precincts, whatever they could rustle up. She would go it alone without them. The Veronicae were to stay campaigning in Wills to ensure she won her seat for parliament.

'Why are you looking so glum?' Veronica asked.

It felt odd to say it to them. 'I was enjoying the cycling,' Aggie replied meekly.

'We'll organise one last big bike rally for you when you get back to Melbourne,' a Veronica promised indulgently. 'On the Yarra on the eve of the election. How's that?'

For a moment, Aggie thought she was talking about the new airline. 'All right,' she agreed. A big rally on the Yarra would be a fun finale. The airline itinerary had her leaving Melbourne this afternoon. 'I'll pack my things,' she said.

'We didn't pay for any checked luggage,' Veronica pointed out. 'You can manage a few changes of clothes on seven kilos of carry-on, can't you?'

• • •

The electorate of Herbert, centred on Townsville, was held by Garry Templeton, a solid backbencher, reliable, uncomplaining. Prime Minister Fitzwilliams had been happy to help his campaign. The Free Drivers Movement speaker had gone on too long, but Templeton had done a splendid introduction for the Prime Minister.

Although nothing bad had happened yet as a result of the Eradicate Feral Animals Day event, Georgia Lambert still felt sick about it. Next election, she would vet these worthy-cause days extra assiduously. Fitzwilliams had forced himself to be a good sport, donned the Dalek helmet thing with the prong and done a surprisingly decent 'Exterminate! Exterminate!' She would kill whoever at Eradicate Feral Animals Day had come up with that idea. No doubt the Labor Party's advertising firm was already cutting it into a new commercial.

What will the next three years have in store for us if the Fitzwilliams Liberals are re-elected? the voiceover would say.

Medicare?

[Cut to Prime Minister] 'Exterminate!'

Education?

'Exterminate!'

The fair go? The Aussie dream?

'Exterminate! Exterminate!'

She could write it for them—or, rather, the bloody idiots at Eradicate Feral Animals Day had written it for them.

She'd never seen such a campaign for mishaps, yet the Prime Minister was soldiering on without complaint. He was on the outdoor stage now delivering a speech to support the local member. Fitzwilliams thrived on this—

'Oh shit!' came the voice of a staffer.

240

Georgia turned. It never paid to ignore that exclamation. 'What is it?'

The staffer was staring at her Genie phone and had both earphones in. 'Oh shit!' she exclaimed again.

Georgia Lambert yanked an earphone out. 'What's the matter?'

'The PM's office just sent this, Ms Lambert,' the staffer stammered. 'They've discovered an extended play version of "We Are Aussie, It's What We Are About". There's a verse we didn't know about!'

Georgia stuffed the earphone into her own ear. It would be quicker to hear what the staffer was talking about than have her explain. 'Play it again,' she instructed.

On the screen came an amateur video of the Jaggernauts in concert, in front of a big Invasion Day banner. The staffer skipped over the first verses. The Jaggernauts were heading into the familiar chorus, but now they sang:

> We are Aussie, it's what we are about.
> We are Aussie, of the terra nullius
> You had no say, took your land away
> Then we tried a genocide
> We are Aussie, it's what we are about.

'The Jaggernauts never told us about this!' the staffer wailed.

'No, they wouldn't, would they,' Georgia muttered. The Jaggernauts had likely improvised this extra verse when they were offered an Invasion Day gig. The lyrics of starving musicians were often flexible in such ways.

The regular version of 'We Are Aussie' was to kick in as soon as Fitzwilliams finished speaking, the backing music as the

Prime Minister mingled with the audience for some up-front-and-personal time. If some stroppy punter from the crowd should unexpectedly have a go at the PM, they could simply crank up the music to drown him out.

They could no longer use 'We Are Aussie'. If this protest version ever got out . . . Georgia did not want to think about the consequences. She took the staffer by the shoulder. 'Go to the sound tech backstage. Tell him to put on something else when the PM finishes.'

. . .

The staffer arrived backstage breathless. The sound tech was an old, overweight guy with tattoos on both arms. The left arm had PUNK written on it; the right had the outline of a heart in red with SID AND NANCY inscribed inside. What thin hair the man still had, he kept spiked up in five prongs atop his head, the remnants of a mostly obliterated army still forlornly trying to stand at attention.

'Sid,' the staffer began, 'we need—'

'My name's not Sid,' the techie interrupted.

'Sorry,' the staffer said. She indicated the tattoo on his arm. 'I thought . . .'

The techie made a rumbling noise. 'It's for Sid Vicious. What do you want? Fitzwilliams is nearly finished.' He was no longer looking at her but watching the PM.

'Excuse me?' she said forcefully to regain his attention. Why did they hire these old fossils? she wondered. This was what came of lifting the retirement age to seventy-two. 'Georgia Lambert wants you to cut the song. When the Prime Minster finishes, don't play the song she gave you earlier. Put on something else.'

'Georgia?' he muttered. 'That the thin one with the glasses?'

'Yes, the thin one with the glasses.' She wasn't sure he'd got the message. 'Don't put on the song she gave you,' she said loudly and slowly.

'Give me what you want, I'll play it.' He held out his hand. There was an anarchist A on the palm.

'I don't have any music!' she exclaimed. 'You're the sound technician. Put something on!'

'Yeah, yeah, calm down.' The technician wasn't going to let this little stress ball wind him up. Where did they get these kids? So young and so uptight. They weren't like anything he recognised from his day. He rummaged in a bag and slotted a stick into the console. The kid was still hovering over him. 'I got it in hand,' he told her. 'Now piss off!'

· · ·

When Fitzwilliams had finished, Garry Templeton got the standing ovation going and the audience was quick to follow his lead. A good crowd, a perfect afternoon. The PM nodded to Templeton to begin the walk-through; Templeton could be trusted to steer him towards the most reliable people to meet. Quentin and Leon fell into step with them.

The first chords of a song rang out—power chords followed by a tiny plink of guitar strings. Fitzwilliams' brow twitched. It was not 'We Are Aussie'.

'Prime Minister!' Quentin nearly gasped. 'That's a bad song to play!'

'Oh God!' Fitzwilliams inhaled, finally recognising the tune. It was The Clash's 'Should I Stay or Should I Go'. That was certainly not a question Fitzwilliams wanted put to the voters at this point of the election.

The Prime Minister reached for a hand to shake and smiled. Hold the smile, he thought. Act as though you are not hearing it.

The Clash put the same question out there again. He tried to exchange a few words with some woman from the business precinct only for her to interrupt and say, 'You shouldn't have that song playing, Prime Minister.'

How many blasted times were The Clash going to repeat the one line? And some of the rest of the lyrics were even worse.

He plunged further into the crowd as if the throng of bodies would block out the music. Did no one realise the mistake up on stage? Australia Post drones were whirling about recording everything. There was nothing for it but to hold his ground and smile.

• • •

The staffer had come hurtling back to the sound technician. 'Are you out of your mind?' she shrieked. 'Turn that song off.'

He looked at her as if he couldn't process what she'd just said. 'That's The Clash,' he said. '*The Clash*,' he repeated emphatically. 'Show some respect, missy.'

The staffer looked at him incredulously and then lunged at the USB stick to pull it from the console. The technician smacked her hand away. 'No one interrupts The Clash at my gigs,' he rumbled.

There was only a moment's hesitation. The staffer thrust the palm of one hand over the techie's face and pushed his head back, groping blindly with her other hand for the USB stick to yank it out.

The heel of her palm hooked the techie under his nose. He growled angrily and twisted his head to the side. Her hand shot upwards and, with his punk instincts afire, he came straight back to nut her one. However, her head wasn't there. Instead, he smashed the bridge of his nose straight into her pointed elbow. His head went woozy with pain and nostalgia. Like being in back in London in '77, he thought, sagging almost contentedly to the floor. Perhaps the younger generation were okay after all.

• • •

The music stopped abruptly. There was a commotion back on the stage. Fitzwilliams heard somebody shouting something about 'blood'. Drones were now buzzing around the hubbub on the stage.

A tiny hand tugged at his sleeve. A small boy was smiling up at him. Fitzwilliams still didn't know what was happening on the stage, but there were undoubtedly cameras still on him. 'Are you going to vote for Ned?' the little fellow asked.

'He's talking about the space station,' his mother jumped in hastily. She cupped a hand around her mouth and spoke softly. 'He wants everyone to vote for her, the Ned Ludd in space— to keep the Aussie astronaut on the space station. We are Liberals,' she added as an afterthought. She looked at her son. 'They're not voting anyone off the space station this weekend, Jason. It's the big Fortuna Friday event. All the astronauts will get to stay on board the station for that.'

Fitzwilliams crouched down by the boy. 'I hope your Ned gets to stay in space.' 'Should I Stay or Should I Go' was still reverberating in his head. The satire shows would have a field day. 'It would be nice to be in space,' he told the boy wistfully. It would be nice to be looking at the planet from afar without feeling you had to be part of it.

CHAPTER TWELVE

The guests on Jim Jarvis's morning radio program still sat facing where the show's formidable host would once have been. Now they saw his empty seat, behind which a portrait of Jim Jarvis hung on the wall, draped in black. It kept guests edgy, the station manager believed. Best not lie to the dead.

The Luddite had the earphones on and that oddly bored look of trepidation guests got as they listened to the show's live feed, its weather and traffic reports, the distractingly mundane build-up to their segment. The station manager had snared the Luddite school kid from the leaders' debate, the one who'd kept her cool when the Prime Minister had lost his and Stanfield had ended up in tears. The rest of the media was treating the kid like a star. The late Jim Jarvis would show her no such deference.

Virtual Jim Jarvis was on fire this morning, having mauled a state cabinet minister and some soppy environmentalist. The Luddite spot was the closing piece for the show. Eight days out from the election and nobody had yet skewered the Luddites. This would be the break-through. Jarvis would nail them and the *Jim Jarvis Show* would be the talking point of the day across all media.

'Many of our listeners have asked that the *Jim Jarvis Show* delve into this so-called Luddite party,' the voice of Jim Jarvis began. 'They've burst onto the political scene and although they talk a lot, not much of it is about themselves. Who are they? Who founded them? Where do they get their money? What's their agenda for our country, a country they wish to govern under an assumed name? Those are just some of the questions hanging over the Luddites. Well, listeners, now is your chance. We have Ned Ludd with us, the young debater we saw the other night who locked horns with our prime minister. Thank you for coming on the *Jim Jarvis Show*.'

That last sentence was Jim's usual signal that civilities were over. The station manager leaned forward.

The young Ned Ludd swallowed and said, 'I apologise, Mr Jarvis, for coming into your studio dressed so eccentrically in all this ... Transylvania paraphernalia, but I'm performing in a school play immediately after I finish this interview.'

The station manager and the producer exchanged looks. What the hell was she on about? The kid was in a regular school uniform. 'Is she stoned?' the producer whispered. The station manager brightened at the thought. Teen Luddite debater stoned at 8.30 am on a school day ... Pow! Chalk up another kill for the *Jim Jarvis Show*.

The kid's bizarre opening gave even the computer program a moment's pause. 'Perhaps we could start,' it said at last, 'with what you consider to be the major issues facing this nation.'

The station manager blinked. Normally, Virtual Jim told his guest what the important issues were.

The kid started describing her wingding national wage idea. Jim Jarvis was unusually content to let her do the talking, asking only probing questions for clarification.

'Something's wrong with Jarvis,' the producer discerned. 'It's like he's—' he searched for the term '—*interviewing* her!' His eyes looked uncomprehending. 'He's letting her have her say!'

The producer was right. Not only that, but Jarvis's voice was softer. It had lost its anger-of-the-people stridency. The station manager couldn't think what was causing it—unless . . . 'Is it possible that the real Jim Jarvis would have supported the Luddites?' he wondered. The question was ridiculous. Jarvis would have loathed the Luddites.

'Let's open the lines for callers now,' Virtual Jim proposed.

The first caller was promising. He denounced the national wage scheme as communism—even worse, it was communism for bludgers. Jim Jarvis jumped in before the young Ned could answer. 'I think you're confused there, caller. In the old communist system, the state owned the means of production. The national wage doesn't propose anything like that. When you use terms like *communist*, caller, you need to use them accurately.'

'What the hell's going on?' the producer asked. Jim Jarvis concerned about throwing labels around? This was the man (or computer program) who'd called the state premier a degenerate corrupt sociopath. (It had been right on only one out of the three). 'It's like the computer has suddenly become PC!'

There was a joke in that line, but the station manager didn't have time for it.

The caller, too, was perplexed. 'But, Jim, this national wage gives money to teenagers for doing nothing.'

'To be fair, caller, it also gives it to all adults, you and me included.'

'*To be fair, caller,*' the producer repeated in disbelief. Since when did Jim Jarvis care about fairness?

Jarvis continued in this polite vein. Eventually even the tone of the callers became courteous. 'If this continues, they'll be singing "Kumbaya" before the show's over,' the producer despaired.

'It's a computer malfunction,' the station manager diagnosed. 'A total malfunction!'

He whipped off his earphones. 'That damned programmer needs to fix this!' The station manager raced from the booth and up the stairs to his office. He thrust his hand into the jumble of his desk's top drawer. That programmer's card had to be in there somewhere.

'Ha!' he cried at last, finding the right card. He remembered it because it had only the programmer's name and contact details. No logo or anything, not even a business name.

The station manager started an email. *URGNET!!* he typed in uppercase alarm. *Your computer program has mal* . . . He peered at the screen. URGNET? He was too agitated to type. Besides, it would feel better to shout at somebody. He picked up his phone.

. . .

The mobile phone on Jiang's desk was ringing. Jiang was across the room playing table tennis. Since he had told Olivia that he was working for the Luddites, she'd been watching him like a hawk. Like a hawk, perhaps, but she was a hawk that didn't know what it was watching for or what to do next, Olivia admitted.

Olivia wasn't a manager who pried into the personal lives of her employees. She was thus somewhat surprised to find she had picked up Jiang's phone and said, 'Hello?' into it without identifying herself or the firm Baxter Lockwood.

'Who's this?' a voice demanded.

'Who do you wish to speak to?' Olivia asked back.

'I want to speak to that programmer—the kid . . . Jiang Luu,' the voice said. It sounded as if he had read the name.

'Jiang is occupied,' Olivia replied primly. Across the room, there were guffaws coming from the table tennis match.

'I don't care whether he's performing open heart surgery!' the voice declared. 'I need to speak with him right away.'

The man was clearly agitated. Olivia felt strangely pleased to hear Jiang having this effect on someone else for a change. Really, she ought to have some sympathy for the man, but she didn't. 'Is this work-related?' she asked.

'Who are you?' the voice demanded. 'I rang Jiang Luu's phone, I want to speak to Jiang Luu. Tell your boyfriend to get his arse over here.'

Boyfriend? The concept made Olivia almost go pale. Having him as a co-worker was nerve-racking enough. 'Jiang isn't available,' she replied curtly. 'If you care to leave a message, I'll have him get back to you.' Why was she doing this?

'Tell Jiang to get over to 2RT right away. Tell him Jim Jarvis has fried his fucking silicon brain. Jarvis has gone all warm and fuzzy and Jiang has got to get over here and fix it pronto. More than pronto, if there's a word that's faster than that. And tell him to answer his own fucking phone next time!'

The call clicked off. The table tennis match finished. Jiang and Sam were returning to their desks. Olivia held out Jiang's phone to him. 'Why would Radio 2RT ring to tell you to get over there immediately? They are not a client of ours. And why do they think you have anything to do with the *Jim Jarvis Show*?'

Jiang laughed; a proper cackle, Olivia thought. 'Because I wrote the program for the Virtual Jim Jarvis. Years ago. Before I worked here.'

Olivia was appalled. Jim Jarvis had been an odious man. Why would Jiang want him to continue broadcasting after he died? 'Your friend on the phone,' she said, getting back to the point, 'wanted you to know that Jim Jarvis has,' she quoted, '*fried his fucking silicon brain*. He says it's your fault and you have to fix it. Pronto,' she added.

Jiang nodded. 'I was wondering when they were going to play that card.'

'Is that the embed program you told me about?' Sam asked. 'What was it? "Transylvania regalia"?'

'Close.' Jiang gave Olivia a satisfied smile.

'I think you need to explain—everything—now,' Olivia told him. 'Erica,' she said, turning around, 'Jiang and I are going to the couch to have a chat. Can you put the kettle on, please? I may need a strong cup of tea.'

• • •

Five minutes later, a cup of tea in her hand, Olivia couldn't get the grin off her face. Jiang was brilliant. Utterly brilliant. 'So, what are you going to do about that phone call?' she asked him.

2028

Jiang picked up his phone, pressed a few buttons. 'Hello, you've reached the phone of Jiang Luu,' he enunciated. 'If your call is from Radio 2RT, I'm under no contractual obligation to do anything for you whatsoever. Anyone else can leave a message.' He put the phone back in his pocket. Olivia erupted in a deep chortle, clapping her hands together delightedly.

When Jiang first created the Virtual Jim Jarvis he'd embedded a sub-program within it. The sub-program was—Olivia still could not believe such a thing was possible—designed to transform Jim Jarvis into a nice guy: someone who listened to others, who wanted to find out more about what other people thought. 'His ego has been recalibrated,' Jiang told her, turning an imaginary dial in the air, 'from near infinity to a modest practically zero.' The sub-program was always dormant within Virtual Jim Jarvis and could only be activated by an audio command—in this case, the words 'Transylvania paraphernalia', a phrase that was never going to come up in the normal course of the *Jim Jarvis Show*. It would only be used long after everyone had accepted that Virtual Jim was the real deal. It would be used when the Luddites needed it.

Seeing Jiang doing Loki the Trickster on someone else—not just someone else, but on the dead Jim Jarvis and 2RT—was magnificent. He was an artist, a maestro. It didn't matter to Olivia that it was Luddite business and that the firm Baxter Lockwood should have absolutely nothing to do with it. This time she'd been on Jiang's side. This time Olivia had played a role in it. It felt good!

Olivia drained her cup and stood up. She threw off her business jacket and began limbering up her arms. 'Come on,' she urged Sam and Jiang, who were still sitting there. 'Get up.'

'What are you doing?' Sam asked.

'Let's have a game of beach volleyball,' Olivia suggested, kicking off her shoes.

. . .

The song 'Should I Stay or Should I Go' was still stuck in Fitzwilliams' head, the musical ghost of disasters past. It had been a relief to retreat to the calm of an observatory. The media had had a feeding frenzy with the story of his young staffer smashing her elbow into the face of a seventy-three-year-old Townsville sound technician, knocking him flat. That wasn't what had actually happened, but it was one of those stories that stayed in the news all the longer if you tried to explain your way out of it. He had visited the geriatric punker in hospital. Just stitches, fortunately, and possible concussion. With a guy like that, the latter was hard to tell.

Georgia Lambert had offered her resignation after The Clash incident. Fitzwilliams hadn't accepted it. How could he hold her responsible? In this campaign, the gods were clearly against them. Besides, it wasn't a good look to lose two campaign managers during an election.

Visiting the Australian Astronomical Observatory was not a natural campaign stop. Hardly anyone worked at the observatory and those who did had so many PhDs that the Prime Minister was too intimidated to talk politics with them. One week to the polls. He needed to be out there scrambling for votes and here he was holed up in an observatory. Fortuna Friday. Something big was going to happen on board the International Space Station and that damned Australian Luddite astronaut would be right there in the thick of it. Fitzwilliams had moved, as planned, to this dignified stronghold. Flanked by white coats with PhDs, he'd make a gracious speech about whatever stunt in space the Fortuna Corporation staged. He would be prime ministerial, out-gravitas-ing the reality TV antics of the Ned in Space. He would need to improvise. Again.

Fortuna Friday wasn't even Friday in Australia. It was Friday over the eastern seaboard of the United States, the world's most lucrative advertising market. It was 10 am Saturday in the eastern time zone of Australia.

The astronomers had put on a little morning tea for the Prime Minister's visit—*little* being the operative word. Scientists always went to great lengths to demonstrate how much his funding cuts had bitten into their budgets. The morning tea consisted of instant coffee and a meagre plate of carrot and celery sticks. Their Spartan fare didn't fool him. If he flung open a few cupboard doors around the place, he was certain he'd find a cappuccino machine and possibly muffins. They were just putting on this no-fat-on-our-budget show for his benefit. God, he could use a proper coffee, he thought, spooning the instant crystals into his cup. He caught one scientist whisking away the plate of celery sticks. They'd only belatedly realised its Luddite connotations. Their intention was to deprive him, not provoke him. He was, after all, still the man with the funding money.

'What do you think the Fortuna Friday event will be?' he asked an astronomer crunching on a carrot stick.

'They've been working on a project called Fortuna Mirror World,' the astronomer replied. 'And by *they* I mean Scott Devonport and Yuri Denisov, the two proper astronauts, not the reality TV contestants. It's a crystal prismatic mirror structure.'

Fitzwilliams didn't understand her further explanation, but he did know Australia was behind in that research area. Crystal prismatics was going to be, among all the other next big things in alternative energy, the next big thing. Fitzwilliams frowned. Only yesterday, he'd announced funding for the refurbishment of a Queensland coal terminal. 'State-of-the-art,' he recalled saying.

It was reassuring, however, to hear this scientist's disdain for the reality TV astronauts on the space station. 'Fortuna's Mirror World will power enormous lasers to transfer energy to photoreceptors on Earth,' the astronomer continued. It seemed a far cry from Fortuna running shoes, Fitzwilliams thought. 'They say they'll use it to bring power to the third world.'

The astronomers had set up an old plasma television in yet another display of their frugal budget. The head of the Fortuna Corporation appeared on the screen. He began to speak, but his material—'a future of progress', 'secure energy for our children' etc.—was too much like one of the Prime Minister's own speeches for Fitzwilliams to concentrate on it. The speech shifted from visionary to showman. 'An historic event . . . an event hearkening a new age of prosperity for everyone,' the CEO announced. Several sports stars flanked him, nodding like backbenchers at his every word. Finally the CEO called over the microphone, 'Scott? Yuri? Are you ready?'

'All systems go, Mr Smallwood,' came Yuri's voice.

'Then . . .' CEO Smallwood paused. 'Go for it!' he shouted, using the famous Fortuna catchphrase.

The TV image now shifted to the crescent moon over New York. The camera zoomed so that the moon filled the entire screen and a dot of light appeared on its dark section. Slowly the dot grew in size, spreading out, and it began to take the form of a familiar shape.

'Oh no!' the astronomer next to Fitzwilliams exclaimed, aghast.

The growing dot had shaped itself into the Fortuna winged running shoe. The Fortuna Corporation logo was illuminated on the surface of the moon! The first act of the new crystal prismatics Mirror World, it now appeared, was not to provide the third world with a much-needed energy source, but to subject the moon to the indignity of product placement.

Fitzwilliams shook his head. The moon being used to display a corporate logo? What statement he could possibly improvise about such a thing that would sound even vaguely prime min-isterial? He simply couldn't bring himself to be enthusiastic. Fitzwilliams suddenly felt so weary that he was grateful for a sip of his instant coffee.

'They can't be allowed to do that!' another astronomer squeaked indignantly.

At least he was in like-minded company here, Fitzwilliams thought. Perhaps he would increase their funding if re-elected.

'What's happening now?' One of them pointed at the screen. The image of the Fortuna logo was dissipating, transforming into something else. 'What's that supposed to be? It looks . . . like a map of the west coast of Australia.'

It hadn't been possible to see this coming, Fitzwilliams consoled himself. 'That,' he informed them all without bothering to sigh about it, 'is the logo of the Luddite Party of Australia.'

He saw their initial amazement and then something he took for pity sweep over their faces. They quickly looked away from him and back at the screen. '*Here . . . be . . . dragons*,' one of them read aloud.

Fitzwilliams closed his eyes. Australia Post media drones would be waiting outside for a statement.

. . .

Paula Perkins, the Ned Ludd in space, felt hands grab her by each arm and sweep her weightlessly across the space station. Yuri and Scott pushed her straight into the only truly private section of the station, a former experiment area turned into a makeshift rant room for *Get Out of My Space* contestants.

Yuri clicked off all the recording devices in the room. 'Hand over your Genie phone and any other device,' he ordered. He frisked her briskly, not trusting her to comply with the demand.

'We know it was you,' Scott stated. 'That was a goddamned Luddite symbol. Your goddamned political party. That's what Mission Control just told us.'

Paula had known it wouldn't take them long to find out. She said nothing.

'You don't mess with the Fortuna logo,' Yuri hissed at her. 'Are you ab-fucking-solutely crazy?'

'It's not said like that, Yuri,' Scott corrected his cosmonaut colleague. 'We say abso-fucking-lutely crazy.'

'What?' Yuri snapped. 'You mean there's a grammatical rule about sticking the word *fuck* inside another word?'

'Well,' Scott hedged, 'I'm not sure it's a rule . . .'

'Then what the fuck are you talking about?' It occurred to Yuri, not for the first time, that he'd been in space with Scott an awfully long time. He turned back to Paula. 'You've jeopardised the mission with your stupid . . .' He couldn't think of an English word to fit.

'You do know Fortuna Corporation is funding this entire mission? You may have killed the hen that lays the golden egg!' he frothed.

'It's a goose that lays golden eggs,' Scott interjected. 'Not a hen.'

Yuri waved his hand. 'The idea works perfectly well with a hen. Neither animal actually lays golden eggs!' he pointed out.

'It's not a concept,' Scott shot back, 'it's a story—and in the story it's a goose that lays the golden egg.'

'Excuse me,' Paula put in, 'aren't you supposed to be berating me?'

'I am just trying to improve your English,' Scott muttered. Sometimes he didn't know why he bothered with the tetchy Yuri.

'Yeah? Well, how much Russian have you learned while up here?' Yuri demanded.

Scott gave him that bewildered look Americans do when someone suggests speaking another language.

'Can we get on with this?' Paula prodded again.

Scott refocused on Paula. 'How did you do it?'

'I copied the laser projection program for Fortuna Friday and sent it to Luddite colleagues in Australia. They modified it and sent it back and I then copied it over the original. Because I have computer access here, I was within the firewall. There was no security to overcome.'

The explanation had been so succinct and calm, the infuriated astronauts felt cheated. Yuri pointed a finger at her. 'You're off the station. I don't care whether the whole planet votes to keep you on, next eviction, I'm going to read your name out.'

'Yeah,' Scott echoed. 'You're abso—' an *f* started to form, but Scott prudently held it back '—lutely off,' he concluded.

'Now get out of here,' Yuri ordered, 'while we try to come up with some way to placate the Fortuna Corporation.'

Paula opened the door, pulled on its frame and glided weight-lessly out of the room. Yuri yanked the door shut behind her.

'You got your phone?' asked Florian, the German *GOOMS* astronaut. He gestured towards the rant room. The profiles of Yuri and Scott were visible through the window in the rant room door.

Paula held out her phone. Florian touched it lightly with his. 'I filmed it,' Florian said. Paula's phone made its contented file-transfer beeping noise.

'But it won't have any sound,' Paula pointed out.

'Hal 9000.' Florian grinned.

'I don't understand the reference,' Paula said apologetically.

'You've never seen *2001: A Space Odyssey*?' Florian was clearly disappointed in her. 'Put the video clip through a lip-reading program,' he spelled out.

CHAPTER THIRTEEN

Fitzwilliams was in the Liberal Party's Melbourne office for the emergency meeting, with Alan Chandos, Donna Hargreaves and Olga O'Rourke checking in by Skype from different locations across the country. The only people there in person with him were Leon and Quentin, Georgia Lambert and Russ Langdon, who'd driven up from Flinders. Judging by the pixilated image of Chandos, wherever he was in Western Australia, the National Broadband Network had yet to roll through.

'I'll deal it to you straight,' Fitzwilliams said when they'd all come on-screen. 'It's my assessment we've already lost the election.' There was no murmur of dissent. They were seasoned enough veterans to know it. Only Leon and Quentin looked shocked. 'We may end up the largest party in parliament, but we'll have lost so many seats, we'll have no mandate in the eyes of the public,' he summed up bleakly. 'It's a hung parliament and the Luddites are going to be players in it.'

'That could be something we exploit,' Georgia Lambert offered. 'People don't like hung parliaments. Campaign the final five days on that. Business, stock markets jittery at the thought of Luddites. Superannuation savings at risk. Economic uncertainty.'

'Fear,' Fitzwilliams commented. 'Is that all we have to offer?' He shook his head. 'If you run a fear campaign out of desperation, as we would be doing now, the electorate can sense it. You're trying to sell fear, but they know you're scared yourself. It doesn't work.'

'You're right, Prime Minister,' Georgia admitted. 'I just thought all options should be on the table.'

Fitzwilliams turned to his cabinet colleagues on the screens. 'We're up against a party that hasn't paid for any advertising and yet they put their logo on the surface of the moon.'

'And hoodwinked the Fortuna Corporation,' Alan Chandos put in. 'Did you see the video of the astronauts conspiring to throw Ned Ludd off the station?' He chuckled.

'No, Alan, I didn't.' Was there anything Chandos didn't find amusing? 'They have danced around us the whole election,' Fitzwilliams resumed with a fresh analogy, 'landing blow after blow, and about all we can say for ourselves is that we're still standing. We haven't laid a glove on them. On top of that, they have someone inside our organisation feeding them information.' He looked at Olga, who shook her head slightly. Even she had been unable to uncover the mole within their ranks. 'We've been outplayed from start to finish. As for the election on Saturday, all we can rely on are the rusted-on voters for both parties. That's about thirty per cent for us, twenty per cent for Labor. Thanks to the Luddites, I'd say about fifty per cent of the electorate can be considered swing voters. No incumbent MP is safe. Even someone sitting on a twenty-five per cent margin in their electorate could go down.'

'What do you want us to do, Prime Minister?' Hargreaves asked.

'If we've lost, let's not throw any more money away. I don't intend to hand over a party with completely empty coffers to the next leader.' Fitzwilliams noted that none of his pragmatic colleagues protested his predicted demise. He would have appreciated at least a stifled objection. 'Pull as many ads as you can, Georgia. For the rest of the cabinet, it's *sauve qui peut* time.'

'You'd better give them that instruction in English, Prime Minister,' Langdon recommended. 'Your cabinet isn't . . .'

. . . *capable of understanding much*, was what Langdon had left unsaid, Fitzwilliams knew. 'I'll tell the cabinet to fall back on their own electorates, save their own seats,' he declared. 'Those who survive, survive. Next, I want each of you to draw up a list of our top backbenchers. The ones who have talent, the ones with potential. If we're going to be reduced to a rump in a hung parliament, we're going to need backbenchers who can tie their own shoelaces without lobbyists doing it for them. I'm making it my mission to hold on to as many of those seats as we can.' His plan for the last week of the campaign was to rescue the best of his backbench. He'd visit each of their electorates. He was going to fight tooth and nail to save the part of his caucus worth saving.

There was silence, but a silence of consent.

'Prime Minister,' Donna Hargreaves said, 'I think you should know Damian Boswell contacted me.'

Boswell? Hadn't he sent his former leadership rival and now ambassador to Russia off to tour the port facilities in Archangel?

'He's resigning as ambassador and coming back. He wanted to know how I would lean if he tilted for the leadership.'

'Senses blood in the water,' Alan Chandos commented, for once without his customary levity.

'It's a nasty, ruthless world you people live in, if you don't mind my saying so, Prime Minister.' Quentin couldn't stop himself from speaking up. 'I mean, you're campaigning your guts out and he ...'

Fitzwilliams found the bodyguard's indignation touching. 'Ours is a ruthless, unsentimental profession,' he agreed. 'Quentin, you're much better off being a bodyguard and dealing with terrorists, madmen and jokers with cream pies.' He turned back to the screens. 'In the last week, we'll mobilise the core and traditional allies such as the Free Drivers Movement.'

'I wouldn't do that, Prime Minister,' Chandos said. 'The Free Drivers attacked the Queen last night.'

Fitzwilliams squinted at Chandos's screen, uncomprehending. The Queen had just turned a hundred and two years old. No one, not even Robespierre, would attack her at this point.

'Alan is making a joke, Prime Minister,' Langdon clarified. 'Last night, the head of the Free Drivers Movement smashed his car into a statue of Queen Victoria. Driving under the influence and he'd disconnected the Autocar system that would have prevented the accident.'

'But a car driven by a motorist can't be started unless the Autocar safety system is on.'

'And there is an illegal device out there to circumvent that nowadays, or so I learned this morning.'

The Prime Minister sighed. 'So what's that . . . two, three criminal charges? Driving under the influence, speeding undoubtedly, disconnecting Autocar.'

'Manslaughter—if he'd rammed anyone other than good Queen Vic,' Chandos contributed.

Georgia Lambert stepped into the void left by their erstwhile ally's implosion. 'Before we head out, everyone remember today is World Try Not to Kill Anyone Today Day. The slogan is Make Murder History. Go for photo ops with police, detectives, social workers.'

'Don't we try to avoid killing anyone on most days?' Chandos asked.

'Yes, but today we're focused on it. It would look good if Australia had a clean sheet.'

'I'll avoid visiting the Free Drivers leader in hospital then,' Fitzwilliams muttered.

• • •

Fiona Brennan felt she already knew the shop. Low Expectations was just as Renard's reports had described it. 'I know who you are,' the owner said gruffly from behind his counter.

'It's not a state secret,' the ASIO chief replied.

'I want you to know that it's not my custom to rent out the top floor for special private meetings.' The owner had actually been flattered by the ASIO director's request to use his premises, but his near decade in the hospitality industry had made him inexperienced at extending any.

'I appreciate your consideration,' Fiona answered.

His eyes narrowed. 'This is a Dickens shop,' he made clear. 'I don't want any of your John le Carré carrying on upstairs.' He threw some oatmeal into the pot of gruel. 'Your man is already there,' he informed her.

Fiona Brennan had arrived early because she wanted Wilson Huang to find her already in place, in control. The Compink Australia CEO had evidently wanted the same thing.

She found Wilson watching a Dickens movie. 'I always had a soft spot for Orlick,' Wilson told her, indicating an actor skulking about on the screen. 'A vicious man, yes, but he's the only character in *Great Expectations* who seems intent on moving the plot anywhere.'

'You like Dickens?' Fiona asked.

'Like Dickens?' Wilson mused. 'What an unusual question. Dickens is more like running a marathon. It has its highs and lows along the way but, in the end, you're just glad it's finally over.'

Fiona laughed. 'I'm here,' she said more seriously, 'to discuss the Renard–Amy situation.'

'The Amy–Renard situation,' Wilson corrected.

'Well?'

'Amy Zhao is brilliant, my most accomplished employee. If Amy has chosen your Renard, then he's a very fortunate man.'

'Renard is very . . .' Fiona had to admit she didn't know Renard particularly well. 'Very nice too,' she said in his defence. She didn't want Wilson thinking Compink Australia had got the short end of this love-between-the-agencies deal. 'Amy is so accomplished, yet she's only a data entry clerk?' Fiona observed.

'Amy Zhao is Compink Australia's deputy CEO,' Wilson informed her proudly, 'and has been so for several years!'

'I see,' Fiona remarked. After a moment, she asked, 'Did you mean to tell me that?'

'Times are changing; I'm embracing a new openness,' Wilson replied with a cavalier wave of his hand. 'Fiona, Compink Australia is only following that time-honoured corporate tradition of trying to make as much money as possible. ASIO doesn't need to bestow as much attention on us as you currently do. But back to the matter at hand: Amy Zhao's happiness is important to me.'

'Renard's happiness is important to me,' Fiona countered. She wasn't going to let Wilson Huang beat her in a contest for Most Considerate Boss.

'Fine. Then we agree to let them enjoy their happiness. A very good decision.'

Fiona Brennan was getting a fair impression of why her agents had never got the upper hand on Wilson Huang. 'If Amy Zhao is your deputy CEO . . .'

'Yes, yes . . . I also gave one of your planted ASIO agents the title of "deputy CEO". It made him think he was in the inner circle. Meanwhile, Amy could get on with doing the real work of deputy CEO. You should probably recall your man. Actually, recall all your spies from my organisation.' Wilson hesitated, 'Except, perhaps, Madeleine Fong. Her work is excellent. I'd like to keep her if I could.'

'Wilson, I can't leave an agent in place at the taxpayer's expense because she does good work for you.'

'She could spy on the Compink China agents infesting my workplace,' Wilson suggested. 'I'll be leaving a few of them in place. Otherwise, they'll just send more.' He favoured Fiona with his most charming smile.

'I'll consider your request,' Fiona replied. She was inclined to believe Wilson was being honest with her. Working with Compink Australia to find out about Compink China's activities did appeal to her. 'Perhaps we should meet here regularly,' she proposed. 'I hear the gruel here is very, well, gruel-like.'

• • •

Just days to the election and it couldn't be any worse. The 2RT station manager held his head with both hands, pulling on what little hair he had left.

'Yes, caller,' he heard Jim Jarvis say, 'but we can't just be against taxes. A solid, dependable tax base is the only way the government can fund the services people need.' It was Virtual Jim Jarvis's new voice of moderation. 'I'm not alive anymore to pay taxes, but I'm sure Radio 2RT is making a lot of money off my show and my expectation would be that 2RT pay a fair rate of corporate tax.'

The station manager slammed a fist onto the desk. 'I'll fucking kill him!' he swore. 'Don't point out the irony in that statement,' he snapped before the producer could speak.

It was a nightmare. The nerd, when the station manager finally reached him, refused to come and fix Virtual Jim Jarvis. He'd also warned that if any other programmer attempted to tamper with the new Jim Jarvis's personality, a sub-program beneath the current one would be activated and transform Jim Jarvis into a Muslim fundamentalist. The show plodded on all week with its new tepid host. Already old foes were cottoning on to the changed field of play. Now that Jim Jarvis wasn't shouting people down, everybody wanted to be on the show, even the fucking Mayor of Sydney.

'I'd rather have an ice pick jammed down my ear than listen to this stuff,' the producer observed. 'Even Radio National is more interesting.'

'We've got to take Jarvis off the air,' the station manager decided.

The producer held up his hands impotently. 'But what do we say? Why are we taking him off? We have a bloody shrine to the man in our foyer with his actual body in it. We can't just give him the sack.'

'I don't know,' the station manager moaned. 'Say he's not well, needs to go on leave.'

'Not well?' the producer exclaimed. 'He's dead!'

The station manager did not speak for almost a minute. 'Let me run this by you,' he said at last, his voice ominously controlled. 'We hire some anarchist kid, some no-good with a chip on his shoulder, tell him he's on work experience for the perpetually unemployed. Then we plant some rinky-dink bomb in our server and blow up Jim Jarvis!'

There was a grin the producer had never seen before on his station manager's face. 'Jim Jarvis dies a second time!' the station manager proposed, his enthusiasm growing. 'A terrorist bomb going off at 2RT to kill Virtual Jim Jarvis! Anarchist suspect! It would be the biggest bloody story in the country!'

The producer considered the idea. Several crimes were involved—including insurance fraud, if he knew his manager. Whether blowing up your own property could lead to terrorism charges was likely a murky legal area. Then there was the framing of some anarchist buffoon. Those things aside, the plan seemed reasonable enough.

'And then we dismantle that fucking shrine in our foyer and stuff Jim Jarvis into the ground where he belongs,' the station manager vowed.

• • •

The Prime Minister sank contentedly into his chair. It was good to be back in his office if only for a few hours. Being the eve of the election, he'd have to head off soon enough to his home electorate of Dobell to cast his vote the following morning.

The end of the race. During the whirlwind final week of the campaign—his last as prime minister in all likelihood—he'd visited the electorates of his twenty best backbenchers. He didn't go to the Sydney fish markets or speak to the troops in Darwin. He shunned the easy photo ops and the hard-hat tours of factories. Instead, he went with his backbenchers to the coal face, where the swing voters were. He gave a speech in a hostile trade union hall. He met with the legions of unemployed in Centrelink offices. He talked with ex-GPs. He fought for votes in the likeliest and unlikeliest places. Most of all, he talked up the local MPs with feeling and commitment. It was the best effort he could have made to save the core of his backbench. And he did it all off script! That afternoon, Quentin and Leon had told him they were proud of him. He was surprised how much it moved him to hear his bodyguards say that.

There was a soft rap on the door and he heard Olga's voice on the other side speaking to Quentin. 'Come in,' he called.

Olga O'Rourke entered the room almost sheepishly, a sheet of paper in her hand. Her normal straightforwardness seemed absent. On the eve of the election, Olga should be in South Australia banging voters' heads together. 'Is something wrong?' Fitzwilliams asked.

'A difficult matter, Prime Minister,' she replied. 'I've narrowed down the list of who could have been feeding information to the Luddites. There are only two possible suspects remaining.'

'Does it even matter now?' Fitzwilliams asked, finding himself oddly uninterested in the question. He still held out hope that the

Liberal–National Coalition would be the largest party in the new parliament, though their ranks would be decimated. The Luddites had routed them in the election campaign. He'd seen the Luddite leader—Nemesis Ned, as he now called her—on TV just minutes ago addressing a throng of cyclists on the Yarra. Thousands of them. 'We aren't passing out how-to-vote cards,' she had proclaimed. 'You all know how to vote. Elect the best people you can to parliament!' The Luddites were going without how-to-vote cards, without scrutineers, without even a party headquarters. Nothing by the book . . . and yet every absurd and unorthodox thing they did worked for them. Fitzwilliams was a seasoned campaigner and they had bested him. If he lived in Wills, he might even vote for Nemesis Ned. You had to respect that level of ability.

He was both surprised and pleased to find that graciousness in defeat was coming so naturally to him. The Luddite mole was only one small facet in the likely rout his government was now facing. Did it really matter who it was?

He could see that it did matter to Olga. He'd set her the task of unearthing the culprit, after all. 'All right, come on,' he said. 'Let's see who it was.'

She handed him the sheet of paper. She had handwritten two names on it. His own was there. And the second name was possibly even more astounding to him. He lifted his eyes to meet Olga's.

'I'm sorry, Prime Minister,' she murmured, giving what struck him as an almost apologetic smile. 'I guess you may call me Ned.'

CHAPTER FOURTEEN

'Olga . . .' Fitzwilliams gazed at her in astonishment. 'Why? If you wanted to be prime minister, you could have told me. We could have come to some arrangement.'

'I did not want to become prime minister, Prime Minister,' Olga replied. 'I wanted to reform the political system.'

'Reform the system?' Fitzwilliams was incredulous. 'With the Luddite Party? With celery sticks and logos on the moon and people marching in the nude?'

By all rights, he should throw her out of the office. He could call Leon and Quentin and have them remove her from the premises. He could pick up the phone and contact his lawyers; God knew they had umpteen punishments on the books for leaking cabinet documents—unless they were documents the government wanted leaked, of course. It was utter treachery what she'd done —whatever it was she had done.

But the rage he should be feeling wasn't there. What he found in its place was . . . what?' Respect for an opponent who'd got the better of him? Olga O'Rourke was one of the few truly first-class minds he'd met in politics. As he held that gaze of hers, what arose in him was not indignation but curiosity. He repeated his original question. 'Why?'

'I will give you a full explanation but I must ask you not to interrupt.' Olga's look remained focused, yet somewhat distant. 'When I was growing up in the Soviet Union,' she began, 'my friends and I knew the Soviet system needed to be completely overhauled and we dreamed of bringing about such a change. But my parents emigrated to Australia in 1985, just as things started to happen in the Soviet Union. A few years later, that process reached crisis point.' Her tone became bitter. 'That drunkard Yeltsin scrambled onto a tank to proclaim a new era and everyone applauded as if a moment of theatre was all that was needed to sweep away seventy years of tyranny and lies. You know the history of Russia from there. Cronyism and corruption, a system worse than it was before.

'I arrived here with the simplistic thinking of a fifteen year old. I reasoned that since communism had made a mess of the Soviet Union, the right-wing parties must be correct. I joined the Young Liberals at the first opportunity and my political activities from there set me on the path to where I am today, elected to the Senate and a cabinet minister in your administration.

'I lost those naive eyes of my fifteen-year-old self. From inside the political system here, I could see it was plagued with problems—problems not so different from what was happening in Russia. There were cronies in our system: mining magnates who thought they were entitled to endless privileges for plundering the nation's resources; casino owners demanding concessions, as if operating roulette tables was the highest calling of civic duty; media moguls of unspeakable greed. Were they really so different from the rogues who swirled around Yeltsin and Putin and now Kharlamov? At least those rogues knew they had to . . .' she paused over the phrase, 'doff their caps to Putin. Here, the scoundrels don't even have the decency to show deference to you, the prime minister.

'Then there was the managerial class of business and bureaucracy here, with their meaningless babble of "total quality assurance", "key performance indicators", "creativity-based solutions". These managers and business elite truly believe they are the engine that powers this country, when all they really do is rebrand dung as Dung Plus or Dung 3.1. In the Soviet Union, everyone knew the system was based on lies. Everyone. Those telling the lies and those hearing them. What shocked me was when I realised that managers here actually believe the nonsense they speak. They call a place a "centre of excellence" and believe it has become so simply by their naming it that.

'Then we have our political system, Prime Minister. Two parliamentary parties obsessed with opinion polls. Focus groups, sound bites, endless fundraising, policies and messages so filtered they have become diluted to almost homeopathic levels. The inanities of question time. It goes on. I came to the conclusion that the system did not need reform, it needed to be brought crashing down and rebuilt from the ground up. The political class was incapable of reform.'

She paused and smiled. 'I realise, given my accent, this speech must sound to your ears like the ravings of a James Bond villain.'

Fitzwilliams had been mesmerised throughout her long dissertation. Had he ever known the real Olga? For all three terms of his government, she'd been his most capable cabinet colleague, his fixer. He also recalled having once told Alan Chandos that Olga had the accent of a James Bond villain. Had bloody Chandos repeated that to her?

'It's all very well to bring a system crashing down,' Olga continued, as if toppling a political regime was a routine matter, 'but it's difficult to ensure that something better takes its place. Revolutionaries are very good at making revolution, seldom good at government; good at capturing a radio station, but hopeless at producing any radio shows worth listening to.'

'What does any of this have to do with the Luddites?' Fitzwilliams was intrigued by the full explanation, but it wouldn't hurt her to get to the point.

'The political parties themselves inevitably develop unsavoury attributes. Our donors would be an example, Prime Minister. There's that expression—' she paused '—about paying the piper and calling the tune. However, the major flaw of our current system is that one party has the role of generating all the ideas to govern and the other party has the responsibility of barking and frothing at them like a pack of rabid dogs. We need an entirely different approach. Everyone in parliament should be there to govern. Everyone should be there to listen to each other in order to decide matters.'

'Is that what the Luddites are then?' Fitzwilliams asked. 'A new model of government, an anti-party party?'

'The Luddites are a different way of doing things. Over several years, I recruited a nucleus of people to the Luddite Party—one hundred and fifty people initially, and I have quietly added more over the years. They were people of ideas. I didn't look for people with my political ideas, but people who were both informed and original thinkers and, most importantly, people who listened discerningly to the ideas and opinions of others. I wanted to remove personal ambition and ego from the political process as much as possible. That was when I hit on the idea of Ned Ludd. Give everyone the same name, then you do not spend your time thinking about who proposed something but, rather, what was being proposed. They all agreed to change their names officially to Ned Ludd.'

'You recruited one hundred and fifty Luddites?' Fitzwilliams queried. 'But two thousand eight hundred and eighty-seven people changed their names to Ned Ludd back then.'

'You remember the figure?' Olga remarked, surprised.

Fitzwilliams shrugged. 'It's a prime number.'

Olga seemed impressed he knew this. 'Most of those people were there as distractors. I knew there'd be a great deal of curiosity around the renaming, so I also recruited a large number of people who thought the name-changing was some sort of postmodern joke and were willing to be part of it.' Fitzwilliams didn't comment. 'If the media wanted to make a story of it, the postmodern joke story would be the one they found.

'With you entering your fourth campaign, the timing was correct for the Luddites. Yours—ours—was a weary government and the opposition was weak. Several years ago, when you had me draft the Demonstration Protection Act—an underhanded act of repression by the way, Prime Minister; I thought it unworthy of you—I deliberately left a loophole within the legislation. That loophole enabled the Luddites to carry out their nude protest march at the start of the campaign. Having the Luddites call the election before you had, and call it in such a starkly revealing way—' she paused, as if considering whether that phrase had worked or not '—made the public curious to know what the Luddites were about, and with Ned Ludd, everyone would know their candidate's name. Also, by encouraging the public to confuse the pollsters, we disrupted the logistical supply of information that both major parties depended on.'

'So everything you've done has been a set-up all along,' Fitzwilliams challenged her. 'The Demonstration Protection Act, the legality of the nude march.' He suddenly found himself both angry and hurt. 'That filmed tennis match where you told me I was old and past my prime and then released it on YouTube!'

'No, Prime Minister,' she corrected him sharply. 'Some child in the next court did that. I simply told you the truth. You're not a young man anymore who can gallop back and forth across a tennis court.' She looked disappointed in him. 'I was trying to improve your game,' she offered, implying he should show some gratitude. 'I never sought to humiliate you.'

'You didn't?'

'No. If you recall, I warned you the Luddites had stolen Alan Chandos's Play as You Go taxation plan. I prevented you from announcing it and embarrassing yourself. I ridded you of the blackmailing Lister St John, sparing you considerable difficulties there. And when you failed to heed Fiona Brennan's warning, I was the one who later reminded you there was a spy within our ranks passing information to the Luddites.'

'But *you* were that spy!' Fitzwilliams protested.

'Yes,' Olga agreed, 'but I was still the one who warned you. In many ways, I continued to do my job for you rather well, even though I was working for the other side.' Fitzwilliams recognised a bizarre work ethic in that answer somewhere. Did double agents pride themselves in doing both jobs well? 'I sought to defeat you, not humiliate you,' Olga concluded.

'But why, Olga? Why didn't you come to me with your ideas for reforming parliament? You were . . . you *are* my closest adviser. I might have listened to you—at least a bit,' he added more honestly.

'Prime Minister, you have a good mind,' Olga observed pensively, 'but as prime minister you put all your mental efforts into keeping the system functioning exactly as it was. It's a system in disrepair, a system manifestly failing to come to grips with serious problems. You did nothing to fix it. You were like Brezhnev.' She looked at him with genuine sadness, as if it hurt her to make that comparison. 'I didn't think you were up to being a Luddite.'

It was true. He wouldn't have listened. It had been his fate— his ambition, really—to push the apple cart along, not upset it. He'd thought of nothing other than keeping it going.

'What about all the other humiliations?' he asked Olga. He couldn't let go of the personal affront so easily. 'What about Ned Ludd in space? What about the celery stick trick on Donna? What about pitting me against a merry-go-round of debating opponents, including a seventeen-year-old schoolgirl?'

Olga shrugged. 'I had nothing to do with any of that. The Luddite candidates have initiative. Besides, those are just engagements in the . . . rough and tumble . . . of a campaign. You cannot claim it is unfair because you did not win those engagements.'

Fitzwilliams found he couldn't muster the will to storm at her. 'How did you do it?' he asked.

'What specifically?'

'How did you organise the whole movement, all those candidates, and yet fly under the radar?' Not even ASIO knew how the Luddites communicated.

Olga had felt she owed him an explanation, but she wasn't going to explain that. The Ghost Post was a secret between her and Australia Post. An undercover postal delivery system. No electronic trail. Envelopes sent and delivered with no one other than the clandestine Ghost Posties knowing how. It was they who kept the minimal but necessary flow of information going within the Luddite campaign. She had set up this special arrangement with Australia Post herself and paid for it from her own savings in cash. There was no record of its activities anywhere.

'You're not going to tell me,' Fitzwilliams observed.

'Need-to-know basis,' Olga replied. 'No one but me needs to know.'

'And now what, Olga? The Luddites win the most seats tomorrow and you become prime minister?'

Olga shook her head. 'No, I told you I never planned to be prime minister. What I planned was to get rid of this current foolishness. I cannot be prime minister. I am . . . tainted goods.' She seemed sad again. 'I've had to do many things in your administration—the Demonstration Protection Act is but one example—that do me no credit. The Luddites in parliament will be a fresh beginning. They could never be seen to have me as their leader.'

Fitzwilliams was astonished to discover that he somehow felt guilty. This traitor had planned her betrayal of him with exquisite precision, had planned it for years. She'd made his carefully-mapped-out final election campaign a torment for him.

Why should he feel he had done her wrong? And yet, when he looked into those sad Russian eyes, he sensed he had.

'Olga . . .' Words were forming on his tongue; he was going to try to cheer her up, he realised. 'It was brilliantly played.'

She visibly brightened at the comment.

'I've never seen a campaign of such genius,' Fitzwilliams continued. 'I only wish Lister St John had been my campaign manager throughout, so he could have shared in this defeat.'

'Really?'

'Really. Garry Kasparov would be proud.'

She beamed at the mention of the chess grandmaster. 'Thank you, Prime Minister. That means a lot to me.'

'What next then?' Fitzwilliams asked, as if it was just a routine question between colleagues. 'What happens tomorrow?'

'Tomorrow, the people decide,' Olga replied. 'We take it from there.' She rose to leave.

'Olga,' Fitzwilliams called.

She stopped at the door.

'Something tells me I shall have rather a lot more time on my hands in the near future.'

Olga merely nodded in agreement.

Fitzwilliams surveyed his opponent. 'If you are free, I wouldn't mind another game of tennis sometime,' he said.

Olga smiled slightly. 'I would very much enjoy that,' she answered. 'When the . . . dust has settled, Prime Minister.'

• • •

Remarkably, the P&C sausage sizzle at the polling station also had celery sticks available. That had to be a good sign both politically for the Luddites and perhaps nutritionally for a sausage sizzle, Aggie thought. She surveyed the sky with displeasure. Drones were pestering all the high-profile Luddite candidates, seeking footage of them casting their votes. That morning, one had followed Aggie to her fruit-and-veg shop. Celery Ned, the one who had debated Donna Hargreaves, had been shown on TV taking her cat to the vet. Another Luddite appeared on the nation's screens going with his daughter to her soccer match (a 1–1 draw).

A drone swooped low and hovered in front of Aggie. She heard the remote studio journalist bark a few questions at her through the drone's speaker. 'My casting a vote isn't a news story,' she told the machine. 'Everyone has to vote. Shoo.' She waved it away.

The Veronicae had finished voting. Tim, in bodyguard mode, led the way to their bicycles. Aggie looked again at the drones buzzing above them.

A Veronica cycled alongside her. 'We can give them the slip if you want,' she suggested.

Aggie gave her an 'I'm interested' flick of her eyebrows.

'We'll park outside this shop I know,' Veronica proposed. 'The drones will stay with the parked bikes. We can head out into the laneway behind the place, cut through a series of shops and find somewhere quiet to watch the election results.'

Aggie looked dubious. 'Disappearing isn't the most responsible thing for a candidate to do.'

'Responsible? You won't be prime minister until what . . . ten, ten thirty at the earliest? No need to start acting prime ministerial just yet. Tim,' Veronica called to the bodyguard, 'let me lead.'

•••

The smarmy face of Damian Boswell, ex-ambassador to Russia, ex-rival to Fitzwilliams for the Liberal Party leadership and possibly resurrected rising star, filled the television screen. He was oozing concern for a prime minister who had served his country well but perhaps too long. The Prime Minister was tired, he thought, the government in need of renewal. Damian Boswell had delivered this assessment with a reluctant half-grimace, a grimace Fitzwilliams could tell was laid atop his smug smile. Boswell was back in the country hoping, no doubt, to deliver the oration at Fitzwilliams' political funeral tonight.

The Prime Minister was mentally prepared for defeat. Liberal seats would be lost tonight, so many he could not continue as leader. He'd accept responsibility, but he would be damned if that pallid-faced Damian Boswell was going to be the beneficiary of his demise.

Network Seven cut to what they called the Lions' Den, where the two most divisive former leaders, one Labor and one Liberal, met in the studio to spew opinion at each other. Fitzwilliams turned the sound off, something he wished he could have done when the rusted old hulks had been in parliament.

It was time for cold political calculation. If Labor won outright, he'd resign and make it effective immediately. If his government won the most seats, but lost its majority, he would announce he was stepping down as PM but wouldn't resign his seat. He wouldn't open an easy by-election route for Damian Boswell to get back into caucus. If the Luddites won enough seats that they had a chance to form government, Fitzwilliams didn't know what he would do—probably ask Olga O'Rourke what she thought best. She was still technically an adviser to him.

When he'd voted earlier that day, the Senate ballot had been an absurdity. Six Ned Ludds were listed one under the other in the Luddite column. As the Ludds didn't go in for middle names, to distinguish between them each Ned had their birth date printed beside their name. One of them, Fitzwilliams noticed, shared his birthday. He'd had to cut short such reverie in the voting booth. It wasn't a good look for the Prime Minister to appear to be taking a long time deciding how to vote.

Word had come of another unexpected development. The online activist organisation Act Out were appearing at polling stations all over the country passing out Say No to How-to-Vote Cards cards. The whole world seemed to be conspiring against anything being political business as usual.

Network Seven cut away from the lions in the Lions' Den. Fitzwilliams turned the sound back on. 'Votes are now coming in and we have our very first numbers to hand,' a host said excitedly. 'They are only from one booth so far. In the seat of Fadden. I'll get this up on the screen. Luddites are currently leading with one hundred and seventy votes. Liberal–National Coalition on one hundred and twenty-five and Labor on eighty-nine. That's a swing of . . .'

Were they really going to give the swing based on an early count in one booth? Such statistics addiction. With the results now coming in, Fitzwilliams would have to set off to the bunker, the election nerve centre of the Liberal Party. He would await the result there before heading to the party HQ, the hall where Liberal activists would be on hand to cheer whichever speech, triumphant or brave-in-defeat, needed to be delivered to the media.

Though he knew his wife hated such things, Beatrice was accompanying him tonight. Her hand touched his elbow now, surprising him. He hadn't noticed that she'd entered the room. 'Ready to go?' she asked.

'Do you have your beeper?' he inquired, recalling the time she had left during his victory speech for a work emergency.

'I got Raul to cover for me this weekend.' Beatrice hesitated. 'I thought you might need some support tonight.'

He recognised the meaning in the sentence. She knew he was finished. She knew he knew he was finished. She might dislike politics, but Beatrice was going to stand by him at his Waterloo. He found himself deeply touched.

'Cheer up,' she said, reading the emotion on his face. 'Watch this.' She gazed at him, a look of pride and admiration etched on her face. Tears welled in her eyes. 'I've been practising that look,' she told him. 'Let Roslyn Stanfield's doe-eyed husband match that!'

'I don't think I've ever seen you do that look before,' he commented, genuinely impressed.

She laughed. 'You've never needed me to do that look before.' She slipped her arm through his. 'Let's go find out how many Neds will be facing you across the floor of parliament.'

He wanted to say something light-hearted, but his gratitude got in the way. 'You did vote Liberal, I hope,' he managed at last.

'I voted Liberal in the lower house,' she replied, smiling. Quentin and Leon fell in beside them as they emerged from the room. 'But only because I'm sleeping with the local candidate.' She hadn't bothered to lower her voice in front of the bodyguards. 'As for the Senate—' she shrugged charmingly '—how I voted is rather my own business, isn't it?'

• • •

One hour into the count. It was going to be a long night in the pub for underemployed freelance camera operators Jesse Pelletier and Gunnar Sigurdsson. Twenty-three Liberal–Nationals elected or leading, twenty-one Labor, twenty-one Luddite. The tension at Labor and Liberal headquarters would be incredible. That made the fact that none of the networks needed Jesse and Gunnar to be there all the more bitter.

At the party headquarters, the networks had dispensed with journalists altogether. Both Nine and Seven were trialling proto-type Roving Roboters: bloody mutant droids (according to Jesse) that rolled around the party headquarters doing the filming and lining up interviews. Roboters were controlled remotely by the studio production team and, through them, the network hosts could speak directly to party spokespeople on the floor. The Roving Roboter's biggest asset over a conventional reporter (other than not needing to be paid) turned out to be their ring of sensitive microphones that could pick up muttered comments from all over the hall floor. In their first hour on the job, the Roving Roboters had already fed the network hosts a steady stream of anxious, abusive and sometimes treacherous sotto voce comments from Liberal and Labor figures.

The Luddite Party had no campaign headquarters and both camera operators had hoped there would be freelance work scrambling around finding individual Luddites to interview on election night. Instead, the networks had turned to Australia Post. Drones were poised, ready to swoop upon anything political happening anywhere. The long professional careers of the two camera operators had petered out completely, the career path equivalent of ending up hopelessly lost in the bush.

They'd headed to Melbourne mostly just to get away from Canberra, where they weren't part of the action. But Melbourne hadn't exactly lifted their spirits. They were in front of a large television screen in a deserted pub watching Labor's Jessykah Underhill being interviewed through a Roboter. The interview was going as mundanely as any interview did with Underhill. Gunnar had predicted she'd say, 'It's a little early to be making predictions,' within the first thirty seconds and been proven right.

The television image suddenly went wonky, the camera having been jostled. Both professionals peered at the screen with renewed interest. The image of Underhill was then completely blocked out. The screen switched back to the network hosts. The camera operators looked at each other in excitement. Someone at Labor headquarters had taken out Seven's new robot camera!

• • •

'What the fuck is going on?' screamed the earpiece of Allison Trang, Network Seven news producer. Though not diplomatically put, it was a fair question from the senior producers upstairs.

The feed from their Roboter hadn't stopped. Something was obscuring its view.

Her chief technician swore. 'It's Nine's Roboter! Network Nine rammed us from behind! And now they've rolled their Roboter between ours and Jessykah Underhill.'

Allison pressed her lips together. 'This could get very ugly,' she predicted.

• • •

2028

PRIVATE FUNCTION read the sign on Low Expectation's door. The owner had even let the Sydney Luddite campaign team set up a viewing screen by the looms. The place was packed. Wine and beer was being poured into the chipped tea mugs.

Amy Zhao surveyed the boisterous Luddite campaign volunteers. She hadn't known any of these people seven weeks ago. Seven weeks ago, she didn't know the Luddites were a real political party. She hadn't met Renard for that matter—Renard, her Luddite lover, whose flat, in the whirlwind of events, she had agreed to move into next week. She took Renard's hand and smiled.

If that wasn't enough of a momentous development in her life for one week, her boss Wilson Huang had more in store for her. When she arrived at Compink Australia on Thursday, Wilson had sacked almost all the ASIO spies employed there. He then announced to the remaining staff that lowly data entry clerk Amy Zhao was now officially Compink Australia's deputy CEO. Amy's first public act as deputy CEO was an obvious one. She informed her stunned co-workers that she was instituting a staff kitchen weekly clean-up roster (and with a democratic flourish put Wilson's name at the top of the list).

And now, tonight, there was the election. In the last half-hour, the Luddites had moved into the lead, but Renard's electorate of Sydney was stubbornly staying Too Close to Call. Everyone was anxious, but the Luddite surge in other parts of the country was putting this partisan Low Expectations crowd in an increasingly raucous mood.

Kate suddenly shouted and pumped a fist at the screen. 'Eden-Monaro has fallen to the Luddites!' she proclaimed. 'Victory!

287

Victory!' she roared like the Prussian army swarming onto the field at Waterloo.

'Congratulations on your campaign, Ned,' came a voice from behind them.

Amy turned and practically gasped. Before her was Loki, her agent in Baxter Lockwood. 'Jiang?' she managed, coming within a whisker of calling him by his codename. 'What are you doing here?'

'I didn't know you knew Jiang,' Renard remarked. 'Jiang, Sam and Mrs Giardino here gave up their own work time to help me campaign in Surry Hills earlier this week.'

'And this is my manager, Olivia,' Jiang added, gesturing to a blonde woman beside him.

'Gave up their own work time.' Olivia chuckled. 'That's one way of putting it.'

'You're a Luddite?' Amy squeaked at Jiang.

'Not just any Luddite!' Sam chortled. 'Jiang was the one who put the Luddite logo on the moon!'

'Helped put,' Jiang corrected modestly.

'And Jiang wrote the "Transylvania paraphernalia" program!' Sam added.

'I've been a Luddite a long time,' Jiang informed Amy. 'I only did the work for you as a sideline.'

Amy was flabbergasted. Olivia, the woman Jiang had introduced, reached over and gave her a hug. 'What was that for?' Amy asked, somewhat bewildered by the embrace.

'I know what it's like to employ Jiang,' Olivia replied.

'Transylvania paraphernalia?' Renard asked. 'That's what Kate had to say on the radio. I never understood what that was about.'

Renard didn't hear the answer. Another roar engulfed the room. Everyone in Low Expectations was jumping about in an explosion of hugging and kissing. Across the screen was written:

Elected—Ned Ludd—Sydney

Luddite Party of Australia—Gain

'Elected!' bellowed Kate. 'We did it!'

'One term only,' Renard declared, pointing a finger at Kate. 'You're the candidate next election. You can run my MP's office until then . . .' His eyes narrowed. 'Are you drinking beer?' he accused.

The voice on the television announced: 'We're going live outside the Sydney electorate headquarters of the Luddite Party . . .'

'Headquarters?' Old Ned asked. 'Does he mean here?'

'. . . to talk to a spokesperson for the Luddites there.'

Old Ned looked around. 'Who's this spokesperson? We're all inside.'

The screen switched to outside Low Expectations. A scruffy-looking man wiped his hands on his apron and intoned: '*It was the best of times, it was the worst of times, it was the age of wisdom, it was the age of foolishness . . .*'

'It's my boss!' Kate cried. The owner of Low Expectations was being broadcast by drones on national television.

'Get out there,' Old Ned coughed at Renard, 'before he recites the whole bloody first chapter at them!'

· · ·

The Luddites had pulled ahead significantly, elected or leading in fifty-seven seats, with the Liberal–National Coalition on forty-one and Labor thirty-seven. The Governor-General would almost certainly be obliged to give the Luddites the first chance to form a minority government.

'Fucking hell!' Jesse declared.

'Yeah!' Gunnar agreed. 'Crazy stuff!'

'No, I meant fucking hell—' Jesse pointed excitedly '—as in, fucking hell, look who just came into the pub.'

Ned Ludd . . . *the* Ned Ludd: Nude Ned, Bicycle Ned, Debater Ned, Dragonbreath Posters Ned had just run into the pub with three others, all of them laughing.

Both men drew their cameras with the speed of gunslingers.

• • •

Was it a workable minority government? Talking heads belaboured the point for thirty minutes while the numbers firmed. Luddite sixty-seven, Liberal forty-seven, Labor forty-three, Independent one. Fitzwilliams' cabinet had been all but obliterated. He couldn't continue as leader, but Fitzwilliams would have to wait for now; it was Roslyn Stanfield's moment to face the camera.

The entry of the defeated leader was traditionally one of the set pieces of election night. The cameras track backwards as the leader moves through the parting crowd, smiling bravely, stopping for a word here and there with a member of the faithful, the audience applauding relentlessly while the more ambitious among them contemplate the personal implications should the leader resign.

Network Seven's Roving Roboter had a good line on Stanfield.

'Fuckers!' Allison heard her chief technician hiss. Network Nine had deliberately rolled their Roboter to block their view again. 'I've had it with them,' the technician snarled. 'Two can play that game!'

'What are you doing?' Allison asked.

The technician threw his Roboter's control throttle forward. 'Ramming speed, Captain!' he shouted.

. . .

'What on earth was that?' Fitzwilliams gaped at the image on the television screen.

Roslyn Stanfield was sprawled on the floor, clutching her knee, what looked like a giant traffic cone bearing Network Nine's logo on top of her. Her stunned bodyguards lifted the thing off her and pushed another machine away. Stanfield was helped to her feet but her left leg gave way when she tried to put weight on it.

'ACL I'd say, from the way she's holding her leg,' Leon assessed. 'Anterior cruciate ligament,' he added for the benefit of those unfamiliar with the abbreviation.

'You're uncommonly well informed on injuries,' Fitzwilliams observed. 'Leon diagnosed Stanfield's hamstring pull just from watching it on YouTube,' he told Beatrice beside him.

'Cruciate?' Beatrice commented. 'Isn't that one of the unforgiveable curses in *Harry Potter*?'

'I think you'll find that was the Cruciatus Curse, ma'am,' Leon replied.

Beatrice turned to Fitzwilliams. 'I was making a joke, but it's reassuring that your bodyguards are ready for anything, even Lord Voldemort.'

On-screen, Stanfield threw an arm over each of her body-guards and used them like crutches to make her way to the stage. Fitzwilliams shook his head. 'Stanfield and Langdon ought to form a party together,' he suggested. 'The Workers' Comp Party.'

Stanfield proceeded to deliver what Fitzwilliams considered to be one of the bravest and most mundane speeches he'd ever heard. Brave because she was clearly in deep pain. Mundane because her gritty resilience summoned only cliché after cliché. She accepted the people's verdict, she thanked the tireless effort of the Labor volunteers who'd campaigned, the mums and dads, the young, the retired, the nurses, the single parents, the . . . You'd have thought the whole nation had risen as one to pass out Labor Party brochures. She would fight to defend Labor's values. This was the party of Curtin, Chifley and Whitlam. This was the party that said the same thing every time it was defeated, Fitzwilliams thought.

With Stanfield done, it would be Fitzwilliams' turn next. He'd make the short trip to the hall where the Liberal faithful were waiting. The ten-minute journey would give the commentators back in their studios time to dissect Stanfield's speech. Stanfield hadn't resigned, so she still must be hoping to cling to the leader-ship. That option wasn't open to Fitzwilliams; too many Liberal and National seats had been lost tonight.

Fitzwilliams rose to his feet. 'Time to do it,' he announced. He didn't want his speech to be trite like Stanfield's. He thought of his improv coach Paul's advice. 'Don't overthink it. Go with what feels right in the moment.' He'd do that, only this time he'd make sure not to drop the f-bomb.

'Prime Minister.' Quentin caught his attention. 'If one of those robot things comes within five metres of you, I'll take a cricket bat to it,' he vowed.

'You don't carry a cricket bat, Quentin.'

'You're right.' He drew a small prod from his jacket. 'I wonder what a taser would do to their internal electronics.'

Though Fitzwilliams planned to go improv, he nevertheless performed the Arrival of the Leader as per the traditional script. He did the walk through the crowd, stopping for a word here and there, smiling, acknowledging the applause. The Roving Roboters, clearly in the doghouse, were conspicuously inert. He accepted the obligatory hugs from those on the podium.

The audience quietened. 'Well,' he began, 'talk about a kick in the teeth.' He hoped Paul his improv coach was watching. Beatrice, to his left, was just warming up her adoring look. 'My thanks to the people of Dobell for re-electing me, but as to the question posed to me on the campaign trail—by The Clash, no less—the answer would have to be: I should go.'

Normally, when a defeated leader resigned, a few of the faithful were obliged to call out, 'No! No!' but Fitzwilliams' jocular tone had puzzled them. 'I'm stepping down as your leader.' Fitzwilliams scanned the crowd. 'But I'll stay on as Member for Dobell because . . . well, I think the next parliament might be a very interesting place after the result tonight.'

There was a smattering of applause, but it seemed uncertain.

'The Luddites certainly put the boots to us tonight,' he summed up. 'I feel like I've been in a ruck and maul with the All Blacks.'

A small part of the audience laughed, hoping this was what was expected of them.

'They're going to think you've been drinking,' Beatrice managed through the clench of her smile. There was a tremor at the corners of her lips. She was suppressing laughter.

'We lost a few excellent MPs tonight,' he told the audience, 'people who made a significant contribution to this nation. And we lost a lot of deadwood too,' he observed more lightly. 'I mean, we had enough deadwood to constitute a fire risk. I reckon tonight was a hazard-reduction burn of our cabinet.'

There was a single guffaw from the crowd. Beatrice, her smile twitching, poked him in the side.

He rallied some gravitas to his voice. 'So now, in all probability, we're the Opposition, the official Opposition. I'm hoping,' he told them, 'that that's a term we won't use very much from now on. Let's make ourselves into something else. Let's be the official Improvers, the official Come-Up-with-a-Better-Idea brigade, the official Are-You-Sure-This-Is-a-Good-Thing-to-Do filter for the government. And if the new government listens and adopts one of those ideas, let's not go frothing to the media calling it a backflip. Reconsidering something because a different point of view is more convincing is a sensible thing to do. Backflips? I wish I could do an actual backflip. I can't touch my toes most days.'

He surveyed the room. The crowd was almost palpably disconcerted. That last bit had been rather tangential. What he'd just said, he realised, was a jumble of what Olga O'Rourke told him yesterday about why she brought the Luddites into being. He hadn't set out to endorse her ideas. It just seemed to slot into the flow of his speech. 'My hope, as I leave you tonight, is that we'll be a party that, instead of scheming to find the quickest route back to power, concentrates its efforts on the sound and just governing of this country. That's the kind of party I hope we'll be in the next parliament. Congratulations to Prime Minister Ned Ludd . . . whoever that may be.'

It took a moment for the crowd to understand that he had finished. The applause rose to the expected level of heartiness. The Speech of the Losing Leader was still a performance piece and this was what was required of them. The applause had a mixed sound to it—some of it angry clapping, some reluctant, some numb, a tiny bit perhaps genuinely enthusiastic.

'They hated that,' Beatrice appraised, giving him a wink, 'but I loved it! It was the right thing to say, Adrian.'

She was looking at him in admiration. She wasn't bunging it on. It was sincere and it was, he realised, hopeful. It made Fitzwilliams think that this campaign, including this particular result, had all been worthwhile, might even be good for the nation. 'I've been PM so long,' he observed at last, 'virtually everyone calls me Prime Minister. Only you and one other call me Adrian.'

'One other?' Beatrice asked suspiciously, as if calling him by his first name should be a level of intimacy reserved only for herself.

'Yes, you and the Transport ACT bus ticket machine when it's shaming fare evaders.' He gave the Defeated Leader's overhead wave to the audience and smiled.

• • •

Although it was a Network Nine Roving Roboter that fell onto the Labor leader, video footage would reveal that Seven had rammed it. Allison Trang and her crew were going to be crucified. 'They could slate us for this,' Allison told her team grimly.

To call 'slating' the latest managerial fad was equivalent to describing a Viking's battle-axe as a fashion accessory. Slating was the disposing of an underperforming or problematic department en masse. If there was a problem in a section, you got rid of the lot of them. No one, regardless of merit or innocence, was spared. The only restraining factor was the so-called Gough Threshold, where the savings brought about by replacing sacked senior staff with junior workers was offset by heavier losses through unfair dismissal claims.

On the control room screen, Prime Minister Fitzwilliams was speaking.

'We could claim the Roving Roboter malfunctioned,' someone suggested.

Allison pressed her lips together and shook her head. 'Maybe if it was made in Australia, but it's German manufacture; no one would believe us.'

'What if we took a coffee and spilled it on the controls?' another proposed. 'Say it shorted out and the Roboter went wild.'

It was a preposterous idea but the only one on the table. 'Anyone got a coffee?' Allison asked.

'Boss! You're not going to believe this!' a technician across the room cried excitedly. 'I've got Jesse Pelletier on the line and he has Ned Ludd! Nude Ned, Bicycle Ned! Ned Ludd! Exclusive!'

Allison's arm froze, the coffee cup poised over the Roboter controls. 'Get the feed direct to our hosts,' she ordered. 'Cut to it the instant Fitzwilliams finishes!' She paused. 'How much money does Pelletier want?' Allison asked perceptively. She'd dealt with Jesse Pelletier before.

'Not money. He wants a permanent job for himself and his camera operator. He's also refusing to throw to the host. He interviews Ned Ludd. No one else.'

Allison grinned. 'Agreed. Tell him we agree to everything. Do it,' she ordered urgently. 'Get ready to cut to wherever the hell Jesse Pelletier is.'

The feed from the Melbourne pub came up on the screen. 'No one's going to slate us if we deliver a Ned Ludd exclusive,' Allison vowed to her team. 'Tomorrow we do a special feature on how our man Jesse Pelletier tracked Ned Ludd down and found the nation's new prime minister!'

'Pelletier was drinking in a bar,' the technician explained, 'and Ned Ludd happened to walk in.'

'We'll tell it slightly differently. Anyway, that's tomorrow's assignment,' Allison said with a dismissive wave of her hand. The PM had finished. 'Tell Pelletier he's on in forty-five seconds. Let the hosts just start blathering their analysis of Fitzwilliams' speech and then we interrupt them.' She raised her fist triumphantly. 'We'll make Jesse Pelletier a hero of journalism. Let them try and slate us after that!'

• • •

Jesse Pelletier drew in a breath. National media with quite possibly the Prime Minister elect. Ned Ludd, wearing a t-shirt with a penny-farthing bicycle on it, was leaning with her back to the bar, facing the camera. On either side of her were the now-famous-in-their-own-right Veronicae. Prime Minister Ned had an arm slung over the shoulders of each. Ned Ludd told him they'd deliberately escaped the drones trailing them, running through shops and laneways until they had tumbled into this pub. Was this his kind of prime minister or what?

Gunnar was working the camera, the bodyguard obligingly holding aloft a pool cue with a microphone taped to it to serve as the sound boom. It was a picture of how journalism ought to look. Jesse didn't even mind that the bartender behind them was photo-bombing the shot.

Gunnar counted him in with his fingers and he was on.

'This is Jesse Pelletier, Network Seven reporter coming to you live from Melbourne, and with me is the person who may well be the next prime minister of Australia, Ned Ludd . . .'

CHAPTER FIFTEEN

Considering he had just stepped down as leader, it struck Fitzwilliams that there was an inordinate amount of politics that needed doing the morning after the election. His first visitor was Russ Langdon, who'd come to tell Fitzwilliams he planned to nominate for the Liberal Party leadership. A few months earlier, Fitzwilliams would have been incredulous at the idea, but Langdon had displayed qualities during the election that Fitzwilliams never suspected were there. Langdon was certainly a better man than Damian bloody Boswell to rebuild the party. As for any others, Alan Chandos wouldn't want the leadership and Donna Hargreaves didn't have the numbers. Langdon was clearly the best choice. Fitzwilliams felt he could offer his support unreservedly to his Minister for Security and Freedom.

'Thank you, Adrian,' Langdon said. 'That means a lot to me.'

Fitzwilliams blinked at Langdon's premature dropping of 'Prime Minister'—he was still technically PM until a new one was sworn in—but, he reflected, he might as well get used to it. 'You shouldn't thank me,' he joked. 'I'm the one who has left you a party holding only forty-seven seats.' Fitzwilliams detected a slight flick of Langdon's eyebrows at the comment. Was forty-seven yet another one of Langdon's blasted prime numbers?

Next in the office were his Treasurer and Minister for Health and Ageing. If he'd been surprised by Langdon's decision, he was astounded by what they had to tell him. The Luddites were offering Chandos and Hargreaves the chance to keep their cabinet posts. 'You have no authorisation to enter into a coalition with the Luddites,' Fitzwilliams informed them both bluntly.

'They aren't asking for a coalition, Adrian,' Hargreaves said. 'They're just asking us—and we intend to accept.'

'They've offered Labor four cabinet posts,' Chandos added. 'All the really capable ones from Labor. At the risk of being immodest, Adrian, they appear to be picking the best brains in parliament. The Luddites are calling it the Conglomerate Cabinet.'

Everyone, it appeared to Fitzwilliams, must have been chomping at the bit to call him by his first name. It irked him that Labor, with four fewer seats, was being offered more cabinet positions than the Liberals, but the Luddites already had Olga onside. Hargreaves and Chandos were really the only other two worth having, he admitted. The Luddites knew what they were doing.

'You're not going to start wearing a celery stick I hope,' Fitzwilliams said, and even Donna laughed.

Around eleven, he received the totally improbable phone call he knew was coming. It was Roslyn Stanfield.

'How's the knee?' Fitzwilliams asked straight away. 'Leon thinks it's your ACL.'

'Leon? Who's Leon?'

'My bodyguard.'

'Well, tell Leon I don't know yet. I'm still waiting in emergency. I've been here since seven am. Something your lot never deals with,' Stanfield muttered. It was the plight of Labor politicians. Liberal MPs could take out private health insurance and nobody would bat an eyelid. Let a Labor leader be spotted in a private hospital and the media would go berserk.

'I know you've stepped down as leader,' Stanfield started, 'but what if instead . . .'

Fitzwilliams closed his eyes, wishing she wouldn't make the offer.

'. . . we formed a coalition. A Labor–Liberal–National coalition would have a solid workable majority.' As if sensing his lack of enthusiasm, she pointed out, 'It's been done before. Winston Churchill and Clement Attlee—the Conservative and Labour Coalition during the Second World War.'

Fitzwilliams couldn't help laughing. 'That was a coalition against the Nazis, not some people wearing celery sticks. Roslyn, if the Labor and Liberal parties joined together, what would be the point of us?' he asked.

'You're right, I suppose.' Stanfield sighed. 'We're going to have to let the Luddites have a go, aren't we?' she observed quietly after a pause. 'Hang on!' she called out before Fitzwilliams could answer. 'Sorry, Prime . . . sorry, Adrian,' she corrected herself. 'Got to go. The doctor just called my name.'

• • •

Fiona Brennan had Geraldine from the Sydney office on the screen. It was the morning of the day after the election, but the counter-terrorism work of ASIO never stopped.

'This is a remarkable story, Geraldine,' Fiona commented. 'They just happened to recruit one of our own undercover agents?'

An ASIO informant embedded within the ranks of an anarchist group had uncovered the bizarre plot. The anarchist group being monitored had proven to be a tepid, mostly boring lot. They did little other than hold meetings and assign mandatory readings to its members, homework about which their agent frequently complained to his ASIO handlers.

This agent, however, had recently been approached by Radio 2RT with a suspicious job offer that he accepted out of professional curiosity. On his first day at 2RT, he did a cursory hack of the station manager's computer, though the agent couldn't really call it hacking; the station manager was someone who left his computer on all day and was prone to long lunches.

He discovered that the station manager had been trawling the dark side of the internet to purchase bomb-making equipment. Over the following days, the ASIO agent easily gleaned further details of the plot. The station manager and the producer of the *Jim Jarvis Show* planned to explode a bomb in their own computer server and pin the crime on the anarchist they'd recently hired. Their intention was to destroy the server housing Virtual Jim Jarvis. They were plotting to murder a dead man!

'It is tempting to let them blow up Jim Jarvis,' Fiona mused; she never could abide the man. 'But someone might get hurt. It is the nature of bombs.' ASIO had security-of-the-nation problems enough without radio stations setting off bombs and blaming non-existent terrorists. 'I suppose we must make an example of them, if only as a deterrent. Let's leave terrorism to the actual terrorists.'

'Deterrent?' Geraldine queried. 'Who would we be deterring? How many people plot to blow up their own computer servers? This lot is completely mad.'

Geraldine had a point. 'This needn't be an ASIO matter,' Fiona decided. 'Build the dossier about the case, then hand it over to local police.' She shook her head. 'What could have possessed them over at 2RT?'

'In radio, Director, I think you'll find it's always about the ratings.'

• • •

The period of indecision after the election had been mercifully brief. Labor had agreed to vote supply to the Luddites. Russ Langdon, the new Liberal leader, hadn't gone as far as that, but he had rammed through the Coalition party room meeting that Donna Hargreaves and Alan Chandos could join the Conglomerate Cabinet. That had not gone down well with some MPs, but it had gone down. Fitzwilliams had been mostly a spectator to these events. Prime Minister Ned Ludd would be sworn in by the Governor-General on Thursday. The Honourable Ned Ludd. It would take some getting used to.

The Prime Minister to be had paid Fitzwilliams a visit. He'd shown her around his office and the cabinet rooms and then taken her to meet with some of the parliamentary staff. She had introduced herself as 'Aggie' but in parliament she would officially be

Ned Ludd, as would all her colleagues. It was going to be difficult to make any sense reading Hansard under such confusing conditions, Fitzwilliams reflected, but then, Hansard often didn't make much sense.

The only feathers Aggie/Ned Ludd had ruffled were those of Fitzwilliams' chauffeur Desmond. Apparently, the new Prime Minister wanted to get about Canberra on a tandem. 'I can't be a chauffeur on a tandem,' Desmond groused to Fitzwilliams. 'It's undignified.'

A phone call from Olga had been a pleasant surprise. Did he want a game of tennis? This invitation from Fitzwilliams' most loyal and disloyal cabinet colleague perked him up considerably. Olga had been a part of his life for so long. Now that she had engineered this Luddite victory so spectacularly, he thought she might never spare him another thought. Instead, here she was proposing to meet on the very same tennis court where they had played that first day of the election campaign, a campaign that now seemed almost a lifetime ago.

They had a coffee first, both players being of an age where caffeine helped considerably before undertaking any activity. 'I am pleased you have decided to stay on in parliament, Prime Minister,' she told him. She was the only person still calling him Prime Minister. 'I was concerned you might stray down that road of so many of your predecessors; ceasing to contribute meaningfully, content to write self-indulgent memoirs and the occasional smug know-it-all opinion pieces for Fairfax or News Corp.'

Fitzwilliams said nothing. He'd been considering writing a little something for *The Australian Online.* 'You can still play a dynamic role in the governing of this country,' Olga informed him and took a sip of her coffee. 'You, Prime Minister, can make it your role to talk sense to the rank and file of Liberal/National MPs and Senators. How politics works is about to change radically and some of them will need your help to understand and adapt to this.' She said this matter-of-factly. She was clearly assuming he was in full agreement with her on what his role should be in this new political order. Perhaps he was.

'But now,' Olga smiled, picking up her racquet, 'to more important matters.' They took their positions on either side of the net. The same group—or at least a very similar group—of primary school students were on the adjacent court. Not being prime minister had its benefits, Fitzwilliams reflected. It no longer mattered if one of the little brats filmed them this time.

Olga won the first game. She was using the same tactic as before, choosing placement over power, wearing him down and making him scramble after every return shot. To start the second game, after Fitzwilliams stretched to his backhand on her serve, he moved almost instinctively to where he knew her return shot would go. When it came, he was there waiting for it on his forehand and tucked it away efficiently in the far corner. So perfect was the shot, so unreturnable, that Olga had not moved a centimetre towards it. She simply watched its trajectory to the opposite corner.

Olga nodded approvingly. 'You are positioning yourself much better than before,' she remarked. 'You have potential in you yet, Prime Minister.'

ACKNOWLEDGEMENTS

Foremost, I must thank the incomparable Irina Dunn for the crucial role she played in bringing this novel to the bright daylight of publication. Had it not been for her encouragement, her efforts, her generosity and, above all, the wisdom of her advice, this book would still be languishing as a stack of A4 sheets with scrawled marginal notes on a shelf I really ought to tidy up some day.

My gratitude also goes to the team at Allen & Unwin, most particularly to Richard Walsh, Rebecca Kaiser, Ali Lavau and Aziza Kuypers. They bring to their work that admirable capacity so needed in today's world of being both very professional and delightfully fun to work with.

And finally, thanks must go to my early readers, Laurie Miller, Susan Kennett, Jan Lingard, Cyril O'Connor, Zhi Yan, and to my international reviewers, my brother Glenn and his friend Joe. It was their laughter and encouragement that made me decide this novel should really be given a go.